DEATH
TAKES
A HAND

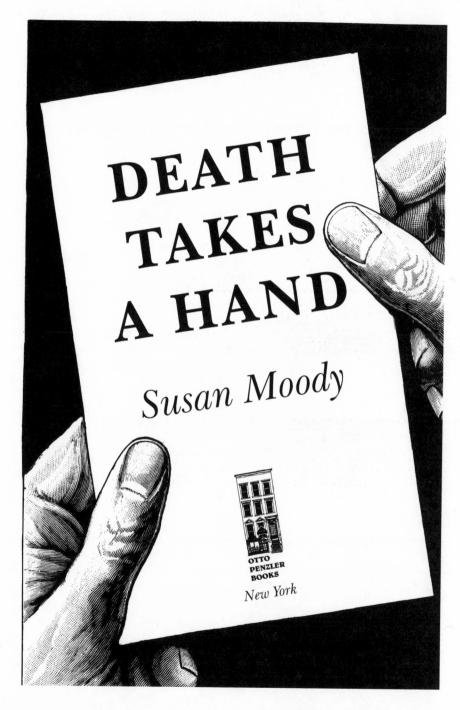

DEATH
TAKES
A HAND

Susan Moody

OTTO
PENZLER
BOOKS

New York

Copyright © 1993 by Susan Moody

First American Edition 1994

Otto Penzler Books

129 West 56th Street

New York, NY 10019

(Editorial Offices only)

Macmillan Publishing Company

866 Third Avenue

New York, NY 10022

Macmillan Publishing Company is part of the Maxwell Communication Group of Companies.

Library of Congress Cataloging-in-Publication Data

Moody, Susan.

Death takes a hand / Susan Moody.—1st American ed.

p.   cm.

ISBN 1-883402-00-X

1. Contract bridge—Study and teaching—England—Fiction.   2. Women detectives—England—Fiction.   I. Title.

PR6063.O575D43   1994

823'.914—dc20   93-32745

CIP

Otto Penzler Books are available at special discounts for bulk purchases for sales promotions, premiums, fund-raising, or educational use. For details, contact:

Special Sales Director

Macmillan Publishing Company

866 Third Avenue

New York, NY 10022

Printed in the United States of America

10 9 8 7 6 5 4 3 2 1

For Julianna Lees, Best Friend,
with gratitude

DEATH
TAKES
A HAND

ONE corpse is usually more than enough. By anyone's standards, three is far too many.

Opening the door of the Macbeth Room and fighting her way through the heavy velvet curtain designed to cut out drafts, Cassandra Swann thought at first that the three of them were playing some kind of joke, pretending she was so late that they had died of old age waiting for her. Automatically she glanced at her watch; she should have been here at eleven and it was now seven minutes past.

Yet the mind is flexible. Even as she took in the time, she was also registering the fact that the mess on the back of Sonia Wetherhead's skull was not some form of bizarre ethnic adornment, that the stuff staining the pink carpet was blood, and that the slumped slack-mouthed figures of old Colonel and Mrs. Plumpton seemed all too realistically lifeless.

Nobody, in other words, was playing games here, though the original intention had been that they should do so. The Broughton Manor Hotel had specifically set this room aside for private lessons, should any of the sixteen punters participating in the Winter Bridge Weekend request them; Cassie was the bridge professional they had engaged to organize the two-and-a-half day event and ensure that it was a success.

Two of the bodies sat square on to the table: they appeared neither to have struggled nor to have tried to run. The third—Sonia's—lay sprawled garishly on the carpet. As though assessing a newly dealt hand, Cassie took in the card table covered in green baize with three chairs set neatly around it, a fourth pulled out as though someone was about to sit down in it. She noted the spread cards and the score pads, each one with a pencil lined up alongside it. She remarked the fallen glass which had rolled under one of the chairs, at the same time storing away the fact that it had probably been empty when it fell since it had left no mark.

Then she opened her mouth to scream for help, before remembering that for this weekend she *was* the help, counting more as hotel staff than as guest. The horror of mouth-to-mouth resuscitation crossed her mind. Although she was certain, just by looking at them, that the three bodies were dead, she nonetheless laid the back of her hand against Sonia's cheek and then, just in case, bent down and listened for some sound from her heart. After all, unlikely though it seemed, she might still be alive. There might remain in that slack motionless body a last fluttering breath which could be coaxed back into life . . .

She did the same with the Colonel. As she leaned against him, he slumped forward until his head struck the table and rested there. Strangely, it was not frightening. His body was warm, solid under his tweed jacket; he looked merely as though he had nodded off. His wife sat at a right angle to him, glassy-eyed and staring, her pillbox—pewter, inlaid with mosaic in a flower pattern—on the baize beside her.

Using thumb and forefinger, repressing a shudder at the feel of the old lady's stubby eyelashes against the tips of her fingers, Cassie drew Mrs. Plumpton's eyelids down over her sightless eyes, as though they were shutters which could hide the unimaginable darkness of death.

Doing so, she unexpectedly recalled her mother's funeral, the sonorous voice of her Uncle Samuel as he spoke of a good woman gone—*Do not go gentle into that good night*—the shake of tears in his voice as he consigned his younger sister to the earth, nothing left of her now but memory. That was more than twenty-five years ago; she had not realized that every detail of the occasion was as vividly imprinted in her mind as though it had happened last week.

She wondered whether Mrs. Plumpton had been good. Or Sonia. What, in any case, did "good" mean? And did it matter? In death, there is nothing to distinguish good from bad, rich from poor, old from young . . .

She looked around the room again. Swagged curtains of damask-rosed chintz hung on either side of diamond-paned windows which afforded a fine view of rain falling across sodden fields in which a few picturesque cows plodded about; pale pink carpet spread to walls which were covered in genuine linenfold paneling of the highest quality; comfortable Tudor-style armchairs sat on either side of a real fire burning warmly on a wide hearth. There was everything, really, that the townie could possibly expect from the country. Especially when he was paying through the nose for it.

While waiting for her, the other three had obviously dealt a hand of cards, played three tricks, and then, for some reason, laid the rest of their cards face up on the table. Aware that she might be tampering with evidence, Cassie turned over the tricks and sneaked a quick look at them before putting them back and studying the four hands, which each contained ten cards. One was laid out as Dummy; the other three were neatly fanned.

A glance at Colonel Plumpton's cards showed that he had had just about enough points to open the bidding. With five diamonds to the Ace in his hand, when his turn came he would almost certainly have bid 1♦; hearing that, Sonia, presumably sitting opposite him in what eventually became Dummy's seat (if the chair which had been pulled away from the table was any indication), would probably have raised him to 5♦, ignoring Mrs. Plumpton's likely bid of 1♥. Having partnered Sonia for a couple of games during an introductory round on Friday, the first evening of the Bridge Weekend, Cassie had already learned that she was a reckless woman, inclined to take risks.

The Colonel would have opened the bidding since, judging by the placing of the second pack to the right of the hand opposite his seat, he must have been the dealer.

A lifetime of playing bridge had trained Cassie to make quick assessments, to notice details: she took all this in during the no more than fifty seconds which had elapsed since she entered the room. She turned and ran for help.

"Weren't you supposed to be there at eleven o'clock?" Detective Inspector Mantripp asked aggressively. For whatever reason, he had clearly decided to treat her as a hostile witness.

"Yes. But I—"

"So why the delay?" He turned his grim gray face to his colleague, Sergeant Walsh. "Dear, dear. I know what *I'd* say if I was paying for an hour's private coaching and the teacher showed up ten minutes late."

"It was seven minutes," Cassie said. "And I already told you why I was delayed."

"Tell me again." He looked over at his sergeant with the expression of a man who's heard the joke before and knows it's a good one.

"I couldn't get my door open."

"Have I got this right?" Mantripp rubbed his hand over his chin and frowned, as though desperate to understand something which was quite outside his experience. Cassie had seldom seen a more barbaric haircut than the one currently stop the DI's head. "The key wouldn't turn: is that what you said?"

"Yes. This is, as you can see, Inspector, a country house hotel." (*"Enjoy the splendor of Elizabethan England in all the comfort of the twentieth century,"* the hotel's brochure said.) "People paying for this kind of ambience don't want too much modernity, electronic key cards and that kind of thing, so although the bedroom doors can be bolted on the inside, you still need an old-fashioned key to get in or out. The lock on my door seemed to have jammed; my key simply wouldn't move."

"And you say no one from Reception answered your telephone calls?"

"That's right. I assumed no one was there."

Though that was not necessarily a logical assumption. The two skeletal harpies who took turns manning the desk during the day had waists the size of Cassie's wrist, and wrists the size of pencils. Definitely not the sort of wrists designed for the weighty task of lifting telephone receivers when they rang, especially not when the call was coming from the bridge pro's room.

"That fits in," Mantripp said grudgingly. "Miss—um—Boanes, on the desk" (*Bones?* What, Cassie wondered, was the other receptionist called? Skin?) "has already stated that at approximately two minutes past eleven there was an—um—altercation in the kitchen which required her immediate attendance." He stared doubtfully at Cassie. "Apparently the chef here is a little temperamental."

"The chef here is way-over-the-top temperamental," Cassie said. "That doesn't stop him from being a superb cook. Last night he served a lamb *en croûte* that was absolutely out of—

"So, receiving no answer to your telephone calls," the policeman interrupted, giving her a frigid stare, "and unable to turn your key in the lock, what did you do then?"

"Banged a bit. Shouted. You know the sort of thing one does."

Mantripp's expression made it plain that he was not in the habit of getting himself locked into hotel bedrooms. Nor shouting. "Yes? And then?"

"Then I looked out of the window."

"And did what?"

"Decided not to try getting out that way."

"Why not?"

"For one thing, it was about twenty feet from the ground. For another, I didn't think I could squeeze through. As you will have noticed, the house was once an Elizabethan manor."

"Yes." His gaze wandered up and down Cassie's figure. He added thoughtfully, "I remember reading somewhere that, on average, the Elizabethans were much smaller than we are."

"Just about everyone in the entire world is much smaller than I am," Cassie said.

"I'm sure you're exaggerating, Miss—um—Swann," he said.

Of course she was bloody exaggerating. She sighed heavily. "Anyway, I decided the best thing was to wait. Eventually someone would realize I hadn't showed up and would come looking. And then I heard one of the chambermaids outside in the passage. I banged on the door and she let me out."

"And down you came to find the—um—deceased?"
"Exactly."

She'd known right from the beginning that this was
going to be a bad day. To start with, it was already ten-
thirty, which meant she'd have to skip breakfast. On top
of that, she had the world's worst headache. All right:
hangover. The hotel had included a party as part of the
integral cost of its weekend package; this had taken
place the previous evening, and everyone was determined to drink themselves stupid to make sure they got
value for their money. Knowing this, the hotel had
sought to minimize costs by providing the best Albanian
paint stripper for them to get drunk on. Cassie had
never been one to hang back when the corks were flying, nor had she done so last night.

In addition to the headache, it was raining.
Staggering over to the window, and in the process
banging her knee painfully on the low Tudor stool at
the foot of the bed, she had stared dismally out at the
wet landscape full of dripping trees and puddled fields.
The sky was overcast, a mass of gray clouds lumbering
from one side of the view to the other with the clear
intent of dumping at least four more inches of water
before moving off over the distant hills. The whole
thing made Cassie very much want to return to her
comfortable bed ("*all our mattresses are fully sprung,*"
according to the brochure), but there wasn't time. A van
was slowly making its way down the damp drive
between leafless trees. It was painted white; over a picture of a weather-beaten dairymaid carrying two wood-

en buckets of milk across her shoulders, bold lettering unequivocally proclaimed that it would not be possible to find higher-quality dairy products anywhere. As she watched, a taxi appeared from below her and overtook the van to go speeding toward the main road beyond the gates.

But the rain was nothing compared to what came next. When she stood on the scales, they registered a five-pound increase since yesterday. *Five pounds?* In twenty-four hours? She bent down and jiggled around with the thing at the side until the dial hand stood at just under zero. When she stepped back onto the scales again, they still showed she'd put on five pounds.

"Fat is a feminist issue," she told herself loudly, but it didn't help much. She had seen them too often on television, the kind of women who wrote books with titles like that. They were always stick insects, the only thing overweight about them being their hair, which they tossed a lot. Why should they worry whether fat was a feminist or any other kind of issue? They weren't the ones who ate like nuns and had spent the entire weekend religiously refusing the hotel chef's amazing desserts in favor of fresh fruit and *still* managed to put on five pounds in a day.

The five pounds niggled at her while she swallowed three paracetamol (how many calories in paracetamol? There was no mention on the side of the box) and stepped into the shower. She tried to tell herself they didn't matter, but she knew they did. To her, anyway.

Only last week her cousin Rose had told her not to be so silly. "You've got a lovely womanly figure," she said kindly, not realizing (or possibly realizing all too well) that only made it worse. "I mean, look at me: no bust, no hips."

"I don't want to look at you, thank you very much," Cassie had said sourly.

"But you're still a size fourteen, aren't you?" (Love that "*still*," Cassie thought, as though it was only a matter of time before all bets were off, all buttons burst, and with a rending of cloth and a clang of broken zippers, she exploded into size 16, a vast pink version of the Incredible Hulk.)

"It depends." Cassie refused to think about the size tags on the last two blouses she'd bought.

"So I mean, it's not as if you're some grotesque obese sort of barrage balloon or something."

"No, it isn't really, is it?" Cassie said.

Rose could bloody talk. She'd never been over a size 10 in her life. As for her twin sisters, Hyacinth and Primula, they could both have made themselves ball gowns out of the average dishcloth and still have enough material left over for matching stoles. Even though the twins were two years older than Cassie's thirty, they still retained the boyish figures of prepubescence. Which was great if you were keen on rose-lipped striplings and perhaps explained why Derek, Primula's husband, was always staring at Cassie's boobs.

Stepping out the hotel shower, Cassie stared at them too. Catching sight of herself in the long mirror attached to one wall was something which at home she usually managed to avoid. Now, faced with herself, she paused. Was that the image of a voluptuous woman, firm-fleshed, splendidly proportioned, magnificent in her nakedness, marble-thighed and snowy-bosomed? Or was it the image of a fat slob?

It was one of those questions whose answer depended on your point of view. It was all very well banging on about beauty being in the eye of the beholder. It was a matter of mood whether this particular beholder saw beauty or bulge. Today, it was definitely bulge. Cassie stepped into the embrace of the supersize bath towel provided by the management (had they known she was coming? Well, of course they had, but had they known what size she'd be when she'd come? Was that why the thing was so huge?) and dried off. She plumped (ha!) for her Nice Gel outfit, since most of the weekend's clientele was over sixty: navy skirt, ladylike shoes, decorous white blouse, and long navy jacket. She dithered a bit over the earrings—the papier-mâché parrots? the silver skulls?—but settled for pearl studs in the end.

Picking up her briefcase, she checked her watch— 10:58: she'd cut it a bit fine, but three minutes was easily enough to get down to the Macbeth Room and still look efficient. Which was the point at which she discovered the darn key wouldn't turn.

"So did you notice anything when you finally turned up?" DI Mantripp said, unnecessarily emphasizing the adverb.

"I noticed three dead people waiting to play bridge with me, if that's what you mean," Cassie said.

"Apart from the—um—deceased." Mantripp breathed hard through his nose, making an unpleasant wheezing sound. "Anything unusual. Anything—um—untoward?"

"Absolutely nothing. It was as though they had simply been struck down as they sat there. Like a plague." Mantripp wrote down "plague," and added a question mark, then looking up and catching Cassie's eye, crossed it out.

"You saw for yourself," she went on. "Nothing'd been disturbed, there was no sign of a struggle." She closed her eyes and unwillingly saw again the three dead, pressed against the inside of her eyelids: Colonel and Mrs. Plumpton, the alabaster obelisk or whatever it was lying beside Sonia's crushed head, the three tricks already played, the cards fanned out on the table. She could have written down the picture cards in each hand, if Mantripp had asked her to, even some of the smaller ones.

"What do you think happened in there this morning, Miss—um—Swann?"

"I've no idea. It looks as though someone calmly walked in, smashed in the back of Miss Wetherhead's skull, and walked out again."

"What about the other two? Why didn't they raise the alarm?"

"Perhaps they had heart attacks or something. I know Mrs. Plumpton had some kind of heart problem and the Col—"

"Simultaneous heart attacks? Come along, Miss—um—Swann: surely you can do better than that."

"I probably can," Cassie said. "I can't honestly see why I should have to, though. You're the one who's supposed to be investigating it, not me. I'm just a bridge instructor." Tired of his belligerence, she leaned her head on her hand. In the room there'd been a smell of blood—and other things; remembering, she felt suddenly nauseous.

"Perhaps you could give us a rundown on the—uh—customers here this weekend," Mantripp said.

"There were fifteen of them." Cassie made an effort to recover herself. "Should have been sixteen but one canceled at the last moment."

"Oh yes?" Mantripp looked bored and rolled his eyes at Sergeant Walsh.

"Look, do you want the details or don't you?" Cassie was in no mood to be condescended to by a man whose barber ought to be had up for offenses against public decency.

"Of course we do."

"Well, then." She took a deep breath. "The group was fairly mixed, as far as their playing ability went. There were two youngish couples, beginners, one from Exeter, one from Luton. There was a solicitor and his wife, both of whom took up the game three years ago, when he retired. There was a woman who owned an antique shop in Hereford; Roy Sowerby, a gardening expert from Surrey; a female publisher called Vicky Duggan." It was easy, really: she had assessed them like a bridge hand, almost mechanically working out their weaknesses and strengths, which ones were losers, which winners. Their point counts, if you liked. "A novelist, Felicity Carridine—"

"My wife likes her stuff," the sergeant said in a quiet voice. He smiled at Cassie from his seat behind Mantripp.

"—and—er—Ned Casaubon." Cassie could have kicked herself for that "er." She saw Mantripp's eyes narrow slightly as she added, a little too quickly, "He's a wine merchant."

"Oh yes?" Sergeant Walsh had counted up names. "Anyone else?" he asked. "You've only mentioned eleven."

"Thomas Lambert: he's a journalist of some kind," Cassie said. "I think that's the lot. Except for the Plumptons, of course, and Sonia Wetherhead. They were all experienced, if not very good, bridge players."

"Bridge over troubled waters, far as they were concerned," said Mantripp. He gave Cassie a cool stare as though daring her to laugh. A waste of time, really: she hadn't the slightest desire to do anything but throw up.

"Excuse me, but I think, if you don't mind . . ." She pushed back her chair, one hand to her mouth.

"I'd like to talk to you again," Mantripp said as she walked toward the door. "Perhaps you'd let my sergeant know when you're feeling better. I want to know anything you can tell me about all these people, even though most of them seem able to provide alibis for each other which would appear to eliminate them as suspects. And I also want to hear about the party that was held here last night."

Ah yes: the party . . .

SHE arrived late, having extended her last teaching session of the day by half an hour in order to run through the scoring system yet again with one of the two youngish couples who had booked in for the weekend— the one from Exeter, she thought, though it might have been the one from Luton; they appeared interchange- able. By the time she had got into her black velvet party frock (which seemed to have shrunk), applied fresh makeup, and found her way to the Othello Lounge, the party was in full swing.

Kevin, the hotel manager, a thin nervous man in a dinner jacket, met her at the door. "Most of them are already tanked up to the eyeballs," he said, peering morosely at his watch.

"More like the hairlines, if you ask me," Cassie said.

"And dinner's not scheduled for another hour." Kevin's hesitant mustache reared and bucked beneath his nose as he moved his upper lip disparagingly about.

"Swings and roundabouts, Kev. If they go on as they've begun, half of them will be out for the count by the the time we get to the table. At least you'll save on food."

He looked at her pityingly. "It doesn't work like that. Haven't you heard of portion control?"

"Not only heard of but spent most of my adult life trying to practice." Cassie moved toward the table where one of Kevin's minions was dispensing the contents of the Albanian bottles.

With a glass in her hand, she surveyed the room. Considering that most of these people had, as far as she knew, been strangers to each other until they had arrived here the night before from all over England, they seemed remarkably matey now. Colonel and Mrs. Plumpton were laughing unrestrainedly with the solicitor and his wife; the Colonel's arm was around the wife's shoulders. The two young couples from Exeter and Luton were discussing Marbella and tax dodges. Felicity Carridine, the well-known romantic novelist, was entertaining the woman who owned the antique shop in Hereford with tales of unscrupulous publishers, while the publisher, who might or might not have been unscrupulous, wagged her fingers about and bobbed her head, shouting "Lies! It's all lies!" every time the famous writer drew breath.

By the fireplace, the gardening expert from Surrey, who had been saturnine on arrival and stayed that way ever since, though his bridge game was pretty sharp, stood listening with Thomas Lambert to Sonia Wetherhead: they seemed to be discussing rhododendrons.

She was wondering why they appeared so acrimonious about it when Ned Casaubon, the wine merchant, caught hold of her elbow. "I was wondering where you'd got to," he said.

Cassie could think of no reply to this that didn't sound simpering; she smiled instead.

"I hope you don't think *I* had anything to do with this," he said, indicating the contents of his glass. "Drink it if you must, but for God's sake don't get it on your hands."

Cassie laughed politely. He was quite fanciable, in his late thirties, she judged, good-looking and very smooth. What interested her much more than the smoothness was the hard edge to his jaw and the bulge of muscle under his well-cut clothes: something about him didn't ring quite true.

"Have you been teaching bridge long?" he said. He glanced swiftly at his watch, as though intending to dash off fairly soon to some more enjoyable entertainment.

"Professionally, about six years."

"What did you do before that?"

"Taught biology in a girls' school."

"Presumably bridge is more interesting."

"I'd do it even if it wasn't," Cassie said. "But yes: since I spend a lot of my time whipping about from one place to another, teaching on cruise ships one week, organizing competitions in the Caribbean the next, it's certainly varied. And I'm just starting to make a reasonable living at it too. What about you?"

"Yes," he said. He smiled at her, showing beautiful teeth.

"What kind of an answer is that?"

"I meant that my life is also varied. Flogging crates of Pomerol to Arab sheiks in Kensington is only a small part of it."

"Tell me," Cass said. "Is your name really Casaubon?"

He seemed momentarily taken aback. "Why should you think it wasn't?" he asked, taking her glass. "Let me find you another drink." He began to steer her across the room.

Sonia Wetherhead blocked his way. Her large unconstrained body was covered like a Peruvian Indian's in layers of woven material, and her once-fair hair, loosely caught up in a species of bun, fell in strands across her wine-flushed cheeks.

"Huh!" she said.

"I'm sorry?" said Casaubon.

"You're a bit of a bastard," she said, conversationally. Her round face had the coarse red look of a farmer's.

"Am I?" Casaubon tried to push past.

"You know you are."

"Sonia, for goodness' sake . . ."

"Don't you Sonia me," Sonia said.

"Why not? It's your name, isn't it?"

"You *bastard*."

"Do you two know each other?" Cassie made disengaging motions. "I'll go and . . ."

"Know?" said Sonia. "Huh!" She shifted her shoulders about.

In the course of the past twenty-four hours, Cassie had learned a certain amount about her, not only from Kevin but also from Sonia herself, with supplements from a glossy magazine which happened to be lying on an oak table in the hotel's Malvolio Snug. Sonia was apparently a well-known weaver, which accounted both for the stuff she was wrapped in and for a kind of brawniness about her upper arms.

She looked directly at Cassie. "Let me warn you, my dear. This man is a health hazard."

"I really don't . . ." began Cassie. Was the woman saying that Casaubon had AIDS? If so, how did she know? What was she: wife? mistress? From the venom with which she spoke, probably ex- either or both of those states. Whatever the relationship between her and handsome Ned Casaubon, it clearly predated this weekend.

"I suggest you get nice Kevin to bring you some strong coffee," Casaubon said patiently, as though used to such behavior.

"I suggest . . . I suggest . . ." said Sonia in a high-pitched voice that was supposed to indicate mimicry of Casaubon, although he had not sounded in the least like that. She danced clumsily on the spot, wagging her head so that more of her hair collapsed. "Have you got round yet to *suggesting* that Ms. Swann here clamber into bed with you?"

"I'm afraid, Sonia, that you interrupted us before I

had a chance to put it to her." Casaubon grinned at Cassie.

"He likes being beaten on the bum," Sonia said loudly. "I put it all down to boarding school myself."

Over Casaubon's shoulder, Cassie saw heads swivel in their direction. The solicitor's wife's mouth was open with astonishment; the young couples were nudging each other. A giggle surged like fermentation through her chest, bubbling and heaving. Across the cinema of her mind flashed an image of a naked cane-wielding Sonia belaboring a figure stretched across an old-fashioned horsehair mattress, large teeth gripping her lower lip as she concentrated on—well, whatever it was one concentrated on when beating someone else for that person's pleasure.

"Don't be tiresome, Sonia." Casaubon spoke sharply, pushing at the woman's shoulder.

"You utter *bastard* . . ." Sonia began to weep, water coming from her eyes in sheets that spread across her cheeks like a flood tide. Behind the tears, her eyes gleamed with real hatred. "Sometimes I think I could easily kill you for what you've done to me . . . toying with my . . . cast aside like an old . . . best years of my . . . used . . . trifled . . . laughingstock . . . don't give a . . ." She rambled on, her big weaver's shoulders shaking.

Kevin appeared, the hair on his upper lip twitching. "Oh dear," he said. He led Sonia away toward the kitchen, saying over his shoulder, "I told you some of them were already pissed."

Casaubon did not seem in the slightest embarrassed about the incident. Nor did he offer any justification. Cassie rather liked that. Perhaps Sonia's party piece was making a scene. Perhaps it did not mean anything at all. Even if it did, it had nothing to do with her.

She saw the wives of the two young couples staring at them; both women were swaying on the spot, like small craft at anchor in a high wind. Mrs. Plumpton was gazing in their direction and at the same time trying to shake pills into her hand from her mosaic-topped pillbox—an unwise move, as it turned out. Behind her, the woman who owned the antique shop in Hereford was staring at the underside of a piece of porcelain she had picked up from the overmantel—one of a pair of simpering shepherdesses in gold-sprigged farthingales or something similar, which Cassie had earlier decided were among the more hideous artifacts which littered the hotel (*"lavishly furnished with heirlooms, many of which have been in the Ryland family's possession for generations"*). On the other side of the room, the Colonel, empty pipe in mouth, examined his empty glass with the air of a man perpetually puzzled beyond belief by the vagaries and contradictions of life.

Felix Ryland, the burly hotel owner, came into the room and began what was clearly a practiced progress from guest to guest, making himself known. He started with the couple either from Exeter or from Luton while Cassie and Casaubon moved over to the drinks table, where they found saturnine Roy Sowerby pouring wine thoughtfully into a large glass. He muttered something at them and moved away.

"You wouldn't believe it, but that chap's a famous gardening authority," Casaubon said.

"I would, actually," said Cassie. "I've read several of his books. He's very sound on vegetables."

"So you're learned as well as beautiful?"

Cassie raised her eyebrows. "God, I hate patronizing men."

Felicity Carridine joined them, booming goatily, "Ah, the bridge teacher. Good evening, madam."

It was a form of greeting to which Cassie was not partial. "I hope you're enjoying yourself," she said politely. The big novelist was an imposing sight. Plentiful black hair hung over and around a face at least half again as big as any face Cassie had ever seen. The flaunting belly had clearly never heard of an aerobics class and the large bum, as Felicity had already loudly explained, was an occupational hazard.

"Enjoy? Enjoy? My dear, what does one enjoy these days? I've eaten it all, drunk it all, seen it all. I'm too fat to exercise and too old for sex. I mean, frankly, I don't know why I keep struggling on." A tremendous sigh shook the novelist's massive chest. "May I say what a very splendiferous dress you're wearing?"

Cassie's instinct was to say that it was out of the question to say anything of the sort. She wanted to be rude, to inquire what kind of a word "splendiferous" was anyway, and why someone who gained a living as a writer should be using it in the first place. Instead, she demurely examined the contents of her glass.

"Thank you," she said.

"Understand that before you saw the light, you used to be a teacher, like me," thundered the novelist.

"I can't imagine we'd have been very similar . . ."

Felicity stared at Cassie's velvet-covered bosom. "If there's one thing I dislike above all others, it's the English schoolchild." The large hot eyes widened suddenly as they caught sight of someone beyond Cassie's shoulder. "Christ, here comes that ghastly woman again. I'm off." There was some purposeful surging toward Thomas Lambert, the journalist.

"Ever read a Felicity Carridine?" Casaubon asked.

"No. Have you?"

"No. I gather the books are tremendously popular. Are you London-based?"

"No—extremely rural."

"Where?"

Before Cassie could answer, the Plumptons appeared. The Colonel's cheeks were empurpled; his white mustache quivered.

"Is everything all right?" Cassie asked, alarmed by his evident perturbation.

"I'll say," he said. "Deeply exciting, as a matter of fact. The wife and I can hardly contain ourselves, if you want to know the truth."

"Really?" The wife looked as though she could contain almost anything, including an atom bomb.

"Yes, indeed." He sipped vigorously from his glass. "Talk about a small world . . ." Patting his pockets vigorously, he took out a yellowed plastic tobacco pouch from one and matches from a second.

"Must you, darling?" Mrs. Plumpton said, her face assuming an expression of intense disgust. "You know I'm allergic to your smoke."

"Come on, old girl, just one," the Colonel said. He began to stuff the pipe's bowl with neat movements.

Mrs. Plumpton turned to Cassie. "Such a dreadful smell, don't you think? And it gets into everything." She waved her hands about in front of her face as though dispersing a cloud of flies.

"Give a chap a break," the Colonel said briskly, carrying on with his preparations.

"It's not just the smell, it's the carcinogens," Mrs. Plumpton said. "I don't want to be a victim of passive smoking." It had been a constant cry over the weekend.

"Just this once, dear." The Colonel went on tamping down tobacco. "Anyway, pipes aren't the same as fags, are they?"

"They smell just as bad," Mrs. Plumpton said. She touched the air near her left breast. "Some water . . . my pills . . ." She wandered away from them.

"It's her heart," said the Colonel, nodding wisely. "A bit dicky. You know how it is. She had something of a turn last night, as a matter of fact. Had to summon the rescue squads." He laughed heartily while the others kept silent, feeling it inappropriate to join in.

The burly man joined them. "Good evening, Miss Swann," he said. "It's nice to see you again." And to Casaubon: "I'm Felix Ryland."

"Aha," said the Colonel, straightening his shoulders militarily. He had set fire to the tobacco and was now busy sucking air through, emitting blue smoke from the corners of his mouth. "Our genial host, I take it."

"That's right." Ryland looked distinctly ungenial.

"Interesting place you've got here, Ryland," continued the Colonel. "Very interesting. Brings back the old days." He puffed vigorously.

"Indeed?" Very much the country squire, Ryland smiled courteously at the old man. "Where would that have been, sir?"

"Ended up in the SIB, for my sins. Been out of it for a long time now, of course, but I still get a few jobs from them. Keeps me in touch, you know. Apart from that, I've been growing roses ever since. And trying to learn bridge, of course, ha, ha."

Ned Casaubon took Cassie's glass from her hand and raised his eyebrows inquiringly at her before moving toward the drinks table.

"What's the SIB?" Cassie said.

"Special Investigations Branch." The Colonel brushed at the lapels of his immaculate blazer, then stared at the woman who owned the antique shop in Hereford as she peered closely at a gold-framed picture on the wall.

"How did you get into that?"

"Started off, if you can believe it, as an artist, rather than a soldier. I was teaching at the Liverpool Art College when King and Country called. You know how the Army thinks: said 'art teacher' on my papers and I was instantly labeled an expert on the subject. Spent my time trying to locate looted art treasures. There was a lot of that going on, during the war." He gave Felix Ryland a stern look. "And don't think that the Nazis were the only buggers at it."

"I'm sure you're right." Ryland looked uneasy, like a guest on his way to a wedding who unaccountably finds himself stopped by some garrulous old sea dog. "Look, I really must be—"

"You look to me as though you might have seen some military service yourself, Ryland," the Colonel continued remorselessly.

Ryland laughed, his eyes on the rest of the party. "Very perceptive, Colonel. I did my stint with the Coldstream Guards. Something of a family tradition.

After I got out, I spent a few years selling insurance at Lloyd's. I was able to buy this place back twelve years ago. Quite an achievement, really: it'd been out of family hands for quite a while." He looked modest. "Hope you're enjoying your stay with us."

"Very much so." Colonel Plumpton nodded vigorously. "One of my little hobbies is antiques, y'know. You've got some interesting stuff here. Love to know a bit more. You've obviously got a very good eye."

"Thank you. I'm—"

"Some fascinating things in your private quarters too."

Ryland narrowed his eyes. "How do you know about my—"

"Absolutely unforgivable, I know, but as I was just telling these good people, the memsahib took queer late last night. Rang Reception, couldn't raise anyone on guard duty, so I made my way to your quarters, since they're only at the end of our passage."

"But wasn't the door locked? I normally turn the key." Ryland looked around at them. "No offense, but in a hotel, where all sorts of people have access to the place, it's a wise precaution, believe me. Not to mention keeping the insurance johnnies happy."

"Must have forgotten last night, old boy," the Colonel said. "I knocked, of course. Opened the door, saw there was no one about and made off downstairs. Frightfully bad form, bursting in like that, but I was getting a trifle panicked. Wouldn't want the old girl pegging out on me. Been together forty-two years now. Don't know what I'd do without her."

For a moment they all fell silent. Before Cassie could

say anything, the Colonel added briskly, "Much appreciate it, Ryland, if you'd give me a guided tour."

"I'd be delighted. Sometime tomorrow be all right?"
Felix Ryland said.

"Perfect."

"Just before lunch, then. Now, if you'll excuse me, I
really ought to have a word with some of the others,"
Ryland said, moving away. "Mustn't monopolize you,
must I?"

Before he could move off, there was a cry from one of
the wives of the two young couples as the other fell slowly to the ground. One of the husbands—possibly her
own—bent over her. "Leave it out, Tracey," he said.

Cassie hurried over. "Do you need any help?"

He looked up at her. "Nah. She'll be all right."

Tracey was the one who had come under protest,
Cassie remembered, the one with absolutely no desire to
play bridge. Looking at the expression on the husband's
face, she thought that unless Tracey did a better job of
keeping up with his social ambitions, she was likely to
find he had become her ex-husband. "I told her to stick
to orange juice," he said now. "But would she listen?"

Roy Sowerby approached, waving his glass about. "I'll
drink to that," he said.

"You look as if you already have," said Cassie.
"Several times."

"It's my only defense," Sowerby said. "What else can I
do when someone like that dreadful weaver woman
insists on lecturing me about the beneficial aspects of
drinking your own urine."

"Better your own than someone else's."

"The woman's obviously entitled to do what she likes

with her bodily wastes, but why does she have to tell me about it?"

"She must think you look like a closet urine drinker."

"Please." Sowerby raised a hand in protest. "I'm already suffering from what I suspect is a peptic ulcer."

"Ulcer? Did I hear the word 'ulcer'?" Felicity Carridine reappeared. "Don't talk to me about ulcers."

"We weren't," said Sowerby.

"Mine's on fire at the moment, thanks to my totally crass American publishers. Do you know what they actually proposed?" At some length, they were told. Cassie had already learned that no conversation with Felicity Carridine ever veered far from Felicity Carridine; by now, everyone in the room already knew the novelist was leaving for Heathrow in the morning, on the first leg of a tour of the United States, in order to promote yet another best-selling Carridine novel, this time a three-generational saga of clogs-and-cobbles love in a northern mill town, with a smattering of lecherous ironmasters and illegitimate babies thrown in.

Casaubon rolled long-suffering eyes ceilingward behind Felicity Carridine's back, and sidled off. Sonia Wetherhead reappeared, looking damp.

"You sod," she said to the writer. "I've just bought a copy of *Life's Tempestuous Sea*."

"Really? How did you think it—"

"You utter bastard," Sonia said.

Felicity was indignant. "What on earth do—"

"You know perfectly well what I mean." Sonia looked around at them. She only needed a jug of custard poured over her, Cassie thought and she would have looked exactly like a poorly shaped plum duff. "You've stolen my plot."

"I beg your pardon."

"The plot of *Life's Tempestuous Sea* is my own life story." Sonia began wagging one of her fingers. "I distinctly remember sitting in the garden at that place where they run writing courses—where was it? Swansea or Swanwick or somewhere—and telling you all about it, and how I was going to turn it into fiction, write a best-seller myself. And you've used everything, all the little details, all that stuff about my father, *everything*, without so much as an acknowledgment."

"Just a minute," the writer blared. "Let's be quite accurate about this."

"That's exactly what I *am* being, you Judas."

"If I may say so, you're somewhat misremembering the facts. What really happened was that, knowing your background, I asked you a few questions about your childhood and before I could stop you, a whole flood of reminiscence came pouring out like a—"

"You dragged it out of me, you bitch, and then used it to—"

"All is grist to the novelist's mill."

"You utter *shit*," Sonia said. "I've a good mind to sue you."

"Try it, my dear." The novelist raised derisive eyebrows in a way which would have infuriated Cassie and certainly seemed to get right up Sonia's nose.

"Don't worry, I shall," she said. "And believe me, I'm not without a certain influence.

"I'm sure that within your own small circle you're very highly regarded."

"People listen to me, you know."

"I'm not surprised, my dear. If you're always this voluble, I doubt if they've very much choice."

"You *bastard* . . ."

On the other side of the room, Felix Ryland was being jovial with the antique shop woman. Near them, Ned Casaubon was chatting with Thomas Lambert, the journalist. Chatting, or quarreling? As Cassie looked on, Casaubon glanced furtively at his watch again. Lambert, a small stocky man in a Marylebone Cricket Club tie, stood forward on the balls of his feet and shoved his jaw toward the taller Casaubon. Ned shrugged indifferently as the other man said something fierce, then turned, his eye sweeping the room until it found Cassie, at which point he broke into a delighted smile and, speaking abruptly to his companion, began making his way toward her.

He was stopped by the publisher, a tiny vivacious woman with very red lipstick and black hair cut close to her head. She laid a hand on his arm and said something emphatic to him; he said something equally emphatic back and shook her off. Vicky Duggan was the one brimming over with enthusiasm for the game but was doomed never to grasp it since she lacked even the most basic card sense. Cassie watched her wander over to Colonel and Mrs. Plumpton and all three turn to look at Casaubon as he finally joined her again.

"Almost dinnertime," he said cheerfully. "We'll be able to choose from the wine list instead of having to drink this muck."

"My teeth feel as though they've been skinned," Cassie said.

"It's a special Albanian teeth-skinning recipe. Someone had the bright idea of bottling it, and *voilà*."

He pushed his handsome face closer to Cassie. "I hope you'll allow me to sit next to you."

Retailing all this to Detective Inspector Mantripp later, Cassie realized that there had been undercurrents and cross-tides rippling through the company of which she had not been aware at the time, though now they seemed to be obvious. It was clear that some of these people knew each other already, might even have come on the weekend together, or as a foursome. But what, for instance, had Colonel Plumpton been so excited about? Why had Sonia been so upset? What connection was there between Thomas Lambert and Casaubon—if that, indeed, was his real name. Or, for that matter, between Casaubon and the publishing lady? And who was the "ghastly woman" referred to by Felicity Carridine? At the time, Cassie had assumed it was a reference to Sonia Wetherhead; looking back, she realized it could not have been, since at that point the weaver was still being plied with black coffee by Kevin, the hotel manager.

"And you didn't notice any of this at the time?" Mantripp asked. He held his head on one side, already incredulous of the answer.

"Not consciously." Cassie shifted about uncomfortably. Since the dreadful discovery in the Macbeth Room and her subsequent interrogation by the police, her body seemed to have become even larger and more ungainly than usual.

"Frankly, it's a bit odd that you didn't. Everyone else we've interviewed seems to have taken on board the fact that Miss—um—Wetherhead quarreled with half the people on the room. Strange that you didn't."

"I did. Of course I did. But there were other things going on too which I didn't . . ." Cassie stared across at the door leading out into the hotel's entrance hall (*"much of the architectural detail dates back to the time of Good Queen Bess"*), in which could be seen uniforms, stretchers, the hideous bustle of sudden and violent death. She swallowed. "You don't think it's relevant to Sonia's death, do you?"

"Why should that surprise you?"

"Because . . . because people like us—middle-class people, I mean—don't usually offer violence to others, nor use violent means to achieve their ends."

"Bit of a class theoretician, are we, Miss Swann?" Mantripp addressed Sergeant Walsh again. "She wants to come down to the station sometime, doesn't she? She'd soon change her assumptions about the middle-class attitude to violence, wouldn't you say?"

The sergeant appeared not to have heard. Cassie swept on, needing words to prevent her thoughts taking over. "If we were boxing promoters, or ruthless businessmen, if the Plumptons had been connected with drugs or Sonia Wetherhead kept a bawdy house, then presumably violence would have been part of our lives and this sort of thing wouldn't be so entirely unexpected, as well as so—so . . ." She stopped talking, turning down the corners of her mouth in an attempt to stop them quivering.

"I take it you'd never met any of these people before this weekend?"

"Never. Except for one."

"Which one would that be?"

"Roy Sowerby was on another bridge course I conducted, sometime last year."

"I think we can forget Mr. Sowerby," Mantripp said. "His presence in the—um—Cymbeline Bar has been vouched for throughout the relevant period."

"That's a relief."

"Some of them obviously knew each other, though. Like Miss Wetherhead and the lady novelist. Or this fellow Casaubon." He fixed Cassie with an eye which was pretty close to beady. "From all accounts he seems to have known both Mr. Thomas Lambert and Miss Vicky Duggan—"

"That's the publisher, right?"

"—the publisher, as well as Miss Wetherhead. And from what you've told us, the Plumptons seem to have been previously acquainted with the solicitor—wotsisname . . ." He snapped his fingers at Sergeant Walsh.

"Joseph Newsome, sir. Of Newsome, Craig, in Swindon."

"I don't know for sure about that," Cassie said. "It just looked like it. I mean, the Colonel had put his arm round Mrs. Newsome, and he wasn't the sort of man who'd do that to someone he didn't know."

"Not even if he was drunk?"

"He was *not* drunk."

She could hear the aggressive note in her voice and thought how easily these two men, weighed down with the cynicism of their profession, had managed to turn an innocent witness like herself into someone potentially culpable for what had happened. Although she had had absolutely nothing to do with it, she nonetheless felt in some way to blame for the deaths. It was not an original feeling, but one which she knew the police, society's moral watchdogs and conscience keepers, were prone to rousing in the average citizen.

"What time did you leave the party?" Walsh asked.

"I don't know. Eleven o'clock. Half past, something like that. I didn't take a lot of notice of the time."

"Did you leave alone?"

"Uh . . . no, as it happens."

"Might one inquire who you were with?"

"The wine merchant. Ned Casaubon."

"Ah."

"We both decided to step outside for a breath of air."

"And did you both go your separate ways, after this breath of air you'd stepped outside for?" Mantripp asked.

"Yes. I'm not much of a night owl." As she said it, Cassie wondered what other kind of owl there might be. A day owl? Since owls were nocturnal by nature, to speak of a night owl was surely tautological.

"And you noticed nothing odd, no cars parked any-where nearby? No figures lurking?"

"Nothing."

Mantripp got up and stretched. His hair, like a som-nolent guinea pig, stirred. "I think that's all, Miss Swann. For now."

In the entrance hall, luggage at their feet, the bridge players were showing an embarrassing degree of dis-gruntlement at the curtailing of their weekend. When Ned Casaubon suggested they get up a collection toward wreaths for the three departed, there was a certain amount of restlessness. Mrs. Newsome, the solicitor's wife, put it bluntly. "I can't see why we should contribute toward a floral tribute—that's the hotel's responsibility, in my opinion, and frankly, I think we should get our money back."

There was a generalized nodding. "After all, they haven't honored their contract with us," Newsome said, in lawyerly fashion. "I fail to see why we should pay."

"Come on," Cassie said. "It's hardly the owner's fault if some madman murders Sonia Wetherhead."

"At the very least, he might have offered us an alternative weekend," said Vicky Duggan, the publisher.

"At a discount," added the antiques woman from Gloucester.

Felix Ryland, tweedy and harassed, appeared. He clapped his hands for attention. "The management apologizes for the disruption," he said loudly, making it sound as though Kevin was too chicken to come out of his office and face them. "Naturally not something one expects to occur. However, we have put our heads together and come up with an offer which may go some way toward ameliorating the situation. Our next Bridge Weekend, under the auspices of the renowned tutor Clyde Ashburn, will be taking place next month, four weeks from now, and we are delighted to offer places on this at a substantially reduced fee to any of you who might wish to take us up on what I'm sure you will agree is a generous invitation."

There were more mutterings. Despite their complaints, most people apparently did not wish to return to a place where death had so suddenly intruded. In the end, Cassie thought, some of them would accept. She wished Clyde Ashburn joy of them.

All in all, it was not one of her more successful weekends.

ALL three of them were dead. Cassie sensed they had given up even before she had brushed aside the exuberant strands of ivy which hung over the cottage porch, inserted the big key which opened the back door and found them. She told herself it wasn't her fault. She'd given them food and water before she left. She'd said an encouraging word or two. But once inside the kitchen, she saw that dead they now indisputably were.

She filled the kettle from the tap and put it on the

ancient Aga. While it boiled she picked up the three
corpses and took them outside to the compost heap.
There was no point denying that as far as houseplants
went, she was the Angel of Death. Vegetables she could
cope with. She was good at those. In the untidy kitchen
garden behind the cottage she raised tomatoes and
courgettes, lettuce, radishes, even *haricots jaunes*, from
seeds she had brought back with her last year from
France. But present her with a philodendron and it gave
up almost without a sigh. Offer her an African violet
(and people did so all the time) and it withered almost
before she'd had time to unwrap it.

She laid the three spider plants to rest among the rot-
ting grapefruit halves, old tea leaves and carrot scrap-
ings. The grapefruit diet hadn't been much bloody
good, she thought morosely, digging them in with a garden fork. By sticking strenuously to grapefruit for a
solid week, she'd managed to gain three pounds and a
nasty rash on the inside of her arms which the doctor
said was an allergic reaction to citric acid.

She looked at the garden burgeoning all around her.
A riot of color, she thought. At least, it would be when
summer came. For the moment it wasn't so much a riot
as a peaceful demonstration. Chocolate-brown rows of
rich earth stretched in parallel lines between where she
stood and the greenhouse; the asparagus bed, left fallow
last year, now lay heaped and waiting to produce this
year's crop; the patch set aside for strawberries had
been composted and fertilized, ready for spring. The
apple trees, the pears, the greengage, which had not yet
produced fruit but might this year: the potential fecun-
dity of it both pleased and excited her. Looking at the

poor spider plants, their etiolated leaves dragging like unbrushed hair over the edge of the compost heap's wooden side, she wondered if she ought to declare the cottage a houseplant-free zone.

Walking back to the kitchen, she reflected that it was this very inability to sustain life in *Aphelandra* and *Dieffenbachia*, poinsettia and Busy Lizzie, which had precipitated her decision to leave teaching. A biology mistress who couldn't even keep a nephrolepis going did not deserve the name. Besides, bridge beckoned, the tantalizing combination of mathematical probability and pure gamble, skill and chance. Nothing—almost nothing—measured up to the thrill she got each time she picked up a new hand of cards; nothing stimulated like a finesse which had worked or holding a low card which was nonetheless a winner.

Whereas biology . . . two years of it had been enough for her to realize that she was not cut out for it, though it was the thought of never having to dissect another frog, never again smelling formaldehyde on her fingers as she lifted some choice forkful of food to her lips, which had finally led to her setting herself up as a bridge professional.

In the six years since then, she had managed to make a reasonably decent living—helped, of course, by being loaned the cottage. Her chief thought on hearing her godfather's suggestion that she caretake it for him, since he planned to remove to France, had been that she would be able to get away from the flat she shared with Primula and Hyacinth. No more hanging up her moderately sized knickers alongside their minute scraps of panties; no more living off kiwifruit because Primula had read somewhere that there was more nourishment in one slice than in the entire vitamin counter at Boots; no more surreptitious smugglings in of pizza because Hyacinth was into nouvelle cuisine and thought that three green beans and a square inch of grilled cod was enough to keep the average biology teacher going.

Back in the cottage, she could hear the telephone bleeping.

Ducking under the ivy, she went into the kitchen and picked up the receiver. If it was one of her cousins, she was prepared to lie about how her weight was, an all too frequent question in their telephonic conversations.

"Cassie!" Primula screamed. "They let you go!"

"Who did?"

"The police! We heard it on the news. Fancy you being involved in those dreadful murders."

"Only insofar as I discovered the bodies."

Primula gave a little shriek. "Don't! I know I would have died right there on the spot if it had been me."

"That wouldn't have been very helpful, would it? Anyway, only one of them was murdered. The other two died of natural causes."

"Oh, Cassie. You're so thrillingly brave. Derek was just saying so."

"Who was?"

"You know perfectly well who Derek is." Even Primula's normally sweet—oversweet, in Cassie's opinion—voice held a tiny edge.

"Of course I do," Cassie said heartily. Primula's husband was a small bearded creature who ran the Yorkshire junior school of which he was headmaster as though it were a military academy. "Thrillingly brave, eh? Is that really what he said?" She doubted it. She and Derek were not exactly soul mates.

"His precise words. Weren't they, Derek?" In the background, a male voice grunted something. "But what did they look like, Cass?" said Primula. "I mean, was there all blood and stuff? Did they just look ordinary? You didn't have to give them the kiss of life or anything, did you?"

"Someone had already given them the kiss of death, Primula."

"But what did they *look* like, sitting there all ready to play bridge?"

"Dead."

"Ca-ass," wheedled Primula. "Tell me."

"You don't really want to know," Cassie said. Any more than she really wanted to tell.

"No. I suppose I don't," said Primula doubtfully.

"Look, Prim, I've been trying to forget all about it but you've brought it all back. If you don't mind, I'm going to go and be sick."

"Sorry, darling. How horribly thoughtless of me to—"

Cassie made some nasty gagging noises and put down the receiver. She smiled. It was only rarely that she had Primula or her sisters at a disadvantage.

She went through into the little sitting room, which smelled of wood smoke and oranges and damp. At the sound of her step, the rubber plant in the hall, a present from cousin Hyacinth, dropped another dead leaf onto the floor. Was it deliberate, a kind of vegetative snook-cocking? Although the central heating was adequate, she put a match to the fire she had laid before setting off for the Bridge Weekend, then sat drinking Red

Zinger and munching gloomily on a carrot. She was going to a wedding next week: she had to lose some weight if she wasn't to see her three cousins exchanging looks, blue eyes glancing off her hips and bust, their minute little short-skirted suits fitted neatly over their nonexistent boobs and hips. God, she hated carrots. Unless they'd been cooked in a very small amount of water, no more than a spoonful to a pound or so, then gently seethed in butter and garlic with a little *crème fraîche* added at the very last moment. Or *carottes Vichy*. She lay back in her big chair and closed her eyes, contemplating the delights of *carottes Vichy*.

But Colonel Plumpton kept intruding. The red face, the popping eyes, the mustache which remained authoritative even in death. What the hell had happened in that room? And who could have wanted to kill Sonia Wetherhead so badly that they were prepared to risk being seen? After all, he could not have counted on the Plumptons to keel over before raising the alarm.

Besides, if bumping the poor woman off was of such overwhelming importance, why not do it when she was alone, in the privacy of her Tudor bedde-chamber? Why do it in the middle of the morning, when the hotel guests were likely to be up and about? An obvious answer came to mind: possibly Sonia had not spent her last night alone, and had thus not been available for murdering.

Putting aside the question of whom she might have spent it with, Cassie realized that the murderer would—supposing him to be one of the hotel guests—have had access to the list of bridge fours she had posted up the night before: he would therefore certainly have known where Sonia would be at a given time the following day. Except that the given time was eleven o'clock, whereas the time narrowed down by the police was sometime between ten-thirty and eleven o'clock; Sonia could have been anywhere. In any case, that was hardly the most inconspicuous moment at which to commit murder.

Or was it?

When you thought about it, on that particular Sunday, the murderer could hardly have chosen a better time. Among the twentieth-century comforts provided by the hotel to blend in with the sixteenth-century discomforts was an indoor swimming pool garnished with palms and other Elizabethan foliage. If the murderer was one of the hotel's guests, he—or she—would have been aware that at eleven o'clock the hotel was offering a mead-tasting session around the pool, which most of the other guests would be attending, while those who were there for the Bridge Weekend would probably have made up their fours already and be playing. Cassie had arranged the tables herself, insisting that the couples from Luton and Exeter split up and play with someone else; more or less forcibly prizing the lady publisher away from Thomas Lambert (who had seemed grateful) and, rather spitefully, perhaps, partnering Ned Casaubon with Mrs. Newsome, the solicitor's wife, whose tendency to forget what was trumps had already caused words to be spoken by both Roy Sowerby and her own husband. The ones from the gardening expert had been sardonic, in keeping with his general demeanor, the ones from her husband were harsh and the cause of a red flush rising in her cheeks.

"What happened to the milk of human kindness?"

Cassie said to Ned, when he sought her out to complain.

"The milkman forgot to deliver," he said. "And in any case, I'm damned if I'm going to waste it on a woman who trumps a trick I've already taken with a perfectly good spade."

"You were a beginner once."

"This woman's going to be a beginner for the rest of her life," he said bitterly.

Beside Cassie now, an asparagus plant wept tiny yellowed leaves onto her arm. A leguminous protest? A cry for help? Absently she brushed them off. As far as the murderer was concerned, it wasn't really that much of a gamble after all. No more than a good bridge player would have been perfectly prepared to take—though there was no reason to suppose that the murderer was necessarily one of the Bridge Weekend lot. There wouldn't have been chambermaids to worry about: the Macbeth Room was on the ground floor of the hotel. The whereabouts of the other guests would have been known. All the killer had to do was to nip through the door, locate Sonia's head (not a difficult task), smash the obelisk down onto it, and nip out again. He (or she) must have known that the Plumptons would also be there; since he (or she) could hardly have expected them both to die on the spot, he must have been disguised in some way (or she, supposing the killer was female).

But how? An IRA-type balaclava? It would have been easy enough to whip on and off again. A Groucho Marx-type combination mustache, false nose and glasses? Ditto. It had to be something like that, something easily removed and concealed about the person so that he could saunter quickly on and join whatever group he (or she—no, assume for the moment it was a man) was supposed to be with.

But why kill Sonia Wetherhead in the first place? Admittedly anyone who'd had to partner her in a bridge game was likely to end up feeling murderous, especially if they'd just gone down four hundred points, as had happened on Saturday to Thomas Lambert, the journalist, when Sonia herself, responding to Lambert's tentative bid of one Spade, had raised him to six when she only held two small Spades in her own hand, leaving him to play—and fail to make—a little slam.

There was, however, a long gap between feeling murderous and actually doing something about it. The woman was irritating, no question about that. But irritation was one of those litmus papers which required a long, slow fuse to ignite; only long-term irritation such as might build up between a married couple could lead to the fatal blade, the blood, the smell, the—

Cassie hastily sipped more of her Red Zinger.

But Sonia wasn't married. Not according to the magazine article Cassie had read. As it happened, she'd picked up a copy before leaving; she intended to read it again and see if it offered any further clues.

Meantime, there was Ned Casaubon. He had clearly enjoyed (if that wasn't overstating the case) some kind of relationship with Sonia in the past. Cassie wished now she had questioned him more closely about it. She also wished she hadn't rather fancied him, despite the crudeness of his chat-up technique. For a moment she tried again to envisage the rakish Ned manacled to a wall, wincing as Sonia's lash caught his naked flesh. It was an image which refused to materialize. And anyway, in spite of the whole ludicrous nature of the thing, and even supposing it was true, one member of the partnership talking publicly about it was not a sufficient motive for murder. And she knew, from reading detective novels, that motive is all. Find your motive and you've found your murderer.

The telephone chirruped again on the windowsill.

"Cassandra Swann," she said firmly into the receiver.

It was Casaubon. Before she could stop herself she said, "Do you *really* like being whipped?"

There was a taken-aback pause. Then he said, "Why do you want to know?"

"I don't really," she said. "I was just wondering if you could have killed Sonia Wetherhead to stop her telling people about your kinky sexual preferences."

"Do I look like a man who'd get pleasure from allowing a lady like poor old Sonia to lay about her with a whip? Or lay about me, for that matter?"

"I don't know what that kind of a man looks like."

"The woman's a fantasist, always was."

"You knew her well, then?"

"Reasonably. As it happens, her mother was my mother's best friend. I've known Sonia most of my life."

"When did you start sleeping with her?"

"Look. I'm not about to discuss such matters over the phone. What I rang up to say was that I shall be coming up your way soon and wondered if we could meet."

"How do you know which way mine is?" Cassie asked.

"I inquired at the hotel desk before I left."

"They aren't supposed to hand out addresses."

"I'll admit they were none too keen to give it to me. In fact, I had to lie to a certain extent, I'm afraid." There was no trace of apology in his voice.

"To how far an extent?"

He hesitated. "I think they may have got the impression that you spent the night in my room."

"*What?*"

"And left behind a pair of valuable earrings which I really had to return to you."

"For heaven's sake," Cassie said angrily. "Do you realize that you're damaging my professional reputation? How do you think I can go back there in May, which I'm supposed to be doing, if they think I'm the kind of person who leaps into bed with any Tom, Dick or Harry that asks?"

"What about any Ned?"

"For one thing, you didn't ask. And for another, I wouldn't have done if you had."

"Listen," he said. His voice was serious now. "I'd like to talk to you about Sonia. There are things about that whole business which really bother me."

"You should be talking to the police. Or," she added, "to your wife."

"Should I?" She could imagine his dark eyebrows rising, the twist of his mouth as he relished her unspoken question about his marital state. "But I'd much rather talk to you first, before I go to the police. You've got what my father used to call a bottom of good sense."

A bottom of—was he getting at her in some way? Implying that she was too fat, making snide comments about the size of her rear end? "Thank you very much," she said coldly.

"You'll allow me to take you out to dinner, I hope."

"I *think* I look forward to that," she said.

As she put down the phone, she was already wondering whether to cook for him at home or lead him toward the best restaurant in the area, choose the most expensive menu money could buy and then let him pay. The Wheatsheaf, on the road to Buckingham, cost an absolute fortune, though they produced a duck which was one of the most delicious . . . She wrenched herself away from thoughts of duck. If she cooked the meal herself, it would be an excuse to make *coquilles St.-Jacques*, using that fantastically simple recipe she had picked up in France last summer. And she could start with *pâté au port*. Totally delectable. On the other hand, once his feet were under her table, he might be difficult to dislodge . . .

She was in the bath when the telephone burped yet again. Cursing, she heaved herself out onto the bath mat, walked through into her bedroom, and picked up the receiver.

"Mantripp here, Miss—um—Swann."

Mantripp? "I don't think I know anyone by that—"

He ignored her. "Just thought you'd like to know you were right."

Ah yes: Mantripp was the policeman. The belligerent detective inspector. "In what sense?" she asked.

"In what sense? Dear me." He spoke to someone in the room with him. "Says, in what sense? Can you credit it?" The someone obviously could, since there was no audible response. "About the *murder*, Miss—um—Swann."

His tone was starting to get to Cassie. "You mean I guessed correctly?" she trilled. "Sonia Wetherhead wasn't just fooling around: she really was dead?"

"I mean, you were right about it being simultaneous heart attacks which killed the other two victims. Colonel and Mrs.—um—Plumpton."

Cassie waited.

"Yes," Mantripp went on weightily. "According to the autopsy, the cause of death in both cases appears to have been acute heart failure, brought on no doubt by the sight of the murder or the murderer—or both."

"Autopsy? Why was that necessary? I mean, surely nobody believes the Plumptons were murdered too, do they?!"

"It's standard procedure in cases of violent death to PM anyone else found at the scene." He paused, squeezing all the drama available from the moment. "What do you say to that, Miss Swann?"

"What *can* I say?" It was difficult to think of any suitable response. "Sounds a bit of a coincidence to me."

It seemed bizarre to be standing there, snowy-bosomed, marble-thighed, dripping water onto the carpet, while below her in the garden late blackbirds hovered over the rows where beans and courgettes, even leeks, would eventually ripen, and at the same time calmly to be discussing the deaths of three people with whom, for a short time, she had been fairly closely connected. She thought of the sonorous way her Uncle Samuel, father of her three cousins, delivered his sermons from the pulpit, rounded syllables rolling down the aisle of his Norman church. *The grass withereth, the flower fadeth* . . . At the end of the garden a winter tangle of lilac bushes stood leafless, and beyond them the bare hills, the darkening sky.

"They were both elderly and a little frail," Mantripp

said pugnaciously. "The Colonel wasn't in the best of health and his wife was on prescriptive medication. According to the police surgeon, the sight of a woman being violently murdered in front of them was undoubtedly enough to cause the kind of agitation which leads to the heart giving out."

"I see."

"I'll speak to you again," said Mantripp.

"Just why did you speak to me in the first place?" asked Cassie. "Surely it's not standard procedure to keep in touch with all those involved in a case like this."

"Not *all*, no. Take care." And Mantripp put the telephone down before she could ask what exactly he meant.

Getting back into the bath and running more hot water, she wondered why he should have telephoned to give her the information. It seemed odd that tiny, sparrowlike Mrs. Plumpton should have succumbed when she was so assiduous about taking her pills, though much less odd that the Colonel should, given his complexion, given the mere fact that he *was* a colonel. In detective novels it was always the red-faced ex-Army bloke who had the heart attack. But hang around.

Cass straightened up, sloshing water onto the bare boards of the bathroom, which she had sanded and then varnished herself, after first decorating them with a stenciled design of vine leaves and fruit plus a tendril here and there for artistic effect.

Hang around. Was it possible that DI Mantripp suspected *her* of murdering Sonia? That he had telephoned in the hope of forcing a confession out of her? Pitilessly piling on the pressure until she broke down and blurted out the details of her hideous crime?

That was ridiculous. She hadn't even been there when the murder took place. She'd been—luckily, as it now turned out—locked in her bedroom. A sudden thought seized her. The damp hair on her neck prickled with horror. If she had been there at the right time, she would almost inevitably have been sitting in the chair Sonia Wetherhead must have been occupying when the murderer struck. Back to the door, just in front of the draft-excluding velvet curtain. West's seat, with Colonel Plumpton opposite her at East, and Mrs. Plumpton occupying the South seat. West was where she always sat when conducting a lesson, and she recalled now that even at the moment of discovery she had been aware of pique, a feeling that it was typical of Sonia, sprawled unbeautifully on the floor, to have taken her place. Could it possibly be—was it conceivable that the intended victim had not been Sonia but herself? Was that why DI Mantripp had told her to take care?

The water seemed suddenly chill. She got hastily out of the bath.

It couldn't be. Who would want to kill her? For heaven's sake, she hadn't done anything. Her only crime, if crime it could be called, was that of ingratitude. She freely admitted that she harbored a certain amount of resentment against her cousins for being so slim, and against Uncle Samuel and Aunt Polly for not being her own parents. Plus the fact that they had produced three minuscule daughters when his sister Sarah, her mother, had been responsible for her. But it was hardly a killing matter.

As for her professional life, she was on good terms with most of her colleagues in the bridge world—not most, she amended hastily: *all*. Financially, the only people who stood to gain from her demise were Rose's eldest son, who was to have the cottage, and Hyacinth's daughter, to whom she'd left her jewelry. Since Richard was in the States, and Georgina had not yet started to walk, it seemed unlikely that either of them could have been creeping about the well-carpeted corridors of the hotel (*"attractive interior decor carefully chosen to enhance the historic nature of the building"*) in the hope of bashing Aunt Cassie about the head and claiming their inheritance.

Another odd thing: although she didn't know much about heart attacks—absolutely nothing, to be precise—it seemed amazingly convenient that two of them should have taken lethal effect at exactly the same time as the stabbing. She went downstairs, still wrapped in a towel, and opened the front door of the cottage. It was cold outside. Not freezing, but chilly enough to make her breath plume out in front of her. If she was quick . . . she ran barefooted across the thick cold grass to her car, parked in front of the wooden lean-to attached to the side of the house. In the boot, her bag stood next to the cartons of bridge equipment she always took with her on these weekends: she'd sold nearly two hundred quid's worth at Broughton Manor Hotel, which was useful extra income on top of her fee. She lifted out the bag and ran with it back into the sitting room, slamming the door shut behind her and hoping her toes wouldn't turn black and drop off with cold.

The magazine with the article about Sonia Wetherhead was lying beneath her underwear. She decided to get dressed before she read it, then pour a slug of something warming into a mug—whiskey with a dash of ginger wine was what she fancied, but the calorific content was too high to be acceptable, not with this darned wedding coming up. Unable to face more Red Zinger, she would make do with Earl Grey—was there such a thing as a slug of tea?—and then go through the article again, see if there was anything in it which could be helpful, provide a lead.

There wasn't. Not that Cassie could see. Loom this, blah that, vegetable dyes, incorporation of natural elements such as leaves and grasses, unique ability, growing international reputation, blah, blah. Nothing about the way Sonia overbid every time she picked up a hand of cards. Nothing about whether her fellow weavers liked or loathed her, her lovers abused or adored her, whether she tended toward drink or drugs or religion.

There was a photograph of Sonia seated at a giant loom, surrounded by hanks of different-colored wools suspended from rods or stacked on shelves. There was another of her, huge in a woven skirt, standing outside the door of her home, described by the magazine as "a former Methodist chapel now converted into her studio, in the tiny Oxfordshire village of Moreton Lacey." No mention of husbands or of children.

She read on:

In 1990, in the face of stiff international competition, she was offered the contract to design a series of tapestries for the Lucille Hagerty Hall, a new exhibition hall built in Southern California by Dr. James L. Hagerty as a memorial to his wife. Using natural products, she created an exciting all-round concept based on the animal and vegetable kingdoms which made a profound statement about the impact of man's reckless destruction of the earth's resources on the vanishing world about us. The panel entitled "The Sea," with its motif of inter-linked curvilinear forms suggestive both of the ocean itself and of the marine life which inhabits it, won a prize at Venice the following year . . .

It looked as though Sonia Wetherhead was something of a loss to the weaving world.

Turning back for another look at the photograph, she noticed the byline: the article had been written by Thomas Lambert. She frowned. Was the fact significant or was it totally irrelevant? From her current perspective, it was impossible to say.

About to pour herself another cup of tea, Cassie decided not to. Milkless tea was one of those tortures to which she subjected herself from time to time and then despised herself for lack of self-confidence. Why didn't she just accept that she and her cousins were built from different blueprints? Perhaps she should try therapy. Or take a new lover. Or, at any rate, *a* lover. For the moment, she would at least have the whiskey she wanted, instead of the tea she did not. She'd save 240 calories by leaving out the ginger wine. Feeling virtuous, she poured a generous measure from the Laphroaig bottle into a glass.

Then she reviewed once more that bridge table surrounded by death. Obviously, they had decided that even though they were only three, they could have a dummy run, an exercise game. Perhaps it was one of several they had played. It was one of her teaching maxims: "The more you play, the more you can say," meaning that bidding was all about telling your partner what you held in your own hand.

Thinking back, it was clear that they had already played three rounds, since three tricks lay on the table. But why should the three of them have then laid down their hands, face up? Had someone come in, engaged them in conversation, turned to leave, and at the last moment seized one of the obelisks on the overmantel and approached Sonia, who, realizing his intent, had risen from her seat, only to fall beneath the savage blows? In that case, why had the Plumptons not raised the alarm? And why choose to kill someone in full view of two witnesses?

Perhaps the murderer had been aware that the two Plumptons would have been bound to get to the Macbeth Room early, in order to run over their cheating codes. She had already worked out that when Mrs. Plumpton wanted a Diamond lead, she would indicate the fact to her husband with a little discreet stroking of the engagement ring on her left hand. Just as he asked for Hearts by a judicious amount of searching in his breast pocket for matches with which to relight the pipe he was rarely without, either lit or unlit. As well as such obvious signals, the Colonel's habit of clutching his head indicated a desire for a Club to be led, and if either of them tapped their teeth with their cards, it meant a good show of Spades. That there were other, more complicated messages being passed between the couple she had absolutely no doubt.

Sonia must also have arrived early: the Plumptons wouldn't have liked that. For a moment Cassie contemplated a scenario in which Mrs. P., balked of rehearsal time with her husband, had grabbed the alabaster obelisk and whacked Sonia on the head, then calmly gone on practicing until guilt caused her heart to give out, the sight of her expiry giving her husband, too, his quietus.

But that was ridiculous. None of it made any sense. Cassie felt suddenly rather sorry for Detective Inspector Mantripp.

ALL morning the telephone rang. The calls that were not from journalists asking for her opinion on everything from the latest budget proposals to astrology were from managers of upmarket hotels pointing out that in view of the fact that Cassie was booked to run weekends at their establishments in the future, they hoped there would not be any recurrence of the—um—unfortunate incident at the Broughton Manor Hotel. Protest as she might that she herself had not yet been arraigned on a murder charge, and in any case was not in a position to prevent such an event as murder, should it occur, none of them seemed really to be listening. Some of them mentioned having read about the deaths in the newspapers. Several simply canceled bridge weekends or evenings which had previously been booked. They gave no explanation. They didn't need to.

The only thing she could think of to do which eased her anger and—yes—fear at the thought that she might lose her livelihood, was to extract a carton of Häagen-Dazs frozen yogurt from the freezer and eat some of it. Quite a lot of it. At least it was fat-free, she told herself. What the *hell* was she going to do? And why should all those hotel managers have been calling her in the first place?

Someone knocked at the front door while she was measuring her wrists. According to the tape measure, they were exactly the same size as they had been three weeks ago when she had last checked them out, although she was positive they'd lost weight since then. She walked through the sitting room and opened the door. The man standing outside it was holding a lot of flowers. He grinned at her.

"Remember me?"

Cassie shuddered theatrically. "It would be impossible to forget you, Mr. Quartermain."

"Please. I told you before. Call me Charlie." He pushed the flowers in her direction.

She looked at them coldly. "What are these?"

"Uh . . . duh," he said. He looked down at them, clutching his forehead as though he had difficulty thinking. "Look like four dozen red roses to me, luv."

"I can see that." Cassie could almost taste the acid in her voice. "Why are you giving them to me?"

"Invite me in and I'll tell you."

"I can't really see why I should, but since you're here..." She turned and led the way into the sitting room.

Charlie Quartermain followed her. He was a big man of about forty. Were she not overly sensitive to the word, Cassie might even have called him fat. Certainly he was circumferentially challenged. He had breezed into one of her bridge evening classes last autumn and made no secret of his admiration of her. The first time he had approached her after the class was over and invited her for a drink, she had accepted because she could think of no polite way to refuse. After that, he simply assumed that the two of them would go off together to the pub. So did everyone else in the class, so much so that she wondered whether he had threatened to duff them up if they did not leave the two of them alone. It would have been very much in character.

What was not in character was her own inability to turn him down. There seemed to be no way to pierce a self-confidence which seemed as massive as his physique. He was a mason, he had told her. Not one of those gits with funny handshakes and an apron, but a master craftsman, a man who dressed stone, restored cathedrals, worked on such arcana as gargoyles and fan vaulting, tympana and capitals.

"Nice place," he said now, looking around the room. His voice was impressively bass; his enormous frame blocked out the light. "Like yer Kauffmanns."

"What?" Cassie despised herself for finding it incredible that a man who looked and sounded like Charlie

Quartermain should recognize an Angelica Kauffmann plate when he saw it.

"Yer plates, luv." He picked one up in his big blunt fingers while she inwardly winced. "You did know they was Kauffmanns, didn't you?"

"Of course I did. They were my mother's."

"I'll bet she's a good-looking bint."

"What?"

"Your mum. I'll bet she's a stunner. Have to be, if she's anything like you."

Cassie gritted her teeth. "Look, Mr. Quartermain—"

"Charlie."

"—why exactly did you come here?"

"Read about you in the paper. And heard about it on the radio."

"*Radio*? What radio?"

"One of those comic news quiz programs where a lot of middle-class ponces take the piss," Quartermain said.

"Oh God . . ."

"Not on, really, is it? So I came to apologize, didn't I?"

"What for?"

"I was supposed to have been at that fancy Bridge Weekend of yours—the one where everyone snuffed it. Signed up and everything, I was. Only at the last minute, see, I was called over to Cologne. Only had time to pack my Y-fronts and I was off."

Snuffed it. Honestly. Angrily, Cassie dumped the roses into a glass vase and filled it to overflowing from the kitchen tap.

"Otherwise I'd have sorted that journalist out for you." Charlie looked at her expression. "I'm sorry, luv," he said. "I really am." He came over to her, close enough so she could smell garlic on his breath. His teeth were those of a deprived childhood: uneven, stained, much filled. "I don't suppose it was all that funny, was it, walking in on those old dears."

"No," she said. "It wasn't funny at all."

"Can't stop thinking about it, I bet."

She nodded, furious with herself as tears tingled behind her eyes.

He took her hand. "It'll pass, luv. Promise you. It's only natural to be upset by something like that but it'll go."

Cassie thought it extraordinary that a man like Quartermain should be the only person who had realized that she might have found the whole business a bit traumatic. *Bloody* traumatic, as a matter of fact. Her chin shook. She sat down in one of the armchairs by the hearth and Quartermain promptly sat down in the other.

"Got the kettle on, have you, luv?" he asked.

"No."

"Good. Then we can have something stronger." He felt in the pocket of the cracked old Barbour jacket he was wearing and brought out a bottle of Mumm's.

"I'm actually quite busy with—"

"Got any glasses?"

"You can't be serious," Cassie protested. "It's only half past eleven and I'm in the middle of—"

"Glasses, darlin'. Where d'you keep 'em?"

Cassie jerked open the cupboard built into one side of the fireplace and snatched out two tall glasses. "Look, Mr.—Charlie: I don't like drinking so early in the day. And I'm in the middle of some fairly important work. I'll have one glass of this stuff with you and then you really will have to go. It's extremely kind of you to drop by and apologize for you absence: as it happened, the weekend worked just as well with fifteen as with sixteen, so no harm was done. At least, until . . . And I'm very grateful for the flowers but there was absolutely no need for you to—"

"Face like an angel," he said softly.

"Sorry?"

"You've got a face just like an angel."

"An *angel*?"

"Yeah. You must have been told that before." As he spoke, he was deftly maneuvering the cork out of the bottle.

An angel? She considered the notion, liking it. She suddenly remembered some paradoxical question Uncle Samuel was fond of discussing: how many angels could dance on the head of a pin? It wasn't something she had considered closely until now. Did angels actually dance? And if so, how—or what? The lambada? The fox-trot? The idea of fox-trotting cherubim and seraphim was almost a contradiction in terms. It was probably more a question of bending and swaying, with a bit of continual praise-chanting thrown in for good measure. "Well, no, not exactly," she said.

"You must know some funny men," said Charlie. "First thing that struck me when I walked into that class-room last September." A wisp of effervescence curled up from the bottle as the cork was eased efficiently out of the neck. He poured champagne into the glasses and handed her one. "Here's to the two of us."

"I presume you mean separately."

"Whichever way you fancy, luv."

Cassie looked ostentatiously at her watch as she tried

to remember the exact calorific count in champagne. It wasn't something she drank that often; it wasn't something she even liked that much.

"Just as well I wasn't there this weekend, if you ask me," Charlie said. "I'm always getting blamed for something, but at least I can't be accused of sticking a knife in poor old Sonia's back."

"You sound as if you knew her."

"Yeah. That's really why I cried off the weekend."

"I thought you said you were called to Cologne."

"I was, but not on the Friday, more like the Sunday. It was hearing from someone that Sonia was going to be around stopped me from going. I didn't want her making scenes all over the place."

"As it happens, she did make one or two."

"Only two? Couldn't hold her booze, that was Sonia's trouble. But not a bad old stick, apart from that. Beats me why anyone should want to do her in."

"How did you happen to know her?" Cassie had already wondered at the smallness of a world where Ned Casaubon's mother should have been the best friend of Sonia's mother, and Thomas Lambert should have written an article about her. In country circles, however, everyone knew everyone else—or knew someone who did. Now it appeared that Charlie Quartermain had also been acquainted with her. Irrelevantly, she wondered whether he'd slept with her? If so, they'd have needed a reinforced bed.

"We worked on something together," Charlie said. "One of those arty-farty projects that do-gooders are always dreaming up. It was her got me into playing bridge. She said it would sharpen my wits."

"Did she indeed?"

He laughed. "Yer. I said, listen, darlin', take more than a pack of cards to put a point on *my* wits, but she said that after you reached forty, yer brain cells had to be stimulated all the time or you'd end up a cabbage. Always hated cabbage, so in the end I went along with it, took up the bridge." Charlie said this in between long gasping drafts of champagne. He wiped his mouth on the back of his hand and said, "Want some more?"

"No, thanks. I've got—"

"Come on," he urged. "Do you good." He poured vigorously, gouts of champagne completely missing Cassie's glass and spattering her knees.

"Have you got any idea why anyone would want to kill Sonia?" Cassie brushed ostentatiously at her skirt. "I mean, she was irritating, no question. But I can't imagine her inspiring sufficient hatred for someone to risk being caught with a bloodied obelisk in his hand."

"Obelisk? Do you mean like they have in Egypt?"

"Except this one was made of alabaster."

"Sure it was Sonia he was after?" he inquired.

Cassie stared at him. Was it her imagination or had he asked the question in a peculiarly sinister tone? After a moment, she said, "If not her, who then?"

She felt again the horror of that moment, opening the door of the Macbeth Room, the two bodies at the table, Sonia's sprawled bulk, the bright poncho with its soaking of scarlet blood. Was it really Cassandra Swann who was the intended victim? Had the murderer made a terrible mistake? And if so, would he (she?) try to rectify that mistake by coming after her again?

"Mr. or Mrs. P.," Quartermain said, shrugging. "He

was an Army man, she'd been a social worker, according to the papers. With jobs like that, they both had plenty of chances of getting up people's noses."

"But the police don't seem to think there was anything suspicious about *their* deaths."

He laughed, holding out one big hand. She could see a curved black line of dirt under each nail. "Bet I could kill you without anyone catching on it was murder," he said.

A thought struck Cassie like a blow: perhaps the murderer was here, in this room. What, after all, did she really know about Quartermain? It was perfectly possible that he was the murderer, that all that stuff about Cologne was so much bullshit and he had come here with the express purpose of eliminating her before she could give vital evidence to the police.

She stood up. "I think you'd better go now," she said, edging toward the door, and to her annoyance, felt her voice shake.

He grinned up at her from the big armchair. "Gawd," he said. "Figure like Venus."

"*What?*"

"Face like an angel and a figure like Venus."

"Thank you. Now will you please—"

The telephone cheeped in the kitchen. She put her glass down on the table and ran toward it.

"Felix Ryland here," she heard, putting the receiver to her ear.

"Have they found whoever was responsible for killing Sonia Wetherhead?" she asked eagerly.

"Afraid not. Not sure they ever will. That police inspector johnny was telling me it seems to be one of those completely motiveless murders. Baffling, really."

"Yes."

"What I'm ringing up about, Miss Swann, is to see if there's any chance of you doing us the most enormous favor. We'd see that you were amply recompensed for your trouble, of course." He waited. So did Cassie.

After a moment he said, "Well, what do you think? Perhaps you need more time to consider it. But I would ask you to get back to us as soon as possible, so that we'd have a chance to notify the punters."

Had she missed some vital question? "I'm not exactly sure what you want me to do." Cassie wished she hadn't drunk two glasses of champagne, though even one was bad enough.

"Next weekend, Miss Swann. Says he's been waiting for two and a half years and if he turns the chance down now he may have to go to the bottom of the NHS waiting list and work his way up to the top again. Could take years, in spite of all this guff about everyone being seen to in a matter of months. Some kind of genitourinary problem, I gather."

"I'm really not quite with you, Mr. Ry—"

"So if you could step in, we'd be enormously grateful." Ryland paused again. "How about it, then?"

"Do you mean Clyde Ashburn's prostate operation finally came through?"

"Thought I just said so."

"And you want me to run the course he was supposed to be organizing next weekend?"

"Precisely."

Cassie could see Charlie Quartermain blundering around her sitting room, picking things up and putting them down somewhere else. She wished he wouldn't.

Although she now realized it was pretty farfetched to see him as Sonia's murderer, she nonetheless wished he'd get himself out of her home and take his champagne with him.

The thought of returning to the hotel only four weeks after the deaths of the Plumptons and Sonia Wetherhead was not exactly magnetic. As for the Macbeth Room, how could she ever go into it again? Even if they'd cleaned it up, even if they'd replaced the pale pink carpet, put new chairs in, a fresh baize-topped card table, she would still know, still remember.

Ryland said, "You do realize that not everyone would give you a chance like this after what happened last time."

"It was nothing to do with me."

"You must have seen the papers, Miss Swann. Or listened to the radio." Bizarrely, he gave a faint chuckle. "The item seems to have caught the popular imagination. I've no doubt you've had cancellations from other hotels."

How did he know that? "And no doubt *you've* had an increase in bookings," she said.

He ignored her tart tones. "I want to show my complete faith in you," he said smoothly.

"And getting a replacement for Clyde Ashburn at short notice has nothing to do with it?" Or is it, Cassie thought bitterly, that I've achieved some kind of celebrity value?

Ryland ignored that too. He said, "Some of the same people who were there on the last—uh—unfortunate occasion will also be attending. After the . . . *pother* last time, it seemed only fair to offer them another go. At a substantial discount, of course." He sounded pained.

"The Potters from Luton are coming. And Ms. Duggan. Mr. Lambert. Mr. and Mrs. Newsome."

"Who did you say before the Newsomes?"

"Lambert. Thomas Lambert. That journalist fellow."

"It'll be frightfully inconvenient," Cassie said slowly. On the other hand, it might give her an opportunity to quiz Lambert about Sonia Wetherhead.

"We'd be most enormously grateful . . ."

"I had other things planned."

"We're fully aware of how much trouble we're putting you to."

"All right," Cassie said in her briskest tone. "I'll do it. Same terms as before, I presume."

"Of course." Ryland sounded pleased.

"Plus a bonus for the inconvenience."

"Uh . . ." Ryland sounded less pleased.

"I'll have to cancel a dinner engagement on the Saturday night," Cassie said.

"Very well, then."

"There'll be a party on the Saturday evening, will there?"

"Yes."

"Right. I'll pack my best frock," said Cassie. And, she thought, a bottle of something halfway decent, get a bit on board before facing the teeth-skinning solution.

"See you then. I say, this is *enormously* good of you, at such short notice."

"I know," Cassie said. Not only was it good of her, it would be good *for* her. She would be able to beard Lambert, ask him if he had any concept of what he had done to her with his stupid articles, point out that people take bridge seriously and murder is not a joke.

In the sitting room, Charlie Quartermain had opened the burl walnut cabinet where she kept her most fragile treasures and was handling an opaque twist-stem glass in a threatening manner.

"Would you mind?" She tried to take it away from him. "That's a Jacobite glass."

"It's a fake," he said. "The other two glasses in there are OK, but this one's a fake. Mind you, I could get you a couple more to make up the set. Got a mate down the market, big into antique glass and such. He could fix you up."

"I don't want to be fixed up," Cassie said. "Those were left to me by my father."

"Blimey. Someone really took him for a ride."

"Look, I wish you'd—"

"Don't suppose you fancy a quick bonk, do you?"

"*What* did you say."

"Sorry. Bit out of order. Should have kept me big mouth shut. It's just, I really fancy you, Cass, and no mistake."

Cassie marched over to the front door and flung it open. A wedge of frozen air pushed in. Outside she could see the frosty grass of the little cottage lawn and, beyond the front hedge, plowed fields, the furrows edged in frost. "Out," she said. "Now. Immediately."

"OK." Charlie looked contrite. "Look, can we see each—"

"OUT."

He stepped out onto the stone step and turned. "Oh. Nearly forgot," he said. He rummaged in one of the pockets of his waxed jacket and pulled something out. "One evening you said you liked these." He handed her a mango.

She watched him walk down the path and tear open the little gate. She listened as the engine of some sleek and powerful car came to elegant life behind the hedge and purred away.

She thought: It's difficult to dislike him. On the other hand . . .

The sun was struggling to break through the winter fog which hung low over the bare fields. There were pearled cobwebs hanging between the posts which held up the porch roof. The air was damp and so still that she could clearly hear Quartermain's car turn the bend in the lane and soar off up the village street. Behind her, the telephone shrilled again and she firmly shut the door before answering it.

"Yes? Cassandra Swann?"

"Charlie Quartermain here, Cass. On the car phone. Meant to say there's a bit of your guttering blown loose. I'll send someone round to fix it."

Cassie took a deep breath. She looked down. Difficult to tell a man to sod off when you were holding his mango in your hand. Besides, she wasn't very good at guttering. It would be useful to have someone deal with it for her. She suspected that among Charlie Quartermain's other irritating qualities was an old-fashioned view on the helplessness of women and thought how insidious a corrupter of feminist principles a man who knew about guttering could be.

"How kind," she said.

Because of the newspaper mentions—including a photograph which made her look like the Michelin Man with boobs—she was diffident about showing up at the wedding, which was to be one of the large and fashionable kind. Luckily those present whom she knew tended not to read newspapers of that type. The ceremony took place in the chapel of the Oxford college where the groom had passed a mediocre undergraduate career some years earlier; the reception was held in the college dining hall.

As Cassie had expected, her cousins were all there. The sight of Rose's emaciated frame wrapped in a tiny fake-fur coat which gave her the appearance of an adorable cuddly toy made Cassie want to spit. Her own coat emphasized her hips, she was sure. As for the twins—Primula in a dear little navy-blue wool dress with red trimmings, Hyacinth in the reverse—they made her feel like a St. Bernard: huge and floppy.

"Cass!" Hyacinth said brightly, kissing the lobe of each of Cassie's ears.

"Darling!" cried Primula. "Don't you look . . . *well!*"

Whether that final word was an exclamation designed to disguise Primula's inability to express just what exactly Cassie looked, or whether she hoped to imply radiant good health, Cassie knew that what Primula really meant was *fat.*

"After all that ghastly publicity," said Hyacinth, "I thought you'd have lost weight with the worry of it. And instead you look so . . ."

"*Well,*" said Primula.

Uncle Samuel was being fey. With the ambitious vicar's eye for a photo opportunity, he gathered his daughters and his niece around him for the benefit of the photographer who was wandering among the wedding guests.

"My garden of delights," he said, putting clerical arms around the four women.

Yes, Cassie thought sourly. Three fragile thin-stalked blooms and one bloody great vegetable marrow. She remembered Charlie Quartermain and felt marginally comforted. When did someone last tell the twins they looked like angels? Probably that very morning. Never mind. It helped to remind herself that not everyone went for the social X-ray look.

At the wedding feast, she found herself placed between Derek, husband of Primula, and a history don, the groom's former tutor. Great. She endured some routine remarks about mixed infants and the government's shortsighted education policies from Derek, then turned to the don, who seemed to be undergoing some species of fit.

"Are you all right?" Cass wondered whether he'd swallowed a bone from the salmon they were eating.

"I am usually," the don said. "But the sight of that fellow over there—" He nodded toward the other arm of the square U of ancient oak around which the guests were seated and Cassie saw Ned Casaubon. She had noticed him earlier, first locked in conversation with a furtive man in morning dress and later chatting to an elderly woman in an expensive suit of fuchsia wool. Now he was sitting next to her cousin Rose, who was apparently liking it.

"What's wrong with him?" Cassie said.

"Man's a charlatan," said the don.

"Really?"

"Look here, happened to bump into him somewhere. Fellow said he was a wine merchant. Asked him what he'd advise to fill one or two of the gaps in our college cellar. I'm on the College Wine Committee—explained our needs, went out and bought what he recommended. Crates of the stuff."

"Gosh."

"Some kind of Australian rubbish. Swore it was the wine of the future but eminently drinkable right now." The don turned large soft eyes on Cass. "Can tell you here and now, in the future I'd sooner accept the advice of a gel from a supermarket wine counter"—his lip curled at the very thought—"than buy so much as a teaspoonful of anything else that fellow recommended. Man displayed a complete lack of oenological scholarship. The college has always prided itself on its cellar, but believe me, our reputation among the other college houses has suffered badly."

"So on the empirical evidence, you'd be prepared to hypothesize that he's not a wine merchant at all?" asked Cassie.

"It's certainly questionable, my dear. Open to debate. Frankly, I'd have got more information from a Brew Your Own Bordeaux kit than *he* was able to offer. Calls himself by some damned highfalutin name too. It's obvious he's much less than he cracks himself up to be."

Which only confirmed Cassie's own opinion.

Look at him, she thought. Smiling like that at Rose. Giving her the eye contact, the accidental brush of the fingers against the hand. There was a certain satisfaction to be gained from the way Casaubon, looking up and catching her cold eye across the hall, suddenly paled, his consternation, even alarm, perfectly obvious. He looked down at his wristwatch.

While not devoting the rest of the afternoon to it, she did spend some time, after the bride and groom had left and the rest of the guests were milling about wondering what to do next, trying to close in on Casaubon. He proved remarkably slippery. Whenever she got to where he had been, he had gone. It was difficult not to suspect that he was avoiding her; the question was: why?

IT was the mixture as before. It always was. Get any group together and you'd find the same combination of the diffident, the know-it-all, the dunce, the clown, the overtalkative and the expert, the latter usually a dark horse easily distinguishable from the know-it-all because he (or she) would not reveal himself until well into the course: "I'm surprised to hear you say that, Miss Swann." (Diffident little cough.) "Naturally I bow to your superior knowledge, but I myself have always used the extended Stayman Convention in those circumstances. As it happens, it came up when I was playing in the European championships only last week . . ."

Cassie glanced around the group as it gathered on the Friday evening for the first friendly rubbers, during which she would move among them, assessing their capabilities, learning them. Some of those present she had already met: the couple from Luton, whose names, she now knew, were Darren and Sharon Potter (or possibly Daron and Sharren). Ms. Duggan, the vivacious red-lipped publisher. Mr. and Mrs. Newsome, he silent, she on the lookout for anyone doing her out of something to which she was legally entitled. Thomas Lambert.

And, of course, Ned Casaubon, alleged wine merchant, hard-jawed charmer, trifler with the affections of vulnerable women. Not that Cassie put herself in that category. It was Rose she was worried about, poor defenseless Rose, whose innocence and lack of worldly wisdom left her a prey to hard-drinking, smooth-talking liars like Casaubon.

The new people came mostly in pairs: two retired couples from Bradford, and a fortyish one from Pevensey Bay, one half of which was heavily overdressed in gold chains and nostril-clenching scent while the other, cruelly thin and salon-blonded, wore silver high-heeled sandals and a lilac shell suit but was otherwise more discreet. There were three singles: a schoolteacher from Derby who reminded Cassie of her cousin-in-law Derek, an excitable former probation officer in her late sixties, and a rather weepy divorcée whose lipstick clung to her teeth rather than to her mouth.

"I had no idea you'd be in charge of this weekend,"

Casaubon said as he and Cassie met in the bar before dinner that evening. "What a stroke of luck."

Oh yeah? "How did you like my cousin Rose?" asked Cassie.

He lifted a quizzical eyebrow. "Rose Seagram is your cousin?"

She wondered what the hell he had to be quizzical about. Unless it was the fact that Rose bought her clothes at the toy counter, whereas Cassie obviously did not.

"As, indeed, are the twins," she said. "How do you come to know them?"

"We're all friends of the groom. I was up at Oxford with him, as a matter of fact."

"Were you avoiding me at the wedding?"

"Good Lord, no," he said. "You know how that kind of function is: full of people you haven't seen for years, who all want to catch up on your news."

She did not believe him. His answer sounded as though he had prepared it against exactly the kind of accusation she had just made. He *had* been avoiding her, whatever he now claimed.

"I thought you were going to drop in and see me," she said. "I thought you were going to take me out to dinner."

"I am," he said. He sounded evasive.

"And you said you were bothered about Sonia's death."

"I was. I still am." Casaubon lifted the lemon slice from his glass of gin and tonic and sucked on it.

"Why?"

He glanced around the room. "Look, before the end

of the weekend, could I fix a date when I could visit you next week?"

Her instincts were to say he could not. After all, the police had the case in hand. And whatever had worried Casaubon previously could not have been that urgent since it was now four weeks since Sonia's murder and the related—presumably—deaths of Colonel Plumpton and his wife.

On the other hand . . . Cassie mentally reviewed the most expensive dishes on the menu at the Wheatsheaf, the crisp-skinned duck, the paper-thin slices of flesh flushing from light brown to the most delicate of pinks, the sauce flavored with cardamom and a dash of Grand Marnier . . .

"Let's do that," she said.

"And I could return those earrings of yours too." He grinned at her.

She gave him a steely stare and opened her mouth to say something even more metallic when the former probation officer appeared. "Oh, Miss Swann," she began. "I can't tell you how much I'm enjoying myself. I lead a very quiet life, you know, pottering about my little house and devoting myself to the garden, so I've looked forward to this weekend for absolutely ages. It's a present from my nephews—to celebrate my birthday—such nice boys, and they know I'd always meant to take up bridge once I retired, and now it's all come so wonderfully true. I'm Flavia Gunn, by the way."

"Let's hope the weekend lives up to your expectations," Cassie said politely, taking the hand which Flavia Gunn had thrust at her. In view of what she had just said, it seemed unlikely to do so: bridge was a cutthroat business, never intended to be a combination of Shangri-La and the Garden of Eden.

"These are such lovely surroundings," sighed Flavia. "So many beautiful things. I love antiques, don't you, Miss Swann? I love to be in an ambience like this, timeless and historic." She turned to Ned Casaubon. "There's such a feeling of the march of history, don't you agree?"

"I'm more interested in the march of dinner," said Casaubon. He looked at his watch. "Isn't it about time they started banging the gong?"

As though on cue, Kevin appeared at the door and spoke to those nearest it, at the same time shifting his arms about.

"The manager's just begun to make cattle-herding gestures," Cassie said. "Shall we go in?"

"What a *wonderful* idea," said Miss Gunn brightly, as though the thought of eating was something quite new which she had not thought of trying until now.

A working lifetime spent being professionally positive, looking on the bright side, absorbing the miseries and peccadilloes of her clients, their crimes and the domestic situations out of which they mostly arose, was bound to leave its mark. It had never occurred to Cassie before that compulsive cheeriness could be as depressing as compulsive gloom.

Casaubon took her arm as they entered the dining room. She shook him off, irritated, then asked herself why she minded, whether she would have objected if she had been, say, Flavia Gunn, frailer, from a different generation. She was not going to pretend she wasn't attracted to Casaubon, in a purely physical way. But that did not mean that she was prepared to trust him, or even that she liked him, or his message, which, reduced to basics, went something like: "*If you're willing, I'm able.*"

Seated beside him, as they and Flavia Gunn ended up sharing a table with the couple from Pevensey Bay, she thought, oddly, of Charlie Quartermain. There was a man secure in his masculinity. His message—"*I want you*"—was as unequivocal as Casaubon's. Lay them both on the line, and one was acceptable, the other was not.

Over dinner, she learned a great deal about the life and times of Miss Flavia Gunn, her three nephews and their five children, her garden, her voluntary work among the elderly, and the man who lived in the cottage opposite hers. While she chatted inexorably on, the rest of them sat in a silence that was not far removed from glum, or exchanged remarks with each other under their breath. The man from Pevensey Bay occasionally inserted a finger between his neck and the chain around it and twisted the thin gold links until they left red marks on his skin.

"So I told them," Miss Gunn said, drawing the cards toward her across the green felt tabletop, "they really mustn't spend their money on me—after all, after a lifetime of working, I do at least have my pension to fall back on, but they all insisted I come—such dear boys, and married to such lovely girls, all of them." She began to put the pre-dealt hands back into their plastic wallets, her eyes, ruthless and predatory as those of a butterfly collector, meantime sweeping around her captive audience of three in her attempt to hold and fix them.

The Potters from Luton exchanged glances. Cassie

knew from experience that they would come to her the minute one of them was Dummy and ask her to change the tables around so that they wouldn't have to endure any more of Miss Gunn's endless monologues. Nor could she blame them. The group was well into the Saturday afternoon session and there was a general feeling that if any of the nephews responsible for Miss Gunn's presence were to show up unexpectedly, he was likely to be lynched.

"Responses to interference bids," Cassie said. "Miss Gunn, are you . . .?"

"Sorry. Talking too much, as usual." Flavia Gunn beamed at her and laid a finger across her own lips.

"At this early stage in the game it is not advisable to use the takeout double," droned Cassie. "If your opponent should open the bidding with your own best suit, then . . ."

Felix Ryland put his head around the door, nodded to Cassie, and withdrew. She knew he hoped she would not delay in bringing the session to a close: the get-together party was to be held in this room tonight, it having been judged tactless to use the Othello Lounge, in view of the events of the previous Bridge Weekend, and a certain amount of preparation was needed to set it up.

". . . own best suit, then your most useful bid in this opening round is to pass."

It was an afternoon much like any other. Normally, Cassie would have found the dawning enlightenment on her students' faces as stimulating as a massage; the imparting of knowledge was in her blood anyway, and to see it grasped by those to whom she imparted was always exhilarating. Today, however, she found her attention wandering. Only a month ago, Colonel and Mrs. Plumpton had sat where one of the couples from Bradford was now sitting. Only a month ago, Sonia Wetherhead had occupied the very chair where the weepy divorcée now sniffed, damp-eyed, over the cards in her hand, hesitating over whether to bid a Heart or a Diamond, although Cassie had twice explained which and why.

Unlike the last time she had been here, it was sunny outside, the bare trees which studded the view looking deceptively springlike. The sky was blue, not the sensual blue of summer but a washed-out pastel version, sprinkled with clumps of smoke-thin cloud. Of the six people who had also attended the previous Bridge Weekend, she wondered how many still suffered in the way she was suffering, unable to rid themselves of disturbing visions: the Colonel slowly tipping forward to lie with his head on the cards; the prostrate bulk of Sonia; Mrs. Plumpton in her chair, one hand reaching toward her pillbox.

None of them, probably, since she was the only person, beyond Ryland himself and the officials of death— the police, the medical team, the forensic experts—who had actually seen the bodies. Certainly not the solicitor's wife: her thin mouth was pursed with satisfaction as she slapped a small Trump down on an Ace and took what must have seemed a certain trick from her opponents. Nor the publisher, whose long red nails clicked slightly against the plasticized surface of the cards each time she played. And definitely not Ned Casaubon, sitting opposite Flavia Gunn with an expression of mild amusement on his face. Since the evening before, he had hardly spoken to Cassie though he had cheerfully accepted Miss Gunn as his partner, and indeed had sat with her at lunch, listening charmingly while she chattered about past case histories she had handled.

"So sad," she was saying now as she sorted her cards. "If they put half the energy into getting themselves a regular job as they do into trying to steal or defraud, they would never land up in prison, never."

"Do you mind?" the male Potter said, glowering ostentatiously at his cards. "I came here to learn some bridge, not to hear a nonstop lecture on the state of Her Majesty's nicks."

Miss Gunn was not put out. "Sorry," she said, smiling broadly. "So sorry. My besetting sin, I'm afraid: talking too much." She looked around at her unenthusiastic audience. "But, you know, some of them come from such deprived homes, surrounded by such ugliness, such a lack of emotional or moral input, that it's no wonder they turn to crime. Some of them are labeled as criminal deviants as young as thirteen or fourteen. The system is disastrous."

"If you ask me, they should all be horsewhipped," the female Potter said unexpectedly. "Give them a taste of their own medicine, I say, instead of all this mollycoddling."

"Bleeding holiday camps, prisons are these days," said her husband. "Tellies, gyms, computers."

"Duvets," said his wife.

"I wouldn't mind a spell inside myself," the husband said. "Get a bit of peace away from the wife and kiddies."

He looked at his female half without affection.

"Oh, but surely you can't really believe that," Miss Gunn said anxiously. "Quite apart from the horror of being deprived of free choice, which is one of the worst aspects of being—uh—*inside*, there's the whole question of recidivism—"

"Three Diamonds," Ned Casaubon said.

"Three Spades," said Sharon Potter.

"—slopping out," said Miss Gunn. "Homosexual abuse . . . drugs. And now the constant threat of AIDS. Believe me, a spell inside our overcrowded prison system is no—"

"Three Spades bid," Sharon Potter said loudly.

"Pass," said Darren Potter. "Your bid, Flavia."

"What?" Miss Gunn looked quickly down at her cards. "Three Dia . . . Dear me, would you mind if we recapped on the bidding? I seem rather to have lost the thread."

Later that evening, emerging from the shower, Cassie unwillingly got a full frontal view of herself in the dressing-table mirror. One of her breasts seemed a different size from the other. She peered more closely: yes, the left-hand one was definitely smaller than the one on the right. Either she was losing weight on one side or she had cancer. She held them both up, one in each hand, and immediately felt depressed. God, they weighed a ton.

She put on black pleated trousers and a matching jacket, fiendishly expensive but flattering, high heels, then dithered among her earrings—the black-and-silver hoops? The cloisonné sun and moon?—before choosing the heavy jet drops which had belonged to Gran. Eyebrows, cheeks, lips, a couple of dabs of something expensive at ear and wrist. She peered at the finished product in the glass. She told herself that she might be big, but by God she was beautiful.

She wished she really believed it.

They were milling around the Prospero Lounge, the noise level already high. For most of them, the events of a month ago meant nothing. They hadn't been there, they had booked this weekend long before, expecting to improve their bridge playing under the guidance of Clyde Ashburn, the noted expert now presumably suffering the indignities of postoperative catheterization. For them, the deaths of three people such a short time ago were no more than a mental frisson.

Kevin, the manager, was looking gloomy. "It always staggers me," he said, shaking his head, "how much they manage to put away in such a short time. Hollow legs, the lot of them. I don't know what Mr. Ryland's going to say when he sees the bills." He reined in his cavorting mustache, pressing it firmly with two fingers.

"Look at it this way, Kev," Cassie said. "Better a load of grifters swilling down his bargain basement booze than no one here at all."

"You've got a point there," he said. "A definite point. After what happened last time, it's a wonder people didn't start canceling."

"Precisely."

Cassie walked across the room, trying not to give the impression she was looking for Casaubon, because she wasn't. She had done that as soon as she came into the room. He was over in one corner, talking to Vicky Duggan, whose red lips and scarlet fingernails gleamed in the light from the fire (*"real log fires in all our public rooms enhance the old-fashioned warmth of your welcome"*).

Cassie worked the room, chatting to both the couples from Bradford, the schoolteacher from Derby, the Pevensey Bay pair, and the divorcée. Despite an unpromising exterior, the schoolteacher proved to be a bit of a wag; the divorcée, eyes now dry, seemed appreciative of his witty sallies.

Thomas Lambert, the journalist, gave Cassie a quick résumé of the country's financial state and quite a few reasons to account for it. Before she could ask him about Sonia Wetherhead, Mrs. Newsome explained in some detail how she got the better of a supermarket manager who had made the mistake of claiming that his weekend special was fresh New Zealand lamb rather than frozen.

Felix Ryland, coming in to do the statutory round of his guests (*"we want you to feel like one of the family during your stay with us"*) told her yet again how enormously grateful he was to her for stepping into the breach. As he spoke, his eyes roamed the room in professional assessment. Cassie supposed that people did not vary much, that after a while a practiced eye could judge pretty accurately how the members of any given group would behave, what their incomes were, what kind of background they came from, which ones were most likely to steal the towels or use the sheets to polish their shoes.

Miss Gunn approached. "What a splendid beano!"

financial circumstances which cause him to throw it open to the public."

Leaning forward, Miss Gunn clutched at Cassie's sleeve. "And the young man over there, the one with the lovely smile. Who might he be?"

"Standing by the fire, do you mean? He's called Casaubon."

"A name with literary associations, I believe."

"I know."

"I have no wish to sound accusatory," Miss Gunn said, "but can it possibly be his real name?"

Cassie laughed. "I asked him that."

"And?"

"He was remarkably evasive."

"Interesting," said Miss Gunn. "I wonder why."

"So did I."

The party was dragging. There was no Sonia Wetherhead to liven things up, no Felicity Carridine to add a touch of the spurious glamour which always accrues even to the only mildly famous. One of the couples from Bradford suggested that they organize some music and start dancing. The only person who greeted this with any enthusiasm was Mrs. Newsome, the solicitor's wife, who clearly viewed it as a way to extract something extra from the management. The thin wife from Pevensey Bay said it was her birthday and she for one intended to get as pissed as a newt.

Hearing this, some of the group decided the occasion warranted the ordering of champagne. Vicky Duggan bore Thomas Lambert triumphantly from the room. Ned Casaubon raised his eyebrows at Cassie and jerked his head toward the door but she pretended she had not seen him. She reminded people that they were to meet at eleven o'clock the next morning and, a little later, quietly slipped out and went up to her room.

Most of them made it the next morning by eleven-fifteen. By eleven-twenty she was able to set up three of the four tables. The only one still to come was Flavia Gunn, no doubt suffering from a hellish hangover. Cassie sat down at the fourth table with Thomas Lambert and one of the Bradford couples, joined in the bidding for the first hand, and then, when she ended up as Dummy, stood up.

"I'll just go up and see if Miss Gunn's all right," she said. "I won't be long."

"All right?" said Mr. Bradford. "I shouldn't think so. The way she was knocking it back last night, I'd guess the old girl's seeing triple this morning."

"She looked as if she was having a good time, though," Thomas Lambert said. He gave Cassie a look from his dark brown eyes and she read in them something of her own sentiments about Miss Gunn. She wondered if he knew there was a large love bite on his neck.

Miss Gunn was on the same floor as the Plumptons had been, in Room 32 ("*all our rooms have extensive views of the rolling Cotswold countryside*"); a DO NOT DISTURB sign had been slung over the handle. Cassie ignored it, knocking vigorously on the door, but there was no reply. When she tried the door, it proved to be locked.

Leaning down, she called through the keyhole. "Miss Gunn! It's Cassandra Swann. Are you all right?"

Again there was no answer.

"Would you like something sent up?" Cassie bawled. "Orange juice? Coffee?"

The room behind the door stayed silent.

She walked down the carpeted corridor. Rolling Cotswold countryside spread beyond the diamond-paned windows; it all looked very cold. The passage right-angled at the end, leading to further views. Halfway down was a service station where a chambermaid sat smoking a cigarette and reading a magazine in a welter of dirty sheets and wet towels.

"Room 32," Cassie said.

"I haven't done it yet. She's put a sign on the door."

"I know. But she's very late for the morning bridge session. It might be a good idea to wake her up—I'm sure she'd be sorry to miss it."

"I'm not really supposed to—"

"Bridge is what she's paid for," Cassie said firmly. "I think we should open the door."

Poor Miss Gunn would be embarrassed, but she could simply tell the others that she'd forgotten to set her alarm clock. There was no need for the rest of the bridge group to know about the undoubted hangover: the splitting headache, the tongue like a hiking sock, the general feeling that death would be preferable to life. Cassie sympathized, having been there herself, yet she felt sure that the older woman would prefer not to miss the final hours of her weekend. After all, she had told them endlessly how seldom she got away from home, how quiet her life was. A hangover might even be judged to be part of the excitement, something to be thought about later, remembered with appreciation.

Together, she and the chambermaid approached

Room 32. The chambermaid knocked loudly before putting her key in the lock and opening the door.

The room was dark, the curtains still closed. It was very neat; despite her overindulgence the night before, Miss Gunn had evidently hung up her dress and her jacket, arranged her underclothes neatly on the Henry VIII-style chair, taken the pins from her hair and laid them on the dressing table. There was a strong hospital smell: it reminded Cassie of the coal-tar soap used at the vicarage during her adolescence.

She stood by the bed. On the table beside it she could make out the shapes of hairbrush, water glass, pillbox, and Bible. The duvet had fallen away, exposing one thin shoulder and an incongruously lacy strap. "Miss Gunn," she said softly, bending over. There was a smell of stale wine, a peppermint whiff of toothpaste. "Miss Gunn."

She put her hand on Flavia's nightdressed shoulder and shook it. Yet her heart was thumping, the blood moaning thickly past her ears with the realization that what she did was pointless. Even as she said again, "Wake up, Miss Gunn," her mind had raced ahead, foreseeing the horrid repetition of the last time she was here: the police, the ambulance, stretchers.

For the shoulder she touched was chill, the skin flaccid under her fingers. She pulled slightly in her haste to remove her hand and the bundled figure in the bed flopped over onto its back to face the ceiling with closed eyes and half-open mouth, from which a trickle of something dark—blood? wine?—had trailed and, sometime during the night, dried. There was a faint popping sound, as though a gas ring had been turned off.

Behind Cassie, the chambermaid gasped as she took in the undeniable fact that Flavia Gunn was dead.

"Oh God," Cassie said. Without further thought, she ran from the room and down the passage toward Felix Ryland's private quarters. She banged on his door and then, when there was no answer, turned the handle, still banging, feeling panic flare along her wrists and at her knees, feeling as she had not felt since the afternoon she came home from school to find Gran dead, that somewhere immediately behind her lay complete disintegration and that nothing would ever again be the same.

"Dearie, dearie me. Remind me not to enroll in one of your bridge courses," Mantripp said heavily. If he was trying to be jovial, he had seriously miscalculated.

"What do you mean?" Cassie injected ice into her tone.

"I mean, it's a pretty lethal kind of instruction you're handing out here, Miss—um—"

"Swann," snapped Cassie. "Cassandra Swann."

He seemed surprised at her bad-tempered reaction. He lifted his hands. "All right, OK," he said aggrievedly. "But you've got to admit it looks bad. Don't you agree?" He looked over his shoulder at Sergeant Walsh, who continued to stare stolidly at the screen of the laptop computer on which he was typing his notes.

"I most certainly do not," Cassie said. "Neither Miss Gunn's death nor those of the three people last month have anything to do with me. I assume you're not suggesting that I personally am responsible for smashing Sonia Wetherhead's head in, are you?"

"Of course not." He grinned without mirth. "Perhaps it's sabotage. Perhaps one of your rivals is trying to destroy your chances."

"Don't be ridiculous. It's merely a bizarre mischance."

"Maybe. But you've got to admit that four deaths in two weekends is going to make people talk."

Cassie made no reply. People already *were* talking. Notably, Mrs. Newsome, the solicitor's wife.

"I certainly shan't wish to repeat this experience," she had said earlier, when Cassie had returned to the Malvolio Snug to break the news of Miss Gunn's death. She had turned to her husband. "It's Miss Swann, Joseph. A young woman to avoid. Make a note of the name so we can be sure not to enroll in one of her courses again."

Others had nodded. "I must say," Vicky Duggan said, apparently speaking for them all. "It's a little too . . . rarefied for my taste." She had looked over at Thomas Lambert. "I mean, one really would prefer to return home in one's car after a weekend like this, rather than in one's coffin."

It was neatly put. The others appeared to agree with the publisher's words.

Lambert, avoiding Vicky's eye, said, "I don't think Cassandra can be held to blame in any way. After all, the weekend was supposed to be run by Clyde Ashburn. If he hadn't backed out, it would have been during *his* course that Miss Gunn—um—died."

"I don't think anyone's *blaming* Miss Swann," one of the Bradford males said. Hidden within his Yorkshire accent was the all too obvious implication that in fact they were.

The final blow fell as she was leaving. The police had come and gone. Miss Gunn had been stretchered away after the police surgeon had pronounced that her death was due to natural causes, aggravated perhaps by an unaccustomed overindulgence in alcohol. Although the body would undergo a postmortem examination, no suspicious circumstances attached themselves to her demise; her medication for a troublesome heart was sitting right beside her bed. People were free to go and most of them had already done so. Casaubon was the only one who had bothered to say goodbye to Cassie.

Now Felix Ryland, not looking at her, said, "I think perhaps we should reconsider the May Bridge Weekend, don't you?"

Cassie felt a sinking in her stomach. While nobody could for a moment suggest that the deaths were her fault, she could see that she was nonetheless going to be tainted with their murky odor. No smoke without fire, people would say. The jokes would fly. She could hear them now.

"Question: What's got several hearts, four hands and is absolutely lethal? Answer: A game of bridge with Cassandra Swann." And so on.

Staring at Felix Ryland while he fiddled about with a pen and reached into the drawers of his desk for things he did not want, so he could avoid meeting her eye, she realized that through the hazard of circumstance the whole professional edifice she had so carefully built up over the past six years, all the planning and forethought, the investment of both time and money, was under threat. Everything she had worked for was going to fly right out of the window.

It would be back to teaching biology. Back to the formaldehyde, the smell of menstruating girls, the teenage spots and adolescent angsts. The staff room, for God's sake.

She thought: He doesn't understand what he's doing to me. Or maybe he simply doesn't care.

She thought bleakly: If this isn't somehow put right, professionally I'm dead meat.

FOR the fourteenth time that morning the telephone rang. If it was another country hotel canceling her Bridge Weekend with them . . . She listened to her own recorded voice explaining that she was not available to take the call at the moment and inviting the caller to leave a message after the tone. This time it was not a hotel. A male voice asked her to verify the story.

Cassie snatched up the receiver, switching off the answering mechanism as she did so. "Which story?" she said.

"That all these people started playing bridge with you and one by one they dropped dead."

"*Whaaat?*"

"Isn't it true?" the voice asked guilelessly.

"It's complete nonsense," Cassie said. "Read the original reports and you'll see I didn't appear on the scene for quite a time after they died."

"What about this latest death—Miss Flavia Gunn?"

"She died in her bed, and I was nowhere near when it happened," yelled Cassie. "Anyway, how did you get hold of my name?"

"How often do people drop dead while you're playing bridge with them?"

"Never. I can't imagine what gives you the idea they do."

He sniggered. "Perhaps you haven't seen the article in the *Mail* this morning."

"I don't take a daily paper," Cassie said. "What's this article say?"

"The headline goes: 'How I Played Cards with Bridge Professional—and Lived.' "

"Very droll."

"So how often do you—"

"Is there a byline?"

"Our correspondent," the voice said, rustling pages. "Thomas Lambert. Do you ever—"

Cassie put down the telephone. The phone immediately rang again.

This time it was David Llewellyn, manager of a hotel near Carlisle where she frequently conducted Bridge Weekends for a well-heeled crowd of sixty-pluses.

"I'm sorry but we'll have to cancel your next weekend," he said.

"Why?" she said pugnaciously, though she knew.

". . . mixed up in this sort of . . . our clients don't care for . . . pride ourselves on our good name," he mumbled.

"But for heaven's sake, I'm not accused of murdering these people," Cassie said. "I merely found them."

"Yes, but after the article in today's paper, you do see, don't you?"

"No, I most definitely do not."

"Our clientele is *very* respectable."

"So am I," Cassie shouted. Most of the time, she thought.

"And a little nearer their own . . . um . . . demise than perhaps you or I are. It's a fact they don't like to be reminded of too overtly."

"I'm not the Grim Reaper, for God's sake," howled Cassie. "I only *found* them."

"Perhaps we can talk again if things are cleared up satisfactorily."

"Get stuffed." Again Cassie slammed down the receiver.

Snow had begun to fall. Already the lawn had taken on the sudden beseeching look of a man going gray too soon. As the evening flattened the countryside, obliterated hedge and cow and furrowed field, Cassie sat beside the open fire, switched on the radio for the six o'clock news, and confronted her problem.

Was she being naïve to think that she had any hope of finding out something which would at least remove any question of her own involvement, however peripheral, in the deaths of Flavia Gunn, the Plumptons, and Sonia

Wetherhead? She was, after all, an average citizen, Ms. Ordinary, with no claim whatsoever to the kind of innate curiosity about her fellow humans which seemed to motivate such amateur sleuths as Miss Marple or that crime-writing one on TV whose neighbors dropped dead every time she exchanged a couple of words with them. What she did have, and needed, was a fierce determination not to let the random perversities of chance snatch her independence from her. There were already a number of cancellations for booked weekends, and undoubtedly others would follow. If this continued, it would mean a drop in income too large for her to be able to survive on bridge alone. One weekend at a hotel like the Broughton Manor brought in more solid cash than two years of evening classes.

Brought up in a conventional middle-class home—insofar as a rural vicarage peopled by Munchkins could be called conventional—Cassie believed strongly in the ability of the police force to maintain law and order and bring the ungodly to book, even though this belief had necessarily taken a bit of a knock over the past year or two, as nearly every month another conviction was over-turned by the courts, and men, unjustly imprisoned on false police evidence, marched bitterly out of the jails. But if she left it to the police, it could take months before they completed their investigations, months in which she would founder. The biology labs loomed—unless she did something about it herself.

Assessing the situation, she decided that though her hand was essentially weak, she nonetheless held one Ace. She had known Sonia Wetherhead alive, while Detective Inspector Mantripp and his team had only been passingly acquainted with her corpse. That being so, even if she found herself covering some of the same ground as they presumably were, and granted that she had none of their resources, she still might hit on some information which could have significance to her but not to them. And if she came up with nothing, she would have lost little but her time.

The problem was where to start. Would it be more useful to drive over to Moreton Lacey, where Sonia had lived, or would it be more effective to start by talking to the people who had evidently known her prior to the Winter Bridge Weekend, such as Thomas Lambert, or Felicity Carridine, the novelist? Such as—oh dear—Charlie Quartermain. And, of course, Ned Casaubon. And if she decided on the latter course, which of them should she opt for first? She tried to defend the way her instincts screamed "Casaubon" on the grounds that any red-blooded female would prefer to arrange a meeting with a handsome, eligible man (or was he? The wife question had still not been resolved) like Casaubon rather than with an overweight egomaniac like Felicity, even supposing the novelist's much-trumpeted publicity tour of the States had ended.

If there was one thing life at the vicarage had taught her, it was the virtue of self-denial. The *supposed* virtue. Cassie had never understood why doing something you disliked improved the soul and Uncle Samuel had always been vague on the point. But old habits die hard, and because she would far rather talk to Casaubon than drive around the countryside in a snowstorm, she had no option but to go for Moreton Lacey, rather than the wine merchant, a decision which left her soul not only one hundred percent unimproved but also distinctly tetchy.

Checking her engagement diary, she saw that apart from an evening class, she would have five days clear before she was due to appear in a charity bridge tournament being held at the Hyde Park Hotel in London—unless that was canceled too.

Five days: it didn't sound like much. On the other hand, murders were seldom random, and still less often were they planned. By careful sifting of any evidence she stumbled across, she might well find out something significant which she could hand on to the police. Mentally she toyed with the classic images of detection: the magnifying glass, the plaster cast of a footprint, the deerstalker, the velvet slipper full of recreational substances. But times had changed for the amateur sleuth. Detection was no longer a matter of railway timetables and mysterious footprints. Besides, she had never stalked a deer in her life and had no intention of starting now. As for cocaine, Sherlock Holmes might not have known how to say no, but she certainly did. Or would, if anyone had ever offered her cocaine—or even a joint—to say no to. When she was at university, the student body had been a staid lot on the whole, particularly the biologists, much more concerned with doing well and finding a job than with such outmoded notions as turning on or dropping out.

But before she did anything else, she wanted to get hold of Thomas Lambert and shake him by the scruff of the neck.

She telephoned the Broughton Manor Hotel and explained to the world-weary voice which answered who she was.

"Oh yes?" It was difficult to tell whether the whiny, indifferent voice belonged to Skin or to Boanes.

"As you can imagine," Cassie said sincerely, "the events of last weekend were a bit of a shock."

"I'll say."

"I thought I ought to write round to the people who were there, not an apology, exactly, since it's hardly my fault if poor Miss Gunn had a fatal heart attack—I mean, you might just as well advise people to avoid your hotel as avoid my bridge lessons, mightn't you?"

There was no answer from Ms. Boanes, if that was who it was.

"So I wondered if I could get one or two addresses from you," Cassie said.

"It's against our policy," said the voice. It was accompanied by a rasping noise, as though a grasshopper was stuck in the receiver. Ms. Boanes (or her colleague) was filing her nails.

"I know that. But you did give out *my* address to Mr. Casaubon, so exceptions can be made," Cassie said firmly. "I'm sure if I pointed this out to Mr. Ryland, he would agree." She knew neither Ms. Boanes nor her friend would want Mr. Ryland to know they had been cajoled into breaking the hotel's rules.

"Which addresses did you want?" the voice asked sulkily.

"All of them," said Cassie. They might come in useful one day. "Dictate them to me."

It might be expensive on the phone bill, but at least she'd be sure of having the addresses she was particularly interested in without drawing undue attention to them.

*   *   *

"Death Takes a Hand." The headline did not exactly scream at her but it spoke fairly loudly from the bottom of page three. Under it was an inaccurate and highly-colored account of the Sonia Wetherhead murder a month earlier, mentioning her by name—at least she presumed that the Miranda Swan named in the article was a reference to herself. She folded it quickly and glanced around the railway carriage, a flush of embarrassment rising in her face. Reason told her that anyone reading it could not possibly know it referred to her and that if they did, they would not necessarily be aware that the woman in the corner seat by the window with a folded newspaper on her knee was that particular bridge pro. No one was taking the slightest notice of her except for a large Rastafarian with his abundant dreadlocks caught up in a tricolored beret of knotted wool, who winked at her. She winked back.

Lambert lived in one of the pleasant thirties houses near West Hampstead station, an area precariously flying the middle-class flag in the midst of the infiltration by less salubrious neighborhoods. The privet hedges around here were trim, even in winter. There was a notable absence of overflowing wheelie bins, ten-year-old cars patched with rust filler, and abandoned supermarket trolleys. Long since divided into flats, these were houses jauntily pretending that the breakdown in standards did not creep ever nearer with every car aerial snapped off, every new piece of graffiti spray-painted on the pavement, every house broken into.

Lambert's flat appeared to be on the third floor. Cassie rang his bell, spoke into the obligatory intercom, pushed open the door when the buzzer sounded. Above her she heard the sound of a door open as he leaned over the top banister to watch her bounding—to start with—up the steep staircase to his flat.

"What a surprise," he said as she puffed after him and collapsed onto a brand-new black leather sofa which sat incongruously among other, shabbier furniture, mostly bookcases, though there was one superb piece, a bowfront commode of inlaid satinwood, on which stood a pair of heavy silver candleholders flanking a piece of ceremonial porcelain. "What brings you here?"

"I wanted you to know," Cassie said, breathing hard, "just how pissed off I am by this article you've written about my Bridge Weekends."

"Oh, come," he said. He stood on the balls of his feet and swayed a little. Today he wore a beige cardigan and matching socks; his shoes were of chocolate-brown suede, the same color as his eyes.

"Come where?"

"I mean, I'm a jobbing journalist; I make my living from writing articles for the press."

"And I'm a professional bridge teacher; I make my living teaching people how to play bridge. Or did until your article came out. You've managed to make me seem both silly and dangerous. Do you have any idea how much damage you've done to my professional reputation?"

"Surely you exaggerate. I mean, why would people—"

"I'm not exaggerating in the slightest. Since that highly amusing piece of yours appeared in the *Mail*, I've had at least half a dozen cancellations and I expect more to follow."

"You know what they say," he said, attempting a smile. "Any publicity is better than no publicity."

"Not in the world of bridge," Cassie said.

"I'm sorry to hear tha—"

"You've managed to endanger the means by which I live, Mr. Lambert, and I very much resent it," Cassie said clearly. "I know most journalists would boil their mothers in oil to get a good headline—"

"Not me," he said. His manner was quick and nervous, like the way he played bridge. "I'm not that sort of journalist at all."

"What sort are you?"

"Much more your cozy sort of chap," he said anxiously. His scrubby beard sagged slightly. "I'm not interested in the cut and thrust of Fleet Street, thank you. I like doing exactly what I do, pottering round the country interviewing craftspeople like Sonia, writing up groups who're restoring single-gauge railway lines in Welsh valleys, or producing clinker-built gaff-rigged Norfolk cruisers by traditional methods—you know the sort of thing. Nothing that would interest the national press, though I have had the occasional bit in one of the Sundays."

"Nothing until now."

"Well, yes. It was originally my girlfriend's fault, really. Not mine at all."

"The old the-woman-tempted-me-and-I-did-eat defense, eh?"

"I was telling her about it and she thought it would make a good filler for the Peterborough column in the *Telegraph*, that sort of thing. I was staggered when the tabloids picked it up."

"And the radio. What fun they had with it on the news quiz," Cassie said bitterly. "How they laughed their public school heads off."

"Honestly, I had no idea . . ."

"So what are you going to do about my business?"

"What on earth do you think I can do?'

"If I could prove that it was nothing to do with me, I might be able to salvage something out of all this. So for a start, you can tell me about Sonia Wetherhead and your relationship with her."

"Relationship?" Lambert squeaked. "I didn't have one. Not as such. Not the way you mean." He stared at her, and added. "Not in any sense."

"Then how come you wrote an article about her for that magazine—I can't remember its name."

"*Rural Life?*"

"That's the one."

"But that's just it; I didn't. Or rather, I did, but it wasn't a personal interview. I had to be in Jersey that week interviewing some old dear who still makes cheeses by hand or some such thing and the editor was agitating for my copy. So I had to do the interview with Sonia Wetherhead over the phone."

"Is that general practice?"

"Absolutely not. My editor would have forty fits if she found out."

"But I read the article. You seemed very familiar with Sonia's work—and her home."

"I am a professional, Miss Swann. Obviously I got most of the info from Sonia herself, and luckily a photographer had gone down the week before and I was sent copies of his pics. A lot of details came from them, to give the piece the kind of cozy feel the magazine likes." He stuck his hands into the pockets of his cardigan and thrust his beard at her. She realized it matched his socks. "That's half the fun, differentiating between the house styles of the various maggies I write for. *Rural Life* is very big on making the reader feel that they too could have been a weaver or a potter or whatever, and lived in a thatched cottage deep in the countryside, if circumstances had been just that bit different. Over three-quarters of our readers live in large cities: did you know that?"

"No, I did not," Cassie said. "Nor did I come here to discuss the readership distribution of your magazine. The point is, I noticed that you and Sonia Wetherhead had a few words at the party on the Saturday, and they didn't seem too friendly."

"They weren't," said Lambert. "She took strong exception to something I'd written in that article, even though I sent her a proof copy before it was published and she'd OK'd it. Very belligerent, she was. To be quite honest, I thought she was going to hit me."

"Are you sure you didn't kill her yourself in order to get yourself into the big time, the national press?"

"Oh, my God," Lambert said. "Is that what the police think?"

"I very much doubt it."

He recovered some, though not very much, brio. "Anyway, I was—um—otherwise occupied at the time the murder is supposed to have taken place. And I have witnesses to prove it."

"Witnesses?"

"Well, just one," Lambert said sheepishly.

"This witness wouldn't by any chance be called Vicky Duggan, would she?"

"Possibly." He fiddled with a loop of loose wool attached to one of the buttons on his cardigan.

"It's no more farfetched to suppose you murdered Sonia for reasons of professional advancement than the idea you're putting round that if you attend one of my Bridge Weekends, you're taking your life into your hands." There was more than a hint of severity in Cassie's voice.

He looked contrite. "I do see that," he said. "I suppose I should have given some thought to the consequences. But I'm afraid I can't help you with Sonia Wetherhead. I'd never met her before that weekend."

"Did you ask her any personal questions in this telephoned interview?"

"How personal?"

"Like whether she had a current lover. Whether she'd ever been married. If she'd ever had children. Anything that might throw some light on who could possibly have killed her."

He jerked at the loose strand. "Not a thing, I'm afraid. That particular mag is much more interested in the work than the worker."

"What about Miss Gunn; had you ever met her before that second weekend?"

"No." The squeak crept back into his voice. He jerked again and the wool came away in his hand. "You aren't suggesting that there was anything odd about *her* death, are you?" The brown button fell off and rolled under the leather sofa.

"No. Just trying to see connections."

But try as she might, Cassie could not see any more to ask him about. So she left.

7

MORETON Lacey was on the very edge of Oxfordshire nudging into Gloucestershire. Most of it was hidden behind a thick curtain of falling snow which whirled against her windscreen in sudden white gusts and lay an inch thick on roofs and branches. A shallow river ran sullenly at an angle to the High Street and was spanned by a stone bridge. Consciously picturesque shopfronts displayed Olde Tyme humbugs and straw dolls, sweaters made of undyed sheep's wool, expensive antiques, woodcraft and potpourri. There was an air about the place of a country reduced to prostitution, emphasizing the tits and bum of its former glory in order to seduce the tourist trade. The idea that in those notional golden olden days, rural England had been populated by humbug-sucking yokels in thick sweaters who spent their time drying rose petals and twisting straws together was off-putting. Even offensive.

Asking directions from the only pedestrian who had ventured out into the weather, Cassie found her way to a back lane which petered out eventually into fields, both grassed and plowed. The Methodist chapel where Sonia had lived stood opposite a fine Queen Anne house of brick and white paint, whose gardens appeared to slope down to a tributary of the stream which bisected the village; they were the only two buildings in the lane.

She got out of her car and ran through flurrying snow to the ecclesiastical door of the building. Cobwebs of considerable antiquity coated the edges and spread funguslike along the imposing hinges, where snowflakes lay caught like albino flies. It didn't need Sherlock Holmes to deduce that the door had not been opened for some considerable time, or to assume further that Sonia Wetherhead was accustomed therefore to enter her home by some other route.

Cassie was about to walk around the side in search of a back entrance when a high fluting voice stopped her in her tracks.

"Can I help you?" it asked, with an upper-class mellifluousness which sent a nostalgic shiver down Cassie's spine and managed to indicate, without any hint of aggression, that the owner would have no hesitation

in calling the constabulary if the answer was unsatisfactory.

"Oh, thank you *so* much," Cassie cried. "I'm looking
for Miss Wetherhead."

"And you are?" An elderly woman in green
Wellingtons, an anorak held like a tent over her freshly
coiffed gray hair, was approaching her from across the
lane.

Cassie was astonished, even appalled, at the ease with
which she found herself lying. At the rectory, the presence of God—omnipresent, omniscient, usually wrath-
ful—had been taken for granted. As a child she had
never understood why He was with her wherever she
went, even into the loo. Didn't He have better things to
do than watch her pee? Growing older, she had decided
that omnipresent or not, God was not a bundle of
laughs, and had ceased to think about Him too much,
though for Uncle Samuel's sake, she had continued to
attend church on Sundays.

Now, glibly stating that she was Midge MacKendrick,
come to see Sonia Wetherhead with a view to commis-
sioning work for a showcase industrial site being
planned in Strathspey (as far away as Cassie could think
of which still sounded plausible), she wondered what
Uncle Samuel would say if he could hear the effortless
way the lies simply sprang from her lips. What *God*
would say, for that matter, for despite her rejection, He
nonetheless still lurked somewhere at the rear of her
mind, an eternal Head Prefect, monitoring everything
she did.

"Strathspey? Oh dear."

"What's wrong?" Cassie said, giving what she hoped

was a Caledonian edge to the syllables, though accents were not her strong point.

The woman hesitated. "I'm expecting some people, but if you'd come in for a moment, I'll explain."

Cassie followed her across the lane and into the Queen Anne house from which she had evidently emerged. At the front door, the woman replaced her Wellingtons with well-polished lace-up shoes and shook the snow from her anorak before showing Cassie into an impeccably upper-class drawing room full of gold-framed pictures and good pieces of furniture. Inlaid cabinets of high-quality porcelain stood here and there; military gentlemen gazed at her from portraits. Cassie immediately saw that God and Uncle Samuel were right: telling lies was self-defeating as well as wicked. There were two bridge tables set up in the big bay window which overlooked the handsome garden, and on a Sheraton side table stood a heavy silver tray with eight cups and saucers and a napkin-covered plate of what looked like homemade biscuits. Clearly her new acquaintance was imminently about to sit down with seven others and play bridge.

Cassie felt a curious twitch in her fingers. If Wordsworth's heart tended to leap up when it beheld a rainbow in the sky, Cassie's did much the same thing when it beheld a pack of cards. She would even play Patience if there was no one else around, just to be holding the cards. The urge to sit down now and shuffle was almost too strong to be resisted.

In front of her, the woman was explaining that Miss Wetherhead had died three weeks previously.

"Died?" Cassie said, as if the news was a shock.

"Most unfortunate," said the woman. She held out a brisk hand. "I'm Lady Comberley, by the way. I'm afraid that, in point of fact, Miss Wetherhead was murdered."

"Murrrderrred!" exclaimed Cassie, still in her north-of-the-border mode. "What on earrrth happened?"

"She was at a Bridge Weekend, and someone apparently hit her over the head. I must say I shall miss her quite dreadfully."

"Good friends, were ye?" Cassie said, sympathetically, Scottishly.

"I wouldn't exactly say that . . ." The older woman paused, a faint flush rising under her skin. "Actually, we were never very good friends, but—and perhaps it seems a somewhat selfish response to such a terrible tragedy—but she was very keen on bridge, and was always ready to make up a four whenever I needed."

Recognizing a fanatic, Cassie wondered why on earth she had landed herself with this Midge MacKendrick caper. How easy it would be to ask questions if she had told the truth right from the beginning. Having established a mutual bond with Lady Comberley through bridge, she would probably have come up with all sorts of juicy gossip about Sonia. Perhaps if she simply came clean and explained . . .

Before she could open her mouth to do so, they heard the clopping sound of a horse's hooves in the lane.

"There goes Giles," Lady Comberley said. She frowned, looking at her watch again. "I must say he's rather late. I'm expecting his mother over to play bridge but she can't leave until he gets home, because of the little boy."

"Lady Comberley," Cassie said, rushing over the

words. "I'm really awfully sorry but I'm not called Midge MacKendrick at all. My name's actually Cassandra Swann."

"How extraordinary." Lady Comberley's head reared back like a gander's.

"My name, do you mean? Or the fact that I didn't use it?"

"The latter, of course."

"The thing is . . ." Cassie began to explain, knowing that as soon as she mentioned the word "bridge" any suspicion Lady Comberley might have felt would melt away. She dwelled at length on the horrors of the press stories, mentioned her loathing of dead frogs and teenage girls, outlined her hopes for independence. "You can see," she ended, "that I had to do something. Otherwise my whole business is going to go right down the drain."

"I do understand." Lady Comberley seemed deeply sympathetic. "I'd have done exactly the same thing myself."

Cassie rather doubted that. "What I really need to know is whether Sonia had any local enemies."

"Anyone who disliked her enough to trek over to this hotel on a Sunday in the hope of bumping her off, you mean?" Lady Comberley's voice was as rich as gravy.

"That sort of thing."

"She certainly didn't get on with everyone. She was a very quarrelsome woman indeed. Take Giles Laughton, for instance, the chap who just went by on horseback. He's had several brushes with Miss Wetherhead in the past. His farm backs onto her garden, or what became her garden, once she'd bought some land from him. Mind you, I'm fond of Giles, known him since he was a boy, but he's not all that even-tempered himself. He and Miss Wetherhead had what I can only call a stormy relationship. Strictly in a business sense, I mean. There wasn't anything else between them. At least . . ." Her voice tailed off. "Not as far as I know."

Which was probably far enough, Cassie considered, though Lady Comberley was much too well bred to keep a watch on her neighbor, or even wish to.

She decided she would have to have a word with farmer Giles. He sounded like a possible suspect, unlikely as it might be that he would, as Lady Comberley put it, trek all the way over to the Broughton Manor Hotel in the hope of finding Sonia available and an alabaster obelisk to hand.

"The problem with poor Miss Wetherhead was that she had an unfortunate habit of . . . well, drinking more than was good for her and then behaving rather badly," Lady Comberley was saying.

"Shouting and being sick sort of badly?" asked Cassie.

"Worse than that, I'm afraid. Saying the most outrageous, the most unforgivable things. Insulting people. The village was not at all sympathetic. Even the rector found it hard to be pleasant . . ."

"But she can't have been so outrageous that someone would have actually murdered her, could she?"

Instead of dismissing the suggestion, Lady Comberley looked thoughtful. "Some of us mind so much more than others about that sort of thing, don't you agree? Perhaps it's a question of insecurity. I wasn't particularly put out by the insults she hurled at me, but some people are very undermined by personal remarks, very wounded."

Tell me about it. Vividly Cassie remembered the horror of the days after Gran's death, the boarding school Uncle Samuel picked out, the sheer awfulness of adolescence. Nobody is entirely secure in those years between leaving childhood and becoming an adult, but when the insults hinge on the way you talk, the way you look, the background you came from . . .

"I certainly wouldn't completely dismiss the idea of someone being angered sufficiently to kill her," continued Lady Comberley. "But not, I think, in the circumstances you've described."

A dark green Rover pulled up in the lane outside and a woman wearing a navy-blue quilted jacket got out. She could have been Lady Comberley's twin sister—quite possibly was—and Cassie deduced that the first of the ladies had arrived for their afternoon bridge.

"And then, of course, there was the business with her former husband and Giles's former wife," Lady Comberley said.

"What business?"

"Oh dear. I really can't go into it at the moment. Perhaps you would care to call later—though it was years ago and can't possibly have anything to do with what happened at the Broughton Manor Hotel."

"I'll talk to you some other time," said Cassie quickly, as Lady Comberley's twin rang the doorbell. "Meanwhile, it might be helpful to have a quick word with Giles Laughton. How do I get to his place?"

Driving between brick barns and long pale sheds along a muddy track splattered with fresh cow droppings, Cassie pulled into a yard in front of what she took to be Laughton's farmhouse. Wisps of straw blew about along with the snowflakes; beneath a covering of snow, plastic sacks of winter feed were stacked against a wall. There was a lot of mud.

Not much of your rural charm here, Cassie thought, stepping from her car into a long-dropped cowpat. Like a well-made meringue, it was crispy on the outside and soft on the inside; unlike a meringue, it oozed green muck when stood on. She cursed, smelling cows. In front of her, the farmhouse, as if cocking a deliberate snook at the fake folksiness of the village, was a crudely modern two-story red-brick affair, strictly lavatorial in design, and devoid of the slightest charm.

Looking around, she knew at once she was on the right track. Excitement filled her. Parked alongside an extensive milking shed was a high-sided white van which proclaimed the information that Laughton's Dairy Farms sold dairy products which were second to none. Beneath them were displayed the brawny arms and healthy smile of the very same bucket-toting milk-maid she had seen pulling away from the Broughton Manor Hotel at more or less the same time Sonia Wetherhead had been battered to death.

Surely it could not be this easy. Briefly, as though assessing a new hand of cards just picked up from the table, Cassie ran over the possibilities. Had Giles Laughton driven over to the hotel, delivered his first-class eggs, his unbeatable milk, then found himself somehow embroiled with Sonia and killed her? Or had he perhaps known, being a near neighbor, that she would be there that weekend and realized this presented him with a perfect opportunity to get rid of her without fouling his own nest?

She shook her head. Too many holes. For instance, why would Laughton have come into the main part of the hotel if the encounter with Sonia had been random? Sonia was hardly likely to have been hanging around the kitchens (though she made a mental note to check this one out). And if the meeting was *not* random but planned, how would Laughton have known where to find Sonia? And even if he had, even if he was familiar with the house—on dining-out terms with Felix Ryland, perhaps—would he really have been prepared to get rid of Sonia in front of two witnesses like the Plumptons, however strong the urge?

She recalled the Macbeth Room as she had seen it that Sunday morning just over a month ago. There was the bridge table, the spread cards, the two dead bodies at the table and the one on the floor . . .

Another possibility struck her. Wild as it might seem, suppose the two Plumptons had died before Sonia ever came into the room. She imagined Giles Laughton, his milk delivered, wandering into the main house to exchange a word or two with his friend Felix Ryland, bumping into Sonia, who either picked a fresh quarrel or revived an old one (the English habit of understatement could well mean that Lady Comberley's remark about "a stormy relationship" in actual fact covered a case of terminal loathing, especially given the "business" of former spouses at which she had so tantalizingly hinted.) Suppose, raging, Giles had followed Sonia into the Macbeth Room, taken in at a glance the two dead at the table, and before he quite knew what he was doing, had grabbed the nearest object and brought it down on Sonia's skull.

Specious, Cassie told herself. Unconvincing. But none-theless possible. The more she considered the events of that morning, the more obvious it was that the killing of Sonia must have been one of those impulsive acts, a spur-of-the-moment event when means and opportunity had provided an unassailable occasion for murder.

"Yes?" A man had appeared. A grumpy, frowning man, clad in the oiled jacket, quilted jerkin, and Wellingtons which seemed to be regulation uniform for country dwellers. Cassie owned versions of all three of them herself, though she tried not to be seen wearing the jerkin.

"Are you Giles Laughton?" she asked.

"Yes. But we're not open, if you've come to look round the farm. Don't open until Easter—didn't you see the sign?"

"I saw it, but I wanted to see you, not the—"

"Why? Who are you?" The frown deepened. If he smiled instead, he'd be quite attractive, Cassie thought. In his early thirties, all that flaming red hair, the kind of forcefulness which she liked . . . Opting this time for honesty, she said, "My name's Cassandra Swann and I teach bridge."

Laughton gave a short barking laugh. "It's my moth-er you want to talk to. Not that there's much you could teach the old girl: she's been playing for the last few centuries, born with a pack of cards in her hand, I always tell her." His voice was attractive, warm, leaning toward the intonation of the landed gentry.

"Actually it's not her I—"

"Just missed her, I'm afraid. She's gone to play bridge with her usual bunch of old biddies."

"I wouldn't call Lady Comberley an old biddy," Cassie said.

"Know her, do you?"

"No. But I—" Cassie raised her voice as he started to interrupt yet again. "I was talking to her just now about Sonia Wetherhead."

That stopped him. He stared at her, his face flushing with some emotion—anger, almost certainly, though she was not sure it was directed at her.

"You did know she was dead, didn't you?" Cassie asked.

"Of course I knew. A place like this, you can't scratch your arse without half the village knowing about it," he said roughly. "But what's it got to do with you? I've already talked to the police about it."

She knew a moment of depression. Her mission was not only vague, it was impossible. What did she think she was doing, racing about Oxfordshire in the hope of picking up some crumb which might have fallen unnoticed from policemen's tables? Moreover, the role of the amateur sleuth which she had temporarily adopted was not what it was in Lord Peter Wimsey's day—the police were not only skilled but had most of today's technology at their disposal. "Yes, but—" she began.

"Who the hell do you think you are anyway?" The frown reappeared, this time accompanied by a scowl.

It was one of those metaphysical questions she had often wished she could answer. "Did you deliver milk to the Broughton Manor Hotel on the Sunday Sonia was murdered?" she said bluntly.

"I've already told the police that one of my men did the milk deliveries that Sunday, since I was bell ringing at the church from ten-thirty until morning service started at eleven o'clock, at which I was reading the first lesson. Isaiah, chapter six, verses one to eight," Laughton said firmly.

"*In the year that King Uzziah died . . .*" Cassie said. Country ways, she thought. This was the real rural England, not all those dried rose petals and turned-beech napkin rings, but this solidity of expectation, this involvement with the community in which you lived, reading the lesson on Sunday, the village fete, fund-raising for the Mothers' Union, the flower show . . .

"Sonia was a gifted woman," Laughton said, staring off at the fields which rose behind his ugly house. "Especially in her ability to make people dislike her. I never met anyone so capable of rousing instant loathing."

"Anyone in particular? Anyone who might have—"

"Everyone in general, really." He sighed, hinting at tender areas beneath his brusqueness. "You couldn't hate her, you had to feel sorry for someone so much at the mercy of her emotions. I certainly don't subscribe to the notion that artistic people are somehow to be excused from showing normal good manners or consideration for others, but there was no denying that Sonia's temperament made her something of a victim. And if you've already spoken to Hilda Comberley, I expect she told you that Sonia and I were constantly at loggerheads."

"She did mention something about a former hus—"

"And she drank too, which she shouldn't have done,"

Laughton continued. "She was one of those people who couldn't touch a drop without becoming instantly leg-less—there's a medical name for it, though I can't remember what."

"Presumably you've got witnesses to vouch for your bell-ringing activities on that Sunday," Cassie said.

Laughton said violently, "Of course I bloody have. And in case you're wondering, I haven't got a twin brother who could have stood in for me. I haven't got the ability to be in two places at once. And I haven't got time to waste on talking to idiotic women who come bothering me with stupid questions."

"Fair enough," Cassie said. "Talking of normal good manners . . ." She smiled at him and watched him, even-tually, flush. "If you ever think of taking up bridge . . ." She gave him one of her business cards and saw him reluctantly put it in his pocket. With amusement, she guessed that he didn't quite have the balls to tear it up in front of her.

Darkness was beginning to fall as the winter evening settled down across the scrubby fields, and a cold sun subsided below the hill which rose behind the house. A faint red reflection shone through Laughton's hair, as though somewhere nearby the jaws of hell had opened, lending him a rakish Byronic air.

Driving away between the cowpats, Cassie told herself that seemed to be that. Although there was still the mat-ter of the two former spouses to ask Lady Comberley about, Laughton had proved to be a dead end, just like Thomas Lambert. Except that Laughton had an alibi and witnesses to prove he was where he said he was, however small the local congregation might be.

Any hopes she'd had of turning up some significant fact which would establish exactly who had killed Sonia Wetherhead were looking fairly slim. Unlike her. Although she was starving, she drove resolutely past a pub with a sign outside it advertising GOOD FOOD, partly because it would be salutary for her to do without dinner and partly because she had learned by experience that such claims usually meant the food on offer was memorably bad.

DRIVING back to her cottage through dark, high-hedged lanes, she thought of Midge McKendrick again. Midge had traveled all the way down from Scotland in order to talk about a wall hanging for the mythical showcase industrial site in Strathspey. At least, had she had any basis in reality, she would have done. According to Thomas Lambert's article on Sonia Wetherhead, Dr. James Hagerty had also commissioned work: did he have any bearing on Sonia's death? It might be worth trying to find out.

Once again she went over the sequence of events. Sonia comes into the room, finds the Plumptons dealing the cards, joins them, plays three rounds with them. Then the murderer enters, says something which causes Sonia to rise from her chair—or perhaps he simply hits her while she's still sitting there. She gets up, staggers about and falls to the floor, dead. The Plumptons, meanwhile, are at first mesmerized by the violence erupting in front of them, then first one and then the other, or both simultaneously, succumb.

Hmm.

As Mantripp had said: Surely she could do better than that.

But how? What other scenario could there be?

Her headlights lit up a fox ambling down the middle of the lane. The pointed head looked back at her over the animal's shoulder, the wild yellow eyes seemed to gaze into hers, then it veered off in leisurely fashion toward the sheltering hedge.

What still puzzled her was why the killer had chosen such an unlikely moment to commit his crime. Most murderers hoped to get away with what they had done. This one could not have relied on the Plumptons to do the decent thing and die, so what precautions had he taken to prevent them from raising the alarm? Or had he bumped them off in some subtle and undetectable way? In any case, how had he proposed to escape?

She was back with the Groucho Marx false-nose-and-mustache bit—and increasingly unsatisfactory it seemed.

And thinking this, she felt a worm of doubt inch its way through the crowded images in her brain. Something . . . some detail which she had noted at the

time but could not quite recall . . . what was it she had
seen or heard which shed some kind of light on things?

She sighed. If it were not for the fact that her livelihood was under threat, she would be glad never to think
of Sonia Wetherhead again. And once the murderer had
been apprehended, she promised herself, she never
would. But until that happened, police or no police, she
might as well keep on trying to unravel the mystery.

It was after eight when she got home. Bullet-biting
time. Pouring herself a strong drink, Cassie rang
through to the school where her weekly evening class
was held and got hold of the Adult Education Officer.

"I need to contact one of my students before classes
start again," she said. It sounded reasonable. "Charles
Quartermain. Could you look him up and give me an
address or phone number?"

The AEO could and did. Refilling her glass, Cassie
made a second call. The androgynous voice which
answered did not sound in the least like Charlie
Quartermain.

"St. Alphege's Vicarage. Can I help you?"

"I think I must have a wrong number," she said. "I
was looking for Char—for Mr. Quartermain."

"He won't be back until next Thursday," the voice
said. Cassie wondered if it knew that prior to his eleva-
tion to sainthood, the unfortunate Alphege had been
viciously pelted with bones by drunken Danes at
Greenwich until he was finally felled by an ax, despite
the intervention of a sober Scandinavian called Thorkell
the Tall. It was one of the more lively scenes from ecclesiastical history rammed down her throat by her Uncle
Samuel and one she had frequently wanted to repeat

with her cousins—stopping short of the ax, of course. The idea of pelting vegetarian Primula with gnawed ham bones had a beauty all its own.

"Thursday," she repeated. The first night of the spring session of evening classes.

"He comes up every Thursday. Goes off to his bridge class and comes back to us," the voice said in kindly fashion.

Cassie wondered where Quartermain spent the rest of the time. "Perhaps you could ask him to telephone me." she said. "My name's Cassandra Swann."

"Ah yes. The bridge teacher."

"How did you—"

"Charlie's told us such a lot about you."

"I wouldn't have thought he had an awful lot to tell."

"We're delighted. Truly delighted," the voice said.

"What about?"

The voice swept on over her question. "I'll certainly tell him you rang."

Putting down the receiver, she felt a rush of heat somewhere in the region of her neck. What the hell was the voice—impossible to decide whether it had been male or female—so delighted about? Somehow she did not think it had anything to do with the fact that Quartermain had taken up bridge. Much more likely that he was making false claims about their exceedingly minimalist relationship.

In a spirit of Christian charity, she told herself she should feel compassion for a man so lonely that he had to fabricate a friendship with a woman he saw once a week standing at a blackboard. Though a woman with whom, she had to concede, he also paid a weekly visit to

the pub afterward. And in whose home he had drunk—
and spilled—champagne. But even so, the fact
remained that there was nothing between them. She
imagined herself turning up to what Derek and Primula
called a supper party with Charlie Quartermain on her
arm. She thought of him picking up Primula's glass ani-
mals or fingering some of Derek's collection of ghastly
pipes. She shuddered.

"Ullo, darlin'."

"Who is this?" Cassie asked in her starchiest voice,
though she knew perfectly well.

"I'm in Rheims," Quartermain said. He wheezed
asthmatically, filling the receiver with chesty noise. "The
vick said you'd telephoned."

"Vick? Oh, you mean the vicar at St. Alphege's?"

"That's the one. What can I do for you?"

"I wanted to talk to you about Sonia Wetherhead."

"What for?"

"I'm trying to—" She stopped. It sounded too Miss
Marple-ish to say she was trying to find out who had
killed the weaver, when there was a team of highly
trained specialists already on the job. "I know I'll be seeing you next Thursday but—"

"But you couldn't wait until then, right?"

"Right," she said uneasily. She hoped he did not
imagine that she was impatient to see him. She was, of
course, but not in the sense he was bound to assume.

"I'll be back in England tomorrow morning," he said.
"I'll drive up. Will you be at home in the evening?"

"Yes. But please don't come up specially."

"Half an hour either side of six. Is that OK?"

"Yes. But I shall be going—"

"See you then," he said. He rang off.

There was snow on his shoulders as he came stooping through the cottage door just before five-thirty. Behind him, the night was filled with whirling flakes. Rubbing his ungloved hands, he made for the log fire roaring in the hearth and stood in front of it, shivering.

"Blimey, it's parky out there," he said. "Blow, blow, thou winter's wind and all that."

She bit back a correction. She had been washing her hair when the doorbell rang, before dressing for the dinner party being given by a couple who lived in the next village and it was wrapped in a green bath towel. Feeling at a disadvantage, she said, "Would you like a drink?"

"Oh, here." He reached into a pocket of his Barbour and pulled out a bottle of champagne, into another and produced a bottle of whiskey. "Take your pick, darlin'."

Did calling someone a form of the word "darling" when you didn't want them to constitute sexual harassment? "I'll join you in a whiskey," she said, "though I do have some of my own, you know," and hoped she did not sound as prim as she felt she did. Something about Quartermain brought out the governessy side of her nature, a side she had never even known she possessed until he had first shown up at her door.

As they sat down opposite each other, the wind howled in the chimney and the flames momentarily sagged before blazing up brighter than before.

Somewhere a window rattled. Quartermain leaned back against the cushions of the sofa and spread his large thighs inelegantly. "Gawd," he said. "It's nice to be home."

"Back in England, do you mean?" Cassie asked, anxious to emphasize the difference between her home and his.

"That's right."

He was wearing a double-breasted suit of some dark striped material and a flamboyant silk tie. She found it unexpectedly difficult to broach the subject of Sonia Wetherhead, even though that was the specific reason for him being there. "What were you doing in Rheims?" she asked politely.

"Is that how you pronounce it?"

"It's how *I* pronounce it."

"Yer, well, I was at a dinner with some mates of mine, wasn't I?"

"You've got a lot of French connections, have you?"

"Not really, darlin'. But I got a lot of French letters, if you're interested." He chuckled coarsely, his big face shaking.

Cassie curled her lip. "About Sonia," she said in freezing tones. "How well did you know her?"

"Well enough for her to get right up my nose, like I said before. I saw a fair old bit of her for a while, because we were both sitting on this committee, trying to raise public consciousness about rural crafts or some such poncey crap."

Cassie expelled an impatient breath.

"My language too ripe for you?" he asked.

"It's not that I'm shocked by the words you use," she

said, not looking at him. "It's just that they seem so unnecessary."

"Sorry, luv."

"Did you and Sonia talk at all?" Cassie said, wishing he were elsewhere, hoping he hadn't arrived expecting she would spend the evening with him. "Did she tell you anything about herself? Anything at all which might have had relevance to her death?"

"Like whether she'd been getting poison-pen letters or death threats over the phone?" he said, laughing so that the buttons strained on his shirt. Horrid glimpses of the hairy belly beneath were revealed.

She averted her gaze. "That sort of thing."

"Poor old Son," he said. "She was an awkward bint, at the best of times. I shouldn't think she had any enemies, as such, except herself, but I don't suppose she had many friends either."

"Can you think of any reason why anyone would wish to kill her?"

"None at all."

"Did she have a husband, a lover, anything like that?"

"There was a husband once. Got lost along the way, I can't remember how. As for lovers, women like Sonia don't stick to one man. She liked it, know what I mean? Plenty of it."

"Are you talking about sex?"

"What else, darlin'."

"Were *you* one of her lovers?"

"Me? Don't be bleedin' stupid. Been savin' myself for you, haven't I?"

"You're exceedingly unlikely to collect the interest on your nest egg," Cassie said tartly.

"We'll have to see how it works out, won't we, luv?"

There was an assurance in his voice which appalled her. He got up and stood by the fire again. Steam rose gently from his large behind. He put his glass down on the exposed beam which served as an overmantel and walked across to the cabinet where she kept her two Angelica Kauffmann plates. Before she could stop him, he had opened it and taken one out, slanting it toward the firelight.

"Gawd," he said, shaking his big head. "I do like these."

"So do I," Cassie said. "So please put them down."

He ignored her. "Interesting woman, Angie was. I mean, when you think about it, this Swiss bint being a founding member of the Royal Academy." He adopted a ludicrous facsimile of an upper-class accent: "When of ah most sacred institooshuns."

"Look, Mr. Quartermain, I really do have to get on." Although she spoke with firmness, Cassie felt a little guilty. After all, the guttering had been done. "Incidentally, how much do I owe your friend for doing the roof?"

"Nothing, darlin'. But if you insist, you could come out to dinner with me one night." He put down the plate, rather harder than Cassie would have liked. "That'd be more than adequate payment, far as I'm concerned."

"I'm perfectly capable of paying my debts," she said, thinking she could hardly imagine a dinner date she would less like to engage in: what on earth would she talk to him about?

"Wossa matter?" he said. "Think you'll run out of things to talk about?"

"Run out?" She raised cool eyebrows. "As a matter of fact, I was thinking I wouldn't even know how to get started . . ."

Apparently he did not hear her. He picked up a silver-framed photograph of Sarah. "Who's this?"

"My mother."

"Good-looking lady," he said. "Like her daughter."

"Thank you."

"Where does she live, then?"

"She doesn't. She's dead."

"How long ago?"

"When I was six," Cassie said briefly.

She had no intention of telling him about the traumatic days after Sarah's death: her handsome father; Gran, who taught her to play bridge; the pub. It was different without Sarah there, but they had managed, the three of them—most of the time. Until her father died, typically, stabbed to death in a brawl with some yobs outside the pub who were trying to kick a policewoman into pulp. That was when Uncle Samuel, whom Cassie had seen only once before, turned up and tried to carry his sister's orphaned child back to the rectory—except Gran wouldn't let him. Not for another two years, when Gran could no longer stop him because she herself was dead.

Perhaps that was why she felt so uneasy with Charlie Quartermain. She'd grown up with men like him—coarse men with huge bellies and big hearts—only to find, when she moved to the rectory, that she ought to despise them for their accents, their clothes, their want of education, their lack of middle-class values.

Quartermain reached forward and put his glass down

on a leather-bound copy of *Le Morte d'Arthur* which had once belonged to Cassie's grandfather. She snatched it off before a ring could form. Conscious that her own behavior was not exactly as recommended by the etiquette manuals, she added quickly, "Would you like a refill?"

He looked at his watch. "Have we got time?"

"We?"

"Yes."

"Time to do what?"

"I've booked a table at the Wheatsheaf," he said.

"For tonight?"

"Yer. Just on the off chance. It'll take us twenty minutes to get there."

"Hang on a minute," Cassie said. "You haven't asked me if I want to have dinner with you. You don't even know if I'm free."

"You are, aren't you?"

"As a matter of fact, I'm not. I tried to explain to you on the phone but you put it down before I could finish my sentence."

"Tell him you can't make it."

"Tell whom?"

"This bloke you say you're going out with tonight."

She stared at him with hostility. "Not only *say* but am," she said. "And even if I wasn't, I certainly wouldn't accept your invitation."

"Why not?"

"For a start, I strongly object to being steamrollered."

He shrugged. "Just thought you'd like to," he said. "Thought it'd take your mind off things."

"That's very kind of you but I am able to look after

myself. And then there's the other point: I don't . . . I can't—" She broke off, unable to come right out and say to his face—his huge crass face with its mouthful of neglected teeth—that even if she were free, it would embarrass her to be seen in public with him. This was Saturday night; the Wheatsheaf was the best restaurant for miles and the chances that someone she knew would be there were very high. Hyacinth, for instance, often ate there, along with her boring second husband, the MP for some minor constituency. So did the ladies with whom she regularly played bridge. Seeing her there with him, they might assume that she and Charlie Quartermain were . . . "As I said, I can't come out with you tonight," she said.

She knew all about the classless society: it was a nice theory but impossible to put into practice. Class did exist. It couldn't be legislated out of the way. It wasn't that she despised Charlie or anything snobby like that. Apart from his behavior, he was obviously a nice bloke: warm, caring, thoughtful. A ruff ♦, she thought, pleased with the joke, and none the worse for that. It was simply that they were poles apart in just about everything that mattered, like education, like—old-fashioned as it might sound—breeding, like expectations.

"Well, how about Thursday night?" said Quartermain. "After class?"

"I don't really—" If she agreed she might be establishing a precedent. On the other hand, she undeniably owed him something for the gutters.

"Come on, Cassie," he said gently. "You'll have to eat sometime that evening and it won't hurt you to eat with me. I promise not to slurp my soup or belch at the waiter, OK?"

She blushed. Had she made her feelings that obvious? Guilt made her say, "All right," and add awkwardly, "Thank you."

When she got home later that night, she found messages on her answering machine. Operating the mechanism—with a certain amount of difficulty, the evening having become bibulous—she heard two more of the voices she had come to expect since Thomas's Lambert's facetious article about the deadly game of bridge had appeared in the *Mail*. Both belonged to hoteliers; both asked her to call them back urgently. She knew what they wanted: to cancel the weekends she was booked to spend as the resident bridge professional. They would just have to ring *her* back, since she was damned if she was going to add insult to injury by footing the bill for a telephone call in which they dispensed with her services.

There was a third message: "Giles Laughton here. I've—er—I've remembered something . . ." Behind him there was a hissing noise suggestive of a heroic goose in the throes of protecting the gates of Rome against barbarian invaders. "Something which might be useful." More hissing, as though the barbarian invaders were actually breaking through. "No!" Giles said forcefully, head turned away. Then, into the receiver again: "Give me a ring." He'd left his number and rung off.

Curious, she lifted the telephone, then realized it was too late to call him now. It would have to wait until the morning.

The morning was soggy, cold; the dead ashes of yesterday's fire lay on the raised stone hearth like a reproach. As though to compensate for two mild winters, this year the temperatures had dropped below freezing shortly after Christmas and remained there ever since. Cassie scattered bread for the birds outside the back door and looked across the lawn to her vegetable garden. Despite the pale sun, the turned furrows of earth were iron hard and frosted with rime. It seemed a long time until the summer's harvest, the bounty of autumn.

She dialled Laughton's number. "Cassandra Swann here."

"Oh yes, hello."

"You left a message to call you."

"Um—yes, that's right, I did."

The telephonic Giles Laughton sounded a very different person from the corporeal one. More hesitant, less belligerent. She wondered if he was still frowning.

She said, "What did you want?"

"It's just that, well, I—er—remembered I still got a key to—um—Sonia's place. I wondered if you would like to—er—"

"Poke round?"

"Something like that."

She wanted to ask who had been hissing during his message and what they were hissing about. Instead she said, "Do we have to ask for permission from the police?"

"I don't know. It's not sealed off or anything." Suddenly regaining himself, he went on: "I'm sure it's completely illegal but it might be useful to you."

"Thank you."

"I'm afraid I was a bit brusque with you the other day.

I told my mother you'd been and she was frightfully impressed. Says you're very well known and I shouldn't have been so rude. So bloody rude is what she actually said."

"I could come over tomorrow afternoon," Cassie said. "I want to see Lady Comberley about something, and if it's convenient with her I could drop in and see you afterward."

"Fine. And perhaps you'd have time for a cup of tea. My mother would love to meet you."

"Thank you." Had it been the mother doing the hissing? "That would be lovely."

"It was bell-ringing which brought them together," Lady Comberley said. She sat straight-backed in an armchair, hands in her lap, ankles neatly crossed, as she must have been taught in her deportment classes sixty years before. "All four of them used to turn out regularly for the church team, the Laughtons and the Wetherheads. Ironic, really, when you think about it."

"In what way, exactly?"

"Well, I mean adultery is one of the Ten Commandments, isn't it?—not *doing* it but *not* doing it, if you see what I mean. And bell ringing is sort of holy, isn't it?"

Cassie thought of the team of bell ringers at Uncle Samuel's church, a grog-blossomed lot whose holiness was very much in question, including, as it did, the local publican, the local poacher, the village Casanova and a City commuter who had done time for fraud. "Is it?"

"It takes place in a church, after all."

"The belfry of a church," Cassie said.

"Not exactly the ideal place for a spot of hanky-panky, one would have thought."

Birds do it; bats do it . . . "Where would you think *was* the ideal place, then?"

"I don't know." Lady Comberley uncrossed her ankles and crossed them the other way. "Some silk-hung boudoir, perhaps, with a huge squashy bed in it, and a silver bucket of champagne to hand. Some Mozart—no, some Elgar playing softly nearby. And the sound of plashing fountains in the distance." She gazed into the wood fire smoking in a small grate. A faint flush colored her face. Was she remembering some long-ago tryst? Some lost lover? "And then," she said dreamily. "After you've—you know—a maid brings in tea with a plateful of tiny cucumber sandwiches, made with thin white bread and left in the fridge all after-noon so that they're cold and a little damp—lovely, after all that sweating and—" She broke off. "*That's* the sort of ideal circumstances in which to conduct an illicit affair, I should think," she said briskly, "rather than some cold church tower with bat droppings all over the place and lots of other people present. Wouldn't you agree?"

"Definitely," Cassie said. Both she and Lady Comberley were conscious of ground somehow shifted: had it been lost or gained?

"And after a bit, people began to bump into Amanda Laughton and Perry Wetherhead in the strangest places—lunching together at the King's Head in Whiteham, for instance. Well, I mean. After that it was only a matter of time."

"Before they split up with their partners?"

"Yes. Sad, really. Giles was absolutely frantic. He blamed Sonia, do you see, for not taking better care of Perry, thus giving him a reason to chase after Amanda. Nonsense, of course. As though committing adultery depended on how well your spouse looked after you. Or loved you, even. I know my own husband was the most loving of men but that didn't prevent—" She broke off. "Anyway, Sonia got annoyed. She went round to Giles's place one evening with a shotgun and fired it at the windows. Nearly caught poor Mercy—his mother—in the knee. Luckily she had just put her feet up on the coffee table, so the pellets went into the sofa instead."

"Heavens," Cassie said. "What did she do?"

"Called the police immediately. She knew it was Sonia, of course, but decided it would be better if Sergeant Ripton had a word with her. I can't say I blame her: last time she remonstrated with Sonia, Sonia started throwing clothes-pegs at her."

"Like St. Alphege," Cassie said.

"Possibly." Lady Comberley looked thoughtful. "Funny, I never envisaged clothes-pegs as something the average saint would have owned. Somehow one doesn't imagine them doing the laundry, does one? Anyway, the whole incident was most unpleasant, especially at Mercy's time of life."

"What happened to Amanda and—er—Perry?"

"Lived together happily ever after, as far as I know. Emigrated to New Zealand or somewhere, to Perry's sheep farm. Mind you, that farm was the cause of the trouble in the first place, if you ask me. Sonia refused point-blank to go out there, said she would never have married him if she'd realized he expected her to start rearing sheep before the ink on her marriage lines was even dry."

"Neither of them bore Sonia any grudge, presumably," Cassie said, trying to envisage a pair of antipodean sheep farmers sneaking round the tiled corridors of Broughton Manor in the hope of bumping Sonia off. As often in the past, she reflected on the peculiarly philosophical acceptance with which country dwellers viewed violence in others, as part and parcel of everyday living, nothing out of the ordinary. Which, in Moreton Lacey, perhaps it was.

"Not in the least. But the reason I wanted to have a word with you is, that the brother of Amanda Laughton—as she then was—plays bridge."

On its own, this revelation hardly seemed worth nearly an hour's cross-country driving. "And . . .?" Cass said.

"It struck me that possibly he was on the same weekend course as Sonia, and, seeing her again, remembered Amanda's grief and decided to take revenge."

"But surely it would be Sonia who had the grief," Cassie said. "It was Amanda who went off with Sonia's husband, not the other way around."

"It comes to much the same thing in the end, my dear, as you will realize when you're my age."

"What was his name?"

"He calls himself Evelyn Charteris, I believe. Or is it Emlyn?"

"You mean that's not his real name?"

"I don't think so. He's an actor of sorts."

"I think I've heard of him," said Cassie. "But there wasn't anyone there with a name like that."

"Pity." Lady Comberley appeared disappointed. "It

seemed so obvious, when one thought about it. Emlyn running into Sonia, the woman who has ruined his sister's life—"

"But she—"

"—picking up some object and bringing it down on her head, just on the spur of the moment, do you see, never intending to kill her. But if he wasn't there, it can't have been him, can it?"

"Not really." It did not seem worth pointing out again that Sonia could hardly be said to have ruined the life of a woman who was living happily ever after on a sheep farm in New Zealand. Cassie was glad she had combined this drive with seeing Giles Laughton; the visit to Lady Comberley was clearly wasted time.

"When one was a gull, one used to go over to Broughton Manor for dances," Mercy Laughton said wistfully. "Carried one's shoes in little bags made of beige linen and changed into them when one got there. They had some wonderful evenings: Violet Ryland was so marvelously inventive. I remember an Oriental evening when we all had to come as Chinamen with pigtails and pajamas and eat with chopsticks. And another one, a Spanish ball in honor of the brave boys fighting in the International Brigade, where we dressed up as flamenco dancers and matadors. Huge bulls' heads made of papier-mâché hanging all round the walls, great jugs of sangria and risotto all over the place."

She pulled at a tumbler of gin which sat stickily on a table beside her chair, then dragged on the cigarette which she was holding in the vicinity of her mouth in a hair grip. Either the smoking or the drinking—or both—had given her voice a strong resemblance to the crunching of broken glass.

"Risotto comes in dishes, Mother, not jugs," Giles said.

Mercy ignored him. "That was a damn good evening," she said. "I remember going out to the greenhouses with Toby Knox-Webber during one of the intervals—you remember Toby, Giles."

"Bit of a sadistic old sod, wasn't he?" Giles said. "Always slapping us kids about, I seem to recall."

"It wasn't so much slap as tickle, in those days," his mother said. "And very nice too. I remember once—"

"That's enough remembering for one afternoon," Giles said quickly.

"Is it?"

"You are rather boring on, you know. Cassandra didn't come here to listen to your risqué past."

"Didn't she?"

"She wants to go and look over Sonia's place."

"I was very interested in what you were saying about Broughton Manor," Cassie said, frowning at Giles.

"Were you? It all changed after the war, of course," Mercy said. "All three of the Ryland boys were killed, you know. It broke their father's heart—he died shortly after Armistice Day, very sad. One remembers it so clearly."

The generations were so closed to each other, Cassie thought. To her, those late-night black-and-white films which occasionally surfaced on TV, of debonair chaps in uniform taking off in primitive aircraft to drop bombs on Dresden, or dancing with girls in roadhouses to the

music of ten-piece bands before flying into the wild blue
yonder to their deaths, were as much period pieces as
Gone With the Wind. But women the age of Mercy
Laughton or Hilda Comberley had *been* those skimpy-
skirted ATS and WRAFS with the oblique vowels and
the puff-rolled hair. All those lost sons, those doomed
brothers and young husbands had been the men they
knew, whereas to Cassie's generation they might have
been courtiers to Henry VIII for all the contemporary
relevance they had.

"It must have been devastating," she said.

"It was. In the end, Violet sold the house to someone
who turned it into a school for daughters of distressed
gentlewomen or some such thing. After that, I think it
was bought by developers, but by then one had really
rather lost touch. Too busy running things here and
coping with the boys—my husband was something of an
invalid, so one was managing the farm more or less sin-
gle-handed." Ice cubes bobbed against the sides of her
glass as she poured gin down her throat. "And you say
that a Ryland has bought it back again?"

"That's right."

"One ought to make an effort to call but one probably
won't," Mercy said perfunctorily. "Which cousin is it?"

"He's called Felix."

Mercy shrugged. "I vaguely remember the name but I
can't remember the face. There were so many Ryland
cousins scattered all over the British Isles: the house was
always crammed with them. Felix, you say?" Her upper
lip was fissured like a cliff face as she reached forward to
touch Cassie's knee. "I'll tell you what, though."

"Yes?"

"Plumpton. Colonel Plumpton. I don't know if it's the same chap but I certainly remember someone of that name during the war, when we were all stationed down in Somerset. Not that he was Colonel then, of course, couldn't have been more than twenty-something. I bumped into him years later in the Strand Palais, dancing the hokey-cokey with some of the boys from the War Office and waving a pair of French knickers around."

"Mother!" Giles said.

"What's wrong with waving?" Mercy said. "I didn't say he was wearing them, did I?" She turned back to Cassie. "Used to be an art teacher, I believe."

"So did the one who died at the Broughton Manor Hotel."

"Must be the same man. Small world, isn't it? I remember once—"

"Why don't I take Cassandra over to Sonia's place before it gets dark," Giles said.

"Just a minute," his mother protested. "I was going to tell her something else."

"What was it?" Cassie said. She liked older people, the accumulation of experience, the memories of times and occasions so different and yet not different at all.

"He's made me forget. Something about Reggie Plumpton. It'll come back to me, I expect."

Giles Laughton reached down and plucked Cassie's hand from her lap to hold it in his. It was a big hand, warm and faintly rasping, like holding a wood file or the branch of a tree. "Come along," he said.

So, meekly, she went.

THE Methodist chapel still smelled of hymnbooks and hopeful worthiness, instantly filling Cassie with an echo of her own adolescence. If there was a single word which summed up her antipathy to the notion of "God," it was guilt, the whole ethos of being made to feel shame for feelings which were a direct consequence of being human and fashioned in His likeness. She remembered her own burgeoning flesh at the age of thirteen, such a contrast to the neat trimness of the

twins, her periods, Aunt Polly's barely concealed embarrassment and even anger. Recalling all the bewilder-
ment, she took a deep breath. Think magnificent, she
told herself; think snowy bosoms.

The ground floor of the former chapel was a single
large room with a perfunctory kitchen at one end and
primitive bathroom arrangements beyond that. Above
the kitchen area was a boarded upper gallery, across the
front of which a text proclaimed in Gothic lettering of
faded gold: THOU LORD SEEST ME.

For Cassie's taste there was too much empty space
between wooden ceiling and living area, too much room
for a vengeful God to lurk, too much opportunity for
worm-chewed beams to fall in retribution on the heads
of those who, like herself, lacked simple faith. However,
she found Sonia's decor sympathetic. In the main it ran
to clutter: chipped mugs full of paintbrushes and pencils, swatches of brightly patterned material, wooden
toys, cracked dishes piled on a stripped pine dresser
mixed up with some really beautiful pieces of antique
hand-painted china, feathers, postcards, pebbles, painted jugs. The furniture was mostly creaking wicker chairs,
pine settles and ancient sofas hidden by woven spreads.
There were baskets full of magazines, wooden trugs
crammed with dried flowers, half an oak barrel stuffed
with balls of wool. Clutter, yes, but organized clutter. In
the middle of the room, a huge table was covered with a
bright cotton bedspread on which were stacked more
magazines, more painted pottery, a cutout cockerel of
black-painted tin, a profusion of candlesticks. Three
withered apples lay at the bottom of a bowl; a lidded jar
of blue earthenware with a bee sculpted on top held

thin honey. Nothing matched, everything blended together.

Across the high arched door which had once admitted the worthy in to pray there was now a huge intricately stringed loom. It held a piece of half-finished work in shades of mulberry and coal. On a smaller loom nearby was a completed throw rug in delicate greens. Between them stood the sort of honeycombed shelving on which wine merchants are wont to display their wares: each diamond shape held hanks of rough wool. There were hundreds of them, in every possible color from bright synthetics—brash pinks and sleazy purples—to gentler earth colors of beige and brown, mushroom and sand. More skeins hung from a long series of brass hooks ranged around the walls.

An oversized desk, laden with orderly papers, and a filing cabinet showed that despite her haphazard appearance, Sonia had been on the ball when it came to matters of business. A faint smell of cigarette smoke lingered, though Sonia had not smoked during the Bridge Weekend on which she had met her death.

Cassie looked around at it all, feeling a kinship with the warm disorder. She said briskly, seeking to dispel the stirring memories of childhood, "Goodness me."

"She was a bit of a magpie, wasn't she?" said Giles.

"I'll say."

He moved uneasily. "It feels strange to be in here without Sonia. Look, I'm sure nobody will bother you if you want to get on with your—er—poking about. I'll just pop over the road and have a quick word with Hilda while you get on with it."

"Where to start." Cassie picked a flat basket full of letters off the table and leafed through the envelopes, most of which were buff and labeled with the names of institutions such as the Gas Board and the Water Authority. There was also one from the VAT office, which meant, if nothing else, that Sonia had been making a fair old whack from her weaving.

"You're the expert." Giles had already sidled back toward the door.

"Maybe. But not in sleuthing."

He waved a vague hand. "See you."

Cassie sat down on a leather-seated swivel chair in front of the desk. There was a great deal of whitish dust about: fingerprint powder, or dribbles from the distempered ceiling miles above her head? Forgive us our trespasses, she thought as she began to search the desk's many pigeonholes.

The God-infested space above her head, the reminder from the gallery front that she was under constant surveillance, the knowledge that the woman who had once lived here was violently dead, all combined to make her feel distinctly ill at ease. Not to mention the fact that what she was doing was probably illegal: entering the home of a murder victim without police permission might well make her an accessory after the fact or something similar.

The pigeonholes provided nothing that held any significance to Cassie: more bills, a few personal letters, mostly written in the same hand, a postcard from Corfu, where someone signing themselves Wanka (or was it Wanda?) was having a *fantastic* time hanging around with these bronzed beach bums, if Sonia would pardon the expression. She pulled one of the letters from its envelope, stifling her guilt at the very idea of reading someone else's correspondence; it was signed "Millie."

Millie, she thought, feeling very much on the ball. Short for Millicent. Not a name you came across these days. Therefore almost certainly from a woman of an older generation. An aunt, perhaps? An elderly cousin? She was quite pleased with this piece of deduction, though unclear about where it led her.

She opened the drawers of the filing cabinet. Each of the green drop files was neatly labeled. She saw one marked with a name she recognized and removed it for closer inspection. The correspondence between Dr. James Hagerty and Sonia Wetherhead was brief, businesslike, impersonal, although he had clearly visited Sonia's chapel at some time since he spoke feelingly of the uplift he had experienced on seeing her at work, and mentioned the oneness with his dead wife, Lucille, which this had afforded him. There were a couple of his visiting cards in the file: Cassie took one and felt efficient.

Another file was labeled STRATHSPEY. She lifted it out and saw letters inside concerning a—help!—wall hanging for an innovative leisure complex which some Japanese firm was proposing to build for the workers at its new industrial site.

Thou, Lord, not only seest me but listeneth in when I am in the midst of telling whoppers and then puttest me to shame.

At least none of the correspondence was signed by someone called Midge MacKendrick. She quickly replaced the file.

Those marked BANK, INSURANCE, TAX, PENSION, and other such uninspiring titles she did not bother to search. The police, after all, had been here before her. If Sonia's financial affairs were of significance, they would have taken note. In any case, such papers could hardly help the investigation—the bumblingly amateur investigation, she reminded herself—which she herself was attempting to conduct. If someone had murdered Sonia for gain, they had chosen a risky way to go about it. Much more likely, as she had already decided, that the thing was a spur-of-the-moment happening, triggered by some action of Sonia's which had brought to a boil a long-festering resentment.

Slowly she worked her way around the room, picking up papers, peering under magazines, shifting baskets and wool, lifting the woven throws, looking behind cushions, uncovering nothing more exciting than a few crumpled tissues and a flustered beetle.

If there were secrets in what passed as the kitchen—a counter with a sink sunk into it, a fridge below and a ceramic hob above, plus a few cupboards housing crockery and pans—it was difficult to see where. There was a goat's milk yogurt in the refrigerator, its sell-by date long passed, and a carton of dairy cream butter. In the crisper, half a pound of mummified organically grown mushrooms lay at the bottom of a blue plastic container, next to some green slime which had once been lettuce leaves. There were a couple of pots of homemade damson jam in one of the cupboards, a green-molded loaf in a white enamel bin marked BREAD in navy lettering, and some packets of herbal tea. There was evidence of field-mouse defecation; spiders had stashed away the gift-wrapped bodies of flies in a couple of cupboard corners; a half-chewed moth lay in a fat-smeared frying pan on the hob. Even granted her unavoidable absence, it did not look as though Sonia had been strong on the domestic front. Wherever she had obtained her physical bulk, it had not been through good home cooking.

There was no packet of sugar to sift through, no flour to sieve. Cassie shook the box of washing-up powder in a halfhearted manner but it seemed pointless. Sonia had not been in the great game, after all, she would have no reason to hide things, she was merely a woman who had met an unfortunate and unexpected end—though just how mere that was had not yet been determined.

Another spider had been at work across the narrow stairway which led to the gallery, as Cassie discovered when she started up the steps. Brushing the strands from her face, she found herself in what had served as Sonia's bedroom. A large divan was covered in Navajo rugs. A dress rail hung with assorted garments of vaguely ethnic origin stood against the wall; beside the bed was a bookcase.

That seemed to be it. Despite the intensely personal nature of Sonia's home, Cassie concluded that there was remarkably little of a personal nature to be found in it. Could the same be said of her own home? Would any hint of the varied elements which made up her own character show up if the cottage were subjected to a similar search? She thought not. Her camouflage was pretty efficient: perhaps the same was true of Sonia's.

She looked at the books beside the bed: works on mystical healing, vegetarianism, the endangered planet. Very worthy, very—to Cassie's mind—dull. On top of the bookcase, which also served as a bedside table, lay a paperback published in the States, entitled *The Holistic Approach to Happiness.*

Groan. She glanced at the author's name—and glanced again to make sure she was not mistaken—Dr. James L. Hagerty. Flipping open the flyleaf, she saw a flamboyant dedication scrawled beneath the title, and a folded sheet of paper.

She could not prevent a glance heavenward before she committed the sin of opening it. And then, phew!

It proved to be a short letter, the words of which, dwelling at some length on Sonia's physical charms, scorched off the page. Whether his approach had been holistic or simply rampant, the letter left no doubt that Dr. Hagerty had experienced considerable happiness both during and immediately subsequent to his encounter with Sonia. Cassie refolded the sheet of paper and replaced it in the book where she had found it, pressed the backs of her hands against her cheeks, and reached into her bag for the doctor's card, which she had abstracted from the files. There was his name and, below it, an address in California. On the back, she saw what she had not noticed before: a handwritten London telephone number.

What did it signify? Apart from the fact that Sonia and James had once got it together in bed, it really meant nothing at all. Or did it? Could Hagerty have fallen madly in love with Sonia and been repulsed? Could he have followed her to the Broughton Manor Hotel and there dispatched her in a fit of unrequited passion? He could. But why would he? If he had homicidal leanings, how much more easily would he be able to fulfill them in the privacy of Sonia's own home. Besides, while it was possible to conjecture that Giles Laughton might be familiar with the inside of the hotel, it was surely beyond the bounds of possibility—or at least very close to them—that Hagerty, an American, was too.

On the other hand, it was the only thing of any kind she had discovered in—she checked her watch and saw that the word Giles Laughton had popped across to have with Lady Comberley had been far from quick—nearly an hour. She picked up Sonia's telephone and heard the dialing tone. Obviously no one had yet got around to disconnecting it. It would do no harm merely to dial the number on the back of Hagerty's card and see what she got.

What she got was a voice saying grudgingly, "Leebing's Hotel, how bay I help you?"

"I'm hoping to speak to Dr. Hagerty," Cassie said. She considered, and rejected, using a disguised voice: for a start there was no need and anyway she was not good at voice disguise. Her Midge MacKendrick had been about as Scottish as an Amazonian nose flute.

"Dr. who?"

"No, Dr. James L. Hagerty."

"There's do Jabes Hagerty staying here, I'b afraid. Have you got the right dunbber?"

"Has he stayed there recently? Perhaps I missed him."

Computer keys clicked, accompanied by the sound of adenoidal breathing. There was a fairly hefty sneeze. "Sorry," the voice came back, heavy with cold. "Dr. Hagerty was with us for a week at the edd of Jaduary. He hasn't beed here sindce."

January. Five or six weeks ago. "Thank you so much," Cassie said.

"Dot at all."

So much for Dr. James Hagerty, widower of Lucille,

commissioner of wall hangings from a now-defunct weaveress, old goat of—if the letter was to be believed—astonishing athleticism. Another day, another dead end. Perhaps she just wasn't much good at detecting. Would it be worth telephoning the California number?

Before she could decide, she had done so. Almost immediately she heard the number ringing and the receiver was lifted. "Dr. James L. Hagerty's residence."

"I—uh—wondered if Dr. Hag—"

The recorded voice interrupted her. "I'm sorry but Dr. Hagerty is currently in Papua New Guinea and will be absent from this office between January 1 and the end of April. His calls are being transferred to Dr. Warren Speisman: if you wish to speak to Dr. Speisman's office, please hold and wait." The recorded voice segued into a plinking xylophonic version of "Somewhere Over the Rainbow."

Cassie could not think of any urgent question she wished to put to Dr. Speisman. She hung up.

She looked again at the dedication written on the fly-leaf of Dr. Hagerty's book. It was dated eighteen months ago. Therefore unlikely to be connected to a recent visit to England. On the back cover, a small picture of the gray-bearded doctor radiated holistic happiness. Cassie reconsidered her original scenario. The widowered Hagerty commissions a woven wall hanging as a memorial to his wife. He travels to England to speak personally with the craftsperson entrusted with the job, experiences at least one night—afternoon? early morning?—of passion with her and departs with glowing memories. But when he returns the following year, instead of the hot smolder he gets the cold shoulder and, understandably miffed, follows Sonia to the Broughton Manor Hotel, where he does away with her.

Whichever way you looked at it, the theory was no better now than it had been a few minutes ago.

Giles Laughton reappeared below, in the main body of the chapel. "Cassandra?" he called.

"I'm up here." She looked down at him, noticing the pink shine of his scalp through his hair. He would bald early.

"Find anything?"

"Not really."

"It all seems so strange, doesn't it?" Giles said. "So unlikely."

"That's it. Unlikely." Cassie made her way down the narrow stairs to the ground floor. "Why kill Sonia at Broughton Manor? Unless it was completely unplanned. In which case searching through her things is really quite unnecessary."

"You look as if you could do with a stiff drink," Giles said roughly. "Want to try the local pub? It's only just down the road."

"Thank you."

They walked in silence down the muddy lane toward the village. There were lights on in Hilda Comberley's house, emphasizing the cold gloom of the evening. Rooks flapped toward bare branches lined up on the near slopes and somewhere sheep muttered. A chill wind worried at their faces as they turned toward the heart of the village past the shuttered tourist traps and the little stone bridges. Smoke fluttered on the evening air, pausing as it emerged from stone chimneys before being whirled away toward the sky.

"Uh—how about dinner sometime?" Giles said awkwardly, when they both had drinks in their hands. He glared at the blue flames of the mock fire in the chimney.

"Me and you?" Cassie was astonished.

"I'm not talking about me and the bloody barmaid, am I?" he said, jerking his head at the sprightly octogenarian in green-framed glasses who was pulling pints behind the bar.

"Um—"

"Nobody's forcing you," he said violently. "I just thought it might be fun."

"Are you always this angry?" Cassie said.

"Angry? Who the hell's angry? I'm certainly not angry."

"That's all right, then."

"So you will have dinner with me?"

Cassie smiled. After a moment of hesitation, he smiled back, as though he were unaccustomed to it. "Did you know you have a dimple on the—um—the left side of your face?" he said, and stared deeply into his pint of Ruddles.

"Give me a ring sometime," she said. "We'll fix something up." Although the thought of dinner with Giles Laughton did not necessarily fill her with ripe anticipation, it was substantially better than dinner with Charlie Quartermain, and possibly even handsome Ned Casaubon. She reflected that she might be glad of a square meal at someone else's expense if she could not very soon detach herself from association with Sonia Wetherhead's death.

HE stood on her doorstep, hands in the pockets of
a gray suit similar to but different from the one he had
worn the first time she had met him. His clean white
shirt bore the kind of crease marks which indicated he
had wrestled it from its packaging that very morning.

"May I come in?" he said. He started forward, confident of being permitted entry. His tie had turned over
and now hung the wrong way round so that she could
read the label—"Pierre Cardin, Pure Silk." Since their

last meeting he had reorganized his hair: today the mousy crop rose neatly from his forehead for several millimeters before veering left in a convoy of separate upright hairs.

Cassie suppressed the feelings of guilt which immediately tried to swarm. God and policemen: they could do that every time. She told herself she was innocent, dammit, and stood back to let Detective Inspector Mantripp enter the cottage. Behind him, glumly, came Sergeant Walsh.

It was colder outside than yesterday. The lawn spread toward the hedge and the lane, stiff as hedgehog prickles, each blade of grass edged with hoarfrost. The sky hung just above the treetops, clouding the bare branches with cold mist. She had been out earlier to collect wood from the pile behind her garage and seen frosted cobwebs slung between the leaves of the privet which marked the edge of her vegetable garden. Not an onion had stirred; arms full of logs, she had wondered whether next year she might not try leeks. All that drainage and vertical piping: it could be a bit of a challenge. But think of the results; think of leek and bacon soup, or leeks seethed in olive oil and basil . . .

Cassie made coffee. Mantripp drank his gratefully, holding the mug in one hand while with the other he sorted through a pile of papers taken from a briefcase of some rigid material. "Dear me," he said. "This weather."

"What exactly can I do for you?" she said, her manner matching it. Although his attitude appeared to have softened in the interval between now and the discovery of the bodies in the Macbeth Room, she was still not prepared to like him.

"I want to go over the events of that day with you again," Mantripp said. He picked up one of the biscuits she had set on a saucer beside the mugs and bit daintily into it.

"I'd hoped you were here to inform me that the murderer had been found."

"I'm afraid not."

"I wish you'd hurry up." Quite apart from the cancellations, Cassie had either Hyacinth or Primula on the phone nearly every afternoon, asking for—although they were too well brought up to come right out and say so—the gory details she had so far refused to provide. So much exposure to her cousins was wearying, a constant reminder of the differences between them.

"To be perfectly honest with you, we seem to have reached an—um—impasse in our investigations."

"You're stumped, you mean."

"We've established without too much difficulty that Miss Wetherhead was—to put it mildly—a bit of an awkward personality," Sergeant Walsh explained. "Easily provoked into verbal abuse."

"In other words, she got up people's noses rather more than the average person," said Mantripp. "Naturally we assumed it must be someone attending the Bridge Weekend who was responsible for killing her, but so far we've been unable to satisfactorily establish both opportunity and motive. Those who were known to have crossed swords with her, such as the novelist Felicity—um—Carotene—"

"Carridine," said Walsh.

"—or the wine merchant, Ned Casaubon." He paused, aware that the sentence lacked something.

"Have you ever read *Middlemarch?*" Cassie said.

"Can't say I have. Never read Felicity Howsyourfather either."

"My wife has," Walsh said, as he had said before.

"That's quite beside the point," said Mantripp. "As I was saying, those with cause, however slight, to murder Miss Wetherhead have all got alibis, and those with the opportunity—about two—had absolutely no reason to want to."

"We've questioned everyone present at least twice and come up with nothing really helpful," said Walsh.

"Established that most of the people in the hotel that weekend had no connection with Miss Wetherhead at all, from Ryland himself on down to the gardener's lad. So we thought it might be appropriate at this stage to go over the entire sequence of events again, take a fresh look, see if we can perhaps stumble across something which we didn't necessarily consider relevant at the time." Coffee mug at his lips, Mantripp looked around the low-beamed room. "Very cozy," he commented. "Very nice."

"I don't know how much I remember," Cassie said. "It's quite a time ago now."

"Never mind," Walsh said. "You'd be amazed at what the human memory can retain."

"And, more to the purpose, reproduce, isn't that right, Walsh?"

"Definitely." Both of them stared at her. Then Mantripp pointed to the nearest chair. "Do sit down, Miss Swann."

At least he had remembered her name.

She sat down at the circular fruitwood table. It had

come from Gran's bedroom over the Saloon Bar; Gran used to keep it covered with a circular crocheted cloth, except on Sundays when the cloth was removed and carefully folded before being put away.

Something tapped her weakly on the shoulder and she turned to find that the philodendron which was Rose's last gift to her had deposited a small yellowed leaf on her sweater and now stood in its pot waiting dumbly for death. She remained unmoved.

"Right," Mantripp said, looking down at a sheaf of xeroxed papers. She could see her own name on the top one; presumably it was a copy of her original statement. "You stated previously that you arrived at the Macbeth Room at approximately eleven-oh-seven a.m."

"Pre*ci*sely at seven minutes past eleven. I checked my watch as I went in."

"And what happened then?"

"I saw the Plumptons sitting at the—"

"Was the door open? Shut? What?"

"It was half open. There was this velvet curtain hanging behind it, inside the room, to keep out drafts. Once you were inside, you closed the door and pulled the curtain across. When I went into the room, the curtain was half pulled, so that anyone opening the door from the passage would have to push against it."

"As though it had been pulled right across until someone pushed at it when trying to open the door from the outside?" asked Walsh.

"That's right." Cassie tried to remember, reliving that last couple of seconds as she entered the room, that moment when she pulled her public persona on over her private self like a tight-fitting jumpsuit, stopped being

Cassie and became Cassandra Swann, Bridge Professional. The diamond-tiled passage had been chill under the soles of her shoes, and as she crossed the threshold her feet were already anticipating the change from their solidity to the yielding softness of the pink carpeting. "And then I saw them, at the table, the two Plumptons."

"That was the first thing you saw?"

"I think so. Though I suppose I must have seen Sonia's feet first, because they would have come into sight before the bridge table. But the body on the floor didn't really register until I was fully into the room."

"And the Plumptons were sitting at a right angle to each other?"

She was about to say that of course they were, they could hardly have got up and changed seats in the interval between her discovery and the arrival of the police. Walsh intervened. "Like we found them, sir."

"So what did you do next?" asked Mantripp. He nipped again at a biscuit and, disconcertingly, a portion of his hair suddenly bent in the opposite direction, like stalks in a field of corn when the wind blows through.

"I knew they were all dead," Cassie said. "You could tell. But even so, I bent down—knelt down on one knee, actually—and laid my head against Sonia's back. I was trying to listen for a heartbeat, you see."

"If you thought she was dead, why didn't you summon help immediately?" asked Mantripp.

"Not that it would have done any good," added Sergeant Walsh.

"It was all so quick . . . I suppose I had some vague idea of being able to—to resuscitate her or something. I touched her face too."

Mantripp square-edged his papers. "You say here: 'It felt perfectly normal.'"

"That's right. Normal body temperature, as though she had simply fallen asleep on the floor."

"Funny place for a nap," Mantripp said.

"I don't suppose Miss Swann really thought she was asleep, sir," said Walsh.

"Especially as there was blood all over the back of her head," Cassie said. "And this obelisk thing on the carpet beside her." Stained, although she was not prepared to say so, with blood and something else, porridgelike, which she took to be brain tissue.

"The murder weapon," said Mantripp. "Now, go back, Miss Swann. Close your eyes, remember coming into the room, one hand on the door, perhaps . . ."

"Yes."

"Was there any other impression you had? Any smell, perhaps? Any sound which you might not have expected to hear?"

Cassie thought about it, then shook her head. "I don't think so. Nothing out of the ordinary. There was the smell of furniture polish, and some reasonably discreet air freshener. And wood smoke from the fire. Tobacco—the Colonel smoked a pipe."

"And it was pipe tobacco you could smell?"

"It was only a vague impression," Cassie said. "I didn't think anything as definite as 'Goodness, what a stink of tobacco,' or 'The Colonel must have been smoking his pipe.'"

"I meant was it pipe tobacco you smelled?"

"I think so."

"Not cigars or cigarettes—"

"Or cannabis," Walsh put in. He appeared to be perfectly serious.

"Something which might give us a clue as to the murderer's identity. Strong odors tend to cling to clothes and hair and leave an impression even after the person has left the room. For instance, were you to inform us that you noticed a slight but definite fragrance of Chanel No. 19 lingering in the room, it might lead us straight to Miss Boanes, the receptionist, who we have already established is a heavy user."

"Of Chanel No. 19, that is," said Walsh quickly.

"It was pipe tobacco, as far as I remember. As for any sounds, looking back, I must have been aware in a vague way as I came into the room that they weren't talking to each other. But if I'd given it any thought, I would have imagined they were simply concentrating on the cards in their hands."

"I'm confused, Miss Swann. Isn't bridge a game for four people?"

"Of course. But if they wanted to practice bidding or something, they might well have dealt out four hands—after all, they were expecting me to arrive at any moment, they weren't planning to play a proper rubber, with only three people there."

"So you came in, saw them there, listened for Miss Wetherhead's heartbeat. What next?"

"I stood up and went over to the Colonel. When I touched him, he—he kind of fell forward."

"So when you first came in, he was sitting upright?"

"More or less. Slightly to one side, I suppose, leaning backward into the angle of the chair, between the arm and the back. And then he slowly flopped toward the table." There had been the scent of Bull Durham about his tweed jacket, and a sweetish smell rising from the sparse hairs combed regimentally across his skull on either side of his parting.

"And Mrs. Plumpton?"

"Next to him, at a right angle. I—uh—I . . . she had one hand on the table, as though she were reaching for her pillbox and her eyes were wide open, staring at her husband. I realize you're not supposed to touch bodies, but I'm afraid I—uh—tried to shut them."

"That's an unusual reaction," Mantripp said.

"Is it?"

"Most people," Sergeant Walsh said, "especially if they're women—not wishing to sound sexist but it's a fact—will start screaming or running from the room in search of help."

"I did it without thinking," Cassie said.

"Pretty cool behavior, Miss Swann."

She stared at him without speaking, seeing not him but Gran, her huge bulk against the grubby pillows, eyes wide and staring. Coming home from school toward the end of the summer term, clattering up the back stairs through the almost solid smell of stale beer from the Public, shouting hello and what's for tea? She wanted to watch something on the telly and knew there'd be the usual argument, Gran being so strict about homework. But Gran wasn't in the kitchen or the living room, and when she had finally burst into her bedroom and seen her there, she'd realized at once that everything, everything was about to be different. Gran had told her about the layings-out in the old days, the bodies she had helped to wash and prepare for funerals, up and down the street;

Gran had said about always closing their eyes for them, that they couldn't really concentrate on being dead until they'd stopped looking at life, about laying pennies on the eyelids to keep them shut if necessary. She had stopped at the door, terror fizzing inside her like Christmas sparklers, then walked across the dusty patterned carpet and done it the way they did in films, finger and thumb down over Gran's cold face, and the eyelids coming down, staying down, no need for pennies . . .

"I've done it before," she said, and her voice sounded tiny, desolate.

"I see." Mantripp cleared his throat. "Then what did you do?"

"I looked at the cards lying on the table." Said like that, it sounded unnervingly blasé.

"Why?"

"I don't know. All this took a few seconds, Inspector."

"Detective Inspector," murmured Walsh. Mantripp's hair swayed to the left again.

"It's so automatic for me to note the cards that I—"

"They were set out on the table the way we found them, were they?"

"Yes." She got up. "I'll show you, as far as I remember."

From the oak corner cupboard attached to the wall, she took out a pack of cards and began to deal them. "I can't remember the smaller cards exactly, but these are the picture cards they had." She sorted through the pack of cards, looking for them, and ended up with a close approximation, as far as she remembered, of the layout of the cards as they had been that morning.

"Very good," said Mantripp. "Very impressive." He looked across at Walsh. "One might even suggest you had a career in the music halls ahead of you, should you care to take it up. Mrs. Marvel, the Memory—uh—Lady."

"Lacks something," Cassie said. "Besides, I'd have thought most music halls were far behind me."

"And me," said Walsh. "Music hall went out years ago."

"Decades," said Cassie. Both of them stared at Mantripp.

He tucked in the corners of his mouth. Then, from his briefcase, he took a folder of photographs and sorted through them, looking for one in particular. "You only made one mistake, Miss Swann." He glanced at one. "You put the 3 of Spades in this hand and it ought to be in *this* one." He reached across and changed the cards around.*

"And these were the three tricks they'd already played," Cassie said. And frowned. "Except that doesn't make any sense at all."

"Why not?"

"Do you play bridge, Inspector?"

"I haven't in the last twenty years or so, and not much before then."

"Because if you look at these cards," Cassie said, pointing to the photograph, "it's obvious that this set laid out in straight rows is the Dummy hand. And since the Diamonds are laid out to the left of the hand, *they* must have been Trumps. Quite apart from the fact that Dummy and partner have ten between them."

"Ten what?"

"Diamonds." Cassie did not add "klunk," knowing that what to her seemed as obvious as daylight could seem impenetrable to the nonplayer. "Winning cards.

* See page 198.

But the cards in these played tricks don't make sense. You see, if Mrs. Plumpton, the person on Dummy's right, led first, as she would have done—"

"Why?"

"—because whoever sits to the right of the Dummy hand always leads first."

"I see."

"—according to these apparently played tricks, she must have led her six of Spades, because it's the first card in this trick." She showed it to them: 6♠ 5♠ 4♥ 3♥. "Mrs Plumpton, having unaccountably won that trick, then presumably led her 8♠. Then the third player, North, on Dummy's left—*ought* to have played his K♠."

"Why?"

"Because Third plays high," Cassie explained. "And he would have hoped to take the trick with the King and then lead another low Spade back to his partner for her to take with the Ace. And then Colonel Plumpton, playing last, would happily have dropped his 3♠."

"Why happily?"

"Because if Spades were led again, he could have trumped, having no more Spades. But nobody played what they should have done," Cassie said, her forehead creased. "Those three were all experienced players. Mrs. Plumpton, leading off, *might* conceivably have played a low Spade; Colonel Plumpton *might* have played something even lower from Dummy, though I very much doubt it, but there is no way that the third hand, whoever held it, would have put *any* Heart down. For one thing, it would not have been following suit, and for another, it wouldn't take the trick, whereas the K♠ would have done."

"Does it mean anything?"

"It has to," Cassie said.

"What?"

"That for some reason, someone—"

"The murderer?" Walsh said.

"The murderer, probably, wanted to make it look as though the three of them had played together before Sonia was killed."

"Why would he want to do that?"

"Something to do with alibis?" Cassie said.

"How do you mean?"

"I don't know. To look as if they'd all been there longer than they said they had?" She thought of Giles Laughton, his statement that he had been ringing bells at ten-thirty. But how could he have been? She had seen the white van from the dairy farm heading down the drive toward the main road at just after that time. Followed by—yes—the taxi which must have contained the exuberant frame of Felicity Carridine.

But the Broughton Manor Hotel was a good fifteen-minute drive from Moreton Lacey church. So either Giles was lying—in which case so was the entire bell-ringing team at Moreton Lacey—or, as he had told her, someone else had been driving the van.

She was surprised at how much she did not wish the redheaded farmer to have been lying. "Did you say you'd spoken to Felicity Carridine?" she said.

"Not yet. There was this tour of the States to finish and then some prearranged holiday down in Florida to join."

"Due back tomorrow morning," Sergeant Walsh said efficiently. "ETA oh-eight-four-five."

"Ay em?" Mantripp said.

Walsh gave him a steady look which lasted for perhaps a count of four before replying, "That's right, sir."

"And then you'll set up an interview?" asked Cassie.

"Right. Leave twenty-four hours for the jet lag, the unpacking of bags. Give the lady time to wash her smalls," Mantripp said, with an unpleasantly sexist laugh.

"Smalls?" said Walsh.

"You know what I mean," Mantripp said impatiently. "Brassiere. Panties. That sort of thing."

"Felicity Carridine does *not* wear smalls," Cassie said. She tried to sound casual. "And you've—um—spoken to Giles Laughton, I understand."

"That's right," Walsh said. "He was ringing bells, with half a dozen witnesses to prove it."

"The bells are ringing for me and my gal," said Mantripp.

After a slight pause, Walsh said, "Is that right, sir?"

The two policemen got up. "If you think of anything," Walsh said heavily.

"Anything at all," said Mantripp.

"However trivial you may feel it to be, please let us know at once, Miss Swann."

"I will. Definitely."

"Good."

When the two policemen had left, she looked down at the cards still set out on Gran's table. Whatever the reason for the three obviously spurious tricks, there was one other inescapable conclusion to be drawn from them.

She wondered if it had any significance.

QUITE what she expected to gain by hanging about the Arrivals gate at Terminal 3, Cassie did not know. Yet the urge to speak to Felicity Carridine had come to her in the middle of the night and been strong enough to propel her early from her bed, despite the frost on the cottage windows, sustain her through the torture of the chill bathroom, and send her hot-wheeling it to Heathrow. All in the hope of snatching a few words with a jet-lagged and possibly hostile Felicity Carridine before the police did.

And having snatched them, what did she hope for? A vital clue leading to the immediate apprehension of the villain? Some verbal slip which would prove conclusively that the novelist dunnit? A confession? Remembering the confrontation between Carridine and Wetherhead at the Bridge Weekend party, the accusations the weaveress was hurling, the antagonism beween the two of them, it did not seem so very farfetched to imagine the big writer picking up one of the alabaster obelisks and crashing it down on Sonia's unsuspecting skull.

Writers are ruthless, Cassie told herself. Almost as bad as journalists. They'll steal anything, plagiarize shamelessly, borrow someone else's idea, someone else's *life*, and forget to return it, show no mercy when on to a good plot. Robin, her godfather, had often told her so, and being one himself, he ought to know.

Perhaps there was truth behind Sonia's claims that Felicity had stolen her story; perhaps she really meant it when she said she intended to sue—and perhaps Felicity, worried about the adverse affect this might have on the sales of *Life's Tempestuous Sea*, had committed murder for the sake of the print run.

And because of the novelist's imminent departure to the States, there had been no time for reflection. The removal of Sonia had to be accomplished without delay. Sonia had accused Felicity at the Saturday night party; by ten-thirty or so the following morning, the weaveress was dead and Felicity Carridine had left the scene of the crime.

The usual disembodied airport voice announced the arrival of the flight from Miami. In the restaurant, Cassie stared gloomily at a magazine, purchased because she knew she would be unable to concentrate on a book. From the fashion pages, a Dachau-slim young woman pouted and sulked in a variety of bathing gear, most of it minimal, all of it impossible for Cassie to imagine ever having the nerve to wear in public. White sand clung to the young woman's thighs, tanned to a mahogany brown in defiance of health warnings about the risk of melanoma; despite the way the swimsuits were cut around the crotch, there was not the faintest suggestion of pubic hair. Perhaps, if you were that ema-ciated, it ceased to grow. Perhaps it had been surgically removed. Perhaps—

But Cassie had more important things on her mind than someone else's pubic hair. Outside the windows, beyond an acreage of gray plastic-topped tables, oil-splashed runways spread in all directions, small vans sped about, planes lumbered into position, exciting that combination of glamour and fear which is the essence of an airport. But all Cassie could see was herself splayed against a blood-spattered wall. Suppose, once she had accosted Felicity Carridine, the novelist turned nasty, produced a gun fitted with a silencer, forced her to go to the nearest WC, and then shot her. Suppose her own suspicions were so near the mark that Felicity, though laughing them off for the moment, later made an attempt to silence Cassandra just as Sonia had been silenced. Cassie determined to announce as early in the conversation as possible that details had been lodged with her solicitor and that in the event of her untimely death . . . but it sounded, even in the spaces inside her own head, ridiculous, like something out of a detective novel written between the wars. She simply could not

envisage the circumstances in which she would enunci-
ate such a sentence, or that she would be taken seriously
if she did so.

Besides, any publicity—according to Robin—was
good publicity. A public row over the rights to the story
of Gossamer Brightway, the heroine of *Life's Tempestuous
Sea*, could only benefit the author and send the publishers rushing to reprint. So as a motive for killing Sonia, it
was counterproductive, worth precisely damn all.

Regretting the impulse which had brought her here,
Cassie was about to leave when there was a stir of anticipation among those waiting at the Arrivals barrier.
Passengers were beginning to trickle out. Feeling that no
harm could be done now that she was here, Cassie took
up a position behind a man waiting for someone who
displayed a placard with the name ITSUBUKI handwritten
on it in capital letters. Once, arriving from a visit to
France, she could have sworn she saw a man bearing a
similar placard inscribed with the word GODOT but by
the time she had extricated herself from the attentions
of a would-be Lothario who had pestered her during the
flight and was now determined to carry her suitcase, the
man had disappeared, leaving her to wonder if she had
merely suffered a literary hallucination.

Felicity Carridine finally appeared from behind the
screens separating the concourse from Customs, pinkly
sunburned, wearing a pair of wide-legged shorts in a
splashy fabric of Day-Glo pinks and greens embellished
with black additions. It was one of the more hideous
examples of an unbecoming garment that Cassie had
ever seen, and for a moment her resolution failed. On
top of which, since their last meeting, the novelist had

grown a beard, a dark springy affair fetchingly streaked with gray.

Carridine caught sight of her, faltered, frowned. A generously cut shirt of lime-green cotton covered the vast authorial torso; even so it was possible to see it heave. "Good morning, madam," he boomed, after a moment. "Fancy bumping into you—are you waiting for someone?" He began to walk toward the gap into the main concourse.

"You," said Cassie, keeping step.

"Me? Why?"

"I wanted to talk to you before the police did."

"Police?" The deep bass voice rose on the word. "Why on earth should the police want to see me?"

"Did you hear about Sonia Wetherhead and the Plumptons?"

"Hear what about them?"

"That they're dead."

Rounding the end of the barrier fencing, the novelist walked into the middle of the concourse and stopped. "*Dead?*"

"Yes."

"All *three* of them?"

"Yes." Somehow Cassie knew that the news was no surprise.

"And the police think *I'm* involved?"

"They certainly plan to question you—as soon as you've recovered from the flight home. The detective inspector spoke of giving you time to wash your smalls."

"Smalls!" trumpeted Felicity. "*Smalls?* Is the man mad?" He ran his fingers over his new beard and stared at Cassie with hot eyes. "Good God, woman. You could house a largish family in a pair of my boxer shorts. It's not a pretty sight, I can tell you."

Irresistibly, an image of Charlie Quartermain forced its way into Cassie's mind. He and the novelist were physically two of a kind—to contemplate either of them in their underwear would require a certain amount of moral strength, bolstered by strong drink. Which reminded her:

"Coffee," she said. "Would you like one?"

"Not really." Carridine stared at her thoughtfully. "I'll tell you what: why don't you drive me home. I seem to remember you live in my direction."

"The other side of Oxford," Cassie said.

"And I'm in Maidenhead, more or less en route. We can talk on the way."

"Fine," said Cassie.

Carridine picked up his bags and followed her to the car park. Settling himself in the passenger seat, he stared gloomily out of the window as Cassie concentrated on finding the exit onto the motorway.

"What a godforsaken island this is," he said. "What with its climate and the tax burden, not to mention the general constipation of its inhabitants, I can't imagine why I stay." He gestured at the concrete view. "Look at that. Last night I was sitting by a floodlit swimming pool with a long drink in my hand and fireflies flitting about and the temperature up in the eighties even though it was dark. Ever been to Florida?"

"No."

"Take my advice, don't delay."

"I've read those Travis McGee books about—"

"Travis McGee? Know him well. Good friend of mine, as a matter of fact."

"But surely John D. MacDonald was the—"

"Know John, do you? Good old John. We were sharing a glass or two just last week."

Cassie rather doubted it since MacDonald had died some years ago. She said, "Look, about Sonia Wetherhead—"

"The woman was insane. A nutter of the purest kind. You could see that simply from the way she wrapped herself in that frightful homespun. Clothes make the man, I always think, and how much more the woman."

What kind of a woman his shorts made *him* was a question which at any other time she would have been eager to explore, but he had carried on. "I mean, anyone who could seriously walk about dressed like a kilim deserves everything she gets."

"Even murder?"

"No, no. Good God, I didn't mean that, of course not. You said she was dead—"

"Murdered," said Cassie.

"But what on earth for?"

"If I knew that I wouldn't be here."

"Tell me, dear lady, why exactly *are* you here?"

Cassie explained about the article Thomas Lambert had written, the subsequent falling-off of her customers, the damage to her professional reputation, the hope that she might find out something which the police had overlooked. "It seems pretty farfetched and hopeless," she concluded, "but I couldn't just sit there and let everything I'd built up over the past few years be destroyed without trying to do something about it."

"Tell me about it!" the novelist exclaimed. "Take *my* business. You wouldn't believe the backbiting, the malicious gossip, the jealousy that one is forced to endure. Just because I'm at the top of my particular tree . . ."

As always, the subject of Felicity Carridine was never far from her namesake's lips.

Cassie interrupted. "What's your real name? I can't sit in a small car next to a man with a beard and call him Felicity." She had never really understood why so many male authors of romantic fiction felt it necessary to hide behind female pseudonyms. And such flowery ones too.

"I don't see why not."

"I don't want to," Cassie said firmly.

"I started life in Cardiff as Naughton Williams, a name, you will agree, lacking in either euphony or romance." Carridine's voice took on the liltingly polished tone of one who has been invited to speak in a hundred provincial libraries, take part in any number of literary panels. "One of the questions I'm frequently asked is how I became a writer and, in particular, a writer of romantic fiction. Like many writers, I had always—"

"The only question I'm asking is whether or not you killed Sonia Wetherhead," interrupted Cassie. Any fears that Carridine—or Naughton, as she must learn to think of him—was going to threaten her with a gun, silenced or otherwise, were obviously ill-founded.

"Killed Son—my good woman, I absolutely *abhor* physical violence of any kind. Besides, why should I wish to do such a thing? I had no grudge against the poor creature, despite her execrable dress sense and her inability to distinguish fact from fiction."

"The last time I saw you, she was accusing you of stealing her plot."

"Which exactly proves my point. Besides, there are only seven plots in the entire universe." The writer paused and assumed a vague expression. "Or is it thirty-six? Whatever the actual figure, the point is that there are too few of them around for anyone to be able to claim exclusive rights. As I freely admitted to *poor* Miss Wetherhead, I may have borrowed one or two details from the extravaganza of information she showered me with, but that is all. As for killing the ridiculous woman, the last I saw of her was as I finished my breakfast in the hotel restaurant, prior to taking a taxi to the airport."

"What was she doing?"

"Standing at the door, talking to someone—I can't remember whom."

"And presumably there were other people in the restaurant at the time," Cassie said dispiritedly. "Who'd remember."

"Far be it from me to consider myself in any way note-worthy," said Carridine modestly. "But I think it likely that someone would be able to vouch for me being there. And only seconds after the Wetherhead woman had gone, one of the receptionists appeared to inform me that my taxi had arrived. She then very kindly wait-ed while I finished the toast and marmalade I was in the middle of consuming, and walked me out to the taxi, where she asked me for my autograph."

"At no time leaving you alone long enough to bump off Miss Wetherhead."

"Precisely. So I think it highly unlikely that the police will be able to drag me off in chains and build a con-vincing case against me. Not," he added darkly, "that that seems to stop them these days. If there's no hard evidence, they simply fabricate it, if the papers are to be believed. Not that you can trust a journalist either. I read a recent review of my latest book which was absolutely scurrilous—the man clearly hadn't read beyond the first paragraph—perhaps not even beyond the first word—and obviously hadn't the faintest idea about life in a mill town at the end of the nineteenth century. Whereas *I* have spent years of my life on the kind of meticulous research my readers have come to expect from me . . ." He launched himself once again into an orgy of self-adulation—"primary sources . . . contemporary records . . . photographs of the period"— while Cassie stared at the rain spitting at the windshield and cursed.

It seemed that no one at all had been in a position to murder Sonia Wetherhead or, if they had, to have possessed any conceivable reason to do so. Yet someone undoubtedly had. And until she knew who, until she could show it was pure coincidence that the murder had occurred during one of Cassandra Swann's Bridge Weekends, she was not going to be able to recoup her lost customers or her professional reputation.

Sometimes she wondered if she really knew what she was doing. Uncle Samuel had voiced the gravest doubts about her ability to make a living from so precarious a field as bridge: she would hate to see him proved right. On the other hand, she had only gone to university, stuck out the three years there, gained her degree, for Gran's sake. Gran, who had insisted that Sarah's daughter should not spend the rest of her life serving behind a bar, who had shown her the advantages of an education, had struggled to comprehend the binary system

and mugged up on Tudors and Stuarts or English literature in the local Islington library in order to help Cassie
with her homework . . . Cassie's career change at the age
of twenty-eight had not been without its conscience-
searching moments: in the end she had decided that
Gran would have approved the switch from salaried staff
to self-employment.

She thought of the bridge sundries business she had
been contemplating buying, the bridge book she had discussed with someone who worked for the publishing house
which produced Robin's novels. Everything had been
going so well and now, thanks to Sonia's murder, everything, like her houseplants, had withered on the stem.

She was not in a position to establish whether
Carridine was lying—that responsibility rested with the
police. Meanwhile, there was very little else she could or
wanted to do to keep him from his business.

"How did you hear of their deaths?" she asked.

He opened his mouth with the obvious intention of
denying that he had, then thought better of it. "My publisher told me," he said. "Naturally one has to keep in
touch when one is constantly on the move—and besides,
I really had to register my complaints about the
arrangements for my reception. In Cleveland, Ohio, for
example, you would hardly credit it but the publicity
people had actually . . ."

Was his unremitting obsession with himself—or,
rather, with Felicity Carridine—as artless as it appeared
to be? Cassie rather thought it was. Behind the façade of
ruthless self-promotion there probably lurked an ego
the size of a communion wafer, she told herself, striving
to be charitable and wishing she did not feel the need.

As Carridine banged on about soulless motels, iceberg lettuce, chat show hosts who had not read his book, and tooth glasses which had been sanitized for his (or her) protection, she tried to remember, to reach back and hook on to the Cassie she had once been. Surely that tough streetwise kid, queen of the William Tyndale Primary School playground, would have felt no compassion for the Naughton Williamses of this world. And anyway, did someone with a string of best-sellers behind them really need anyone else's sympathy? Or was the whole Carridine persona an elaborate piece of self-parody?

Whatever complicated psychological reasons lay behind Carridine's need to reassure himself that he existed—and obviously Freud would have made something of the fact that he hid behind a female pseudonym, though whether it would have been the same thing as he would have made of Mary Ann Evans hiding behind the name George Eliot was open to debate—she herself had better things to do than carry on interrogating a bearded novelist who was dressed in a pair of shorts which merited a mandatory custodial sentence.

By a natural process of thought—George Eliot—*Middlemarch*—The Key to All Mythologies—she remembered Ned Casaubon. He had telephoned the evening before and asked her to have dinner with him, once again hinting at revelations to do with Sonia Wetherhead. She had agreed to meet him but now wondered whether there was any point. Whatever information he possessed, she was already wearily convinced that it would simply lead once more to a blank wall at the end of a blind alley.

The only cause for satisfaction she could see was that

during all the chafing years she had spent as a biology teacher, she had never once yearned to take up amateur detection as an alternative profession. Just as well: she was obviously a complete nonstarter as a sleuth.

"Personally, I should imagine that whoever killed the woman did so on the spur of the moment," Carridine said.

"That's exactly what I—"

"No self-respecting novelist—and let's face it, we all think we're self-respecting, ha, ha—would *dream* of setting a murder in a country house and then letting the murderer sneak in from outside." He brooded briefly. "Or did Agatha Christie? Than whom none could be more self-respecting . . . anyway, it rather strains credulity to imagine that someone planned this murder, by all accounts. Therefore, all you have to do—"

"Not me."

"—all the *police* have to do is look for the one person who had not bargained on meeting Sonia Wetherhead at the Bridge Weekend and hey presto! another case successfully concluded for Inspector Bloodhound."

"But surely none of those present could have known beforehand who would be coming. Except the hotel staff, of course. So that still leaves everything wide open, doesn't it?"

"Absolutely." The novelist laughed cheerily. "Which is precisely why Felicity Carridine writes romantic fiction and not crime novels."

"Oh, is *that* why?"

"Though, believe me, I've had plenty of requests from my publishers to do exactly that. Only a few weeks ago the senior editor took me out to lunch at Le

Caprice and positively *begged* me to consider a series of period crime novels, based in a—"

"Let me guess: a mill town at the turn of the century and featuring an innocent girl detective, daughter of poor but proud parents, called Clematis Silksmooth or something similar?"

Carridine stared at her, his expression awestruck. "This is uncanny," he said. "How in the *world* did you know that?"

Oh God.

Cassie felt distinctly queasy. Even in these days of bottom lines and percentage increases, were publishers really so devoid of sensitivity that they could contemplate such a notion? "Just a gut feeling," she said.

Carridine lived in a grandly thirties house hung about with balconies and conservatories, with a garden which sloped down to the river. He invited Cassie in and, always keen to see how the other half spent its considerable income, she accepted. But despite the man's eccentricity of attire and personality, the house was standardly comfortable. Passing open doors, Cassie saw polished bureaus, glass-fronted cabinets full of objets d'art, photographs in silver frames, pieces of modern sculpture, wide soft sofas, large numbers of books, coffee tables covered in magazines, flowers, copies of the owner's works and silver cigarette boxes.

In the large kitchen, Carridine made coffee, and searching noisily through a walk-in larder, came out with a tin containing biscuits. Tearing off the lid, he bit vigorously into one and pronounced it too soggy.

"Forget those," he said, and threw the tin away. He peered into a capacious fridge. "At least there's fresh milk. Thank God for Mrs. Wicksteed, my treasure."

Did people really still talk about treasures when they meant people whom they paid to come in and clean their houses? Cassie drank the coffee and through the kitchen window watched two drakes waddle across Carridine's immaculate lawn, feeling superfluous, anxious to get away.

When she finally said she should leave, Carridine led her toward the hall. At the door of the drawing room, he paused, then walked into the room, Cassandra following. "Most kind of you," he said. "Driving me back here, I mean."

"Not at all."

He looked embarrassed. "Look, I'm not going to pretend I write great literature or anything of that kind, but if you'd accept one of my books, I'd be more than happy to sign one for you." He examined a framed hunting scene hanging on the wall, not meeting her eyes.

His humble air seemed genuine. Perhaps beneath the capacious persona of Felicity Carridine there still lurked the modest personality of Cardiff-born Naughton Williams. "I'd like that," Cassie said, frantically trying to remember the titles of his books in case he asked which one she'd prefer.

"Any title you'd prefer?" he said.

"Uh—" Inspiration came to her as she stared into the cabinet of polished yew which stood beside her. "I haven't had a chance to read *Life's*—um—*Tempestuous Sea* yet. Have you got a copy of that?"

"Ah, my latest." Beaming, Carridine picked a thick

book up from one of the piles on the coffee table. He signed it with a flourish, dotting the *i*'s of his pseudonym with small circles. "I think you'll enjoy it."

"I'm sure I will." Cassie coughed. "I *know* I will."

Behind Casaubon's head lounged a large philodendron at which Cassie was trying hard not to stare. The fourth leaf down was dangling in withered mode, yet she could have sworn that when they arrived a couple of hours ago, it had been a healthy green.

Casaubon, brandy glass in hand, turned to look behind him. "Why are you looking so cross?"

"It's that philodendron," Cassie said.

"I never met a woman who glared at plants before," he said. "What's it done?"

"Contracted some incurable disease," Cassie said. It was worrying, really. You could get away with a black thumb in the privacy of your own home without too many repercussions but the ability to blight public houseplants at ten feet was not likely to win her many friends.

"Has it? I can't say I've ever got really worked up about things in pots." He put both elbows on the table and leaned toward her. He said, "I need your advice, Cassie."

The remark did not ring quite true. "If you hadn't come on that Bridge Weekend, you'd never have met me," she responded tartly. "Who would you have asked advice from then?" Until then, they had talked desultorily, mostly about Cassie and her attempts to build up a career and a living for herself as a bridge player, in which he seemed intensely interested.

"That's just it: it's about that weekend that I need to talk to you."

"Go on."

He said dramatically, "I was the last person to see Sonia Wetherhead alive."

"In that case, I'm surprised the police haven't arrested you for murder."

"Apart from the murderer, of course," he said. "My problem is that I haven't told the police."

"Isn't there some frightful penalty for withholding information?"

"Perhaps my input is entirely immaterial, I don't know." He smoothed back his hair, looking worried.

"Tell me about it," Cassie said.

"I was coming down those back stairs at the hotel," said Casaubon. "If you remember, once you reach ground level the passage either continues straight ahead, toward the main part of the hotel, or turns left."

"Toward the Macbeth Room . . ."

"Exactly. And the swimming pool: I was planning to do a few lengths, work off my breakfast before we started playing bridge again. The door of the Macbeth Room was obviously open, because I could hear the Plumptons talking."

"What were they saying?"

"I couldn't hear precise words, just murmurings."

"Was anyone else with them?"

"That's just it. I couldn't hear a third voice but I know someone else was in there—and this, Cassandra, is why I haven't gone to the police yet, because it's so intangible. Cops like to deal in facts, not feelings, and I can't explain why I knew there was someone else in the room

with the Plumptons except to say—well, the murmurings had a kind of polite edge. I mean, they weren't the
sort of murmurings you'd expect between husband and
wife; they were more . . . *social*."

Cassie knew exactly what he meant. "But you didn't
hear another voice?"

"Nothing. And then I saw Sonia standing straight
ahead of me down the passage, at the door of the dining room, talking to someone."

Which only confirmed what Felicity Carridine had
said.

"I wanted to have a word with her about her behavior
the night before," continued Casaubon, "so I waited at the
foot of the stairs. I could still hear the Plumptons, this
time a bit more clearly—Mrs. Plumpton said, 'Your trick,'
and there was a small noise, as though she'd slapped the
last card down in a fit of pique. Then Sonia saw me and
called out in that loud voice of hers, perfectly normal, as
though she hadn't made a complete fool of herself—and
me—the night before. She said she was about to join the
Plumptons for a quick run-through before you came
down for the lesson, they'd arranged it the previous
evening, and why didn't I make up the four." He paused.

"Yes. What then?"

"I said I couldn't because I wanted a swim. When she
reached me—you know how long that passage is—I
walked with her along the other passage toward the
Macbeth Room." Taking a gulp of his brandy, he grimaced. "I said I'd see her later, and went on toward the
pool while she—she went into the room."

The two of them stared at each other. "Goodness,"
Cassie said.

"He must have been in there," said Casaubon. "He must have been waiting for her."

"But the Plumptons were there. Surely they'd have called out something."

"Unless they'd collapsed by then."

"Why on earth should they have done that?"

"Or perhaps they hadn't collapsed, they were just waiting for her."

"That passage is tiled, isn't it?"

"With those little black and white Victorian diamond shapes—they'd have been able to hear us coming."

"But when I got there, the cards had been dealt and three tricks played. The murderer can't have arrived by then. Sonia must have come in, sat down and played at least three tricks before he showed up. So you can't have been the last person to see her alive, if it's any comfort."

"It's not much, frankly. I let her go into that room alone." He made a motion suggestive of being about to bury his head in his hands.

"Come on," Cassie said. "Don't let's get too melodramatic about this. You couldn't possibly have known what was going to happen."

"But if I'd looked in and seen the Plumptons dead I would never have—"

"They must still have been alive. What time was this?"

"About ten twenty-one."

"You're very precise."

"I'm always checking the time—haven't you noticed?"

"I had, yes." He'd already done it at least half a dozen times during the evening. It was a mannerism which irritated Cassie, implying as it did that he had better things to rush off to, or else that he was bored. Or both.

"It's a habit we simple mu—we *wine* merchants get into." He laughed without veracity. "Don't want to miss the next consignment of—um—Château Lafite."

"I can see you wouldn't."

"Anyway, I looked at my watch when I saw Sonia. It said ten-nineteen then—it can't have taken us more than a couple of minutes for her to finish her conversation, reach me, say whatever we said, and get as far as the door of the Macbeth Room."

"A minute can be a long time."

"Long enough to murd . . . except you say the Plumptons must still have been alive at that point."

"I can't see how else a hand would have been dealt and three tricks played. Eccentric she might have been, but Sonia would hardly have sat down with two dead people and started a game of bridge on her own."

"I suppose not. What do you think I ought to do?"

"I don't know why you're asking me," Cassie said. "But obviously I think you ought to tell the police."

"It's not going to help much with their inquiries."

"You don't know that."

"Won't I look like a bit of a prat for not coming forward before?"

"Yes."

"Well, then . . ."

"Better a prat than an accessory to murder—by possibly allowing a killer to get away with it. Why didn't you tell them at the time?"

"Ridiculous, isn't it? We're brought up to regard the police as the guardians of the law, yet the minute I get within feet of one, I start to panic and feel guilty, even though I haven't done anything. At least—nothing they'd be interested in." He grinned at her.

She was not going to give the flirtatious little rejoinder he so obviously expected. He had proved to be an amusing dinner companion, but that did not prevent her from feeling a certain wariness in his company; something about him did not hang together, though she had not yet worked out what. When he had telephoned the night before, she had been pleased to accept his invitation. Nonetheless, she was glad she had arranged to meet him at the restaurant rather than allowing him to pick her up. If he drove her home she would be forced to ask him in for a coffee and it might prove difficult to get rid of him after that: he came across as someone with an unshakable belief in his own attraction for women.

What she had learned, during the earlier part of the evening, about Sonia had only reinforced what she already knew: Sonia was a difficult woman with a strong sexual urge, who had not grasped any subtlety of technique in dealing with other people and was thus constantly being rebuffed by them. Whether that had contributed in any way to her death it was difficult to determine; if at all, it could only have been peripherally. It was, after all, hard to imagine that the murderer, incensed by Sonia's abrasive manner, would have reached for the nearest obelisk in a drastic attempt to smooth feathers which had been ruffled.

Casaubon raised his eyebrows at her and called the waiter over to order another brandy.

"Look," he said. "I want to clear something up. That business between Sonia and me."

"All that bondage stuff?" Cassie asked brightly. "It's really nothing to do with me."

"Of course. But just for the record, it happened years ago, when we were kids. Our families spent three weeks together in Cornwall one summer—I don't think it stopped raining for more than half an hour the entire holiday. The parents went out in the evening quite often but we didn't always want to tag along." He shrugged. "Adolescents: you can guess what happened."

"Easily."

"I must say it was bloody marvelous. We found one of those sex manuals in my parents' room and tried a whole lot of things out." His voice trailed wistfully away. "I don't know that it's ever been that good again . . ."

"Poor you."

"And one of the things we tried out was slapping each other around. Sonia's never let me forget it."

"Why are you telling me all this?"

"Just to clear the air. It's better to be honest, don't you think?"

Is it? Cassie was not sure. For one thing, she suspected that whatever Ned Casaubon was being, it was not entirely honest, either about himself or about his job. For another, in her brief incarnation as Midge (Midge? Where on earth had she dredged up a name like that?) MacKendrick, she had felt a rush of freedom from her everyday persona such as she had never experienced before. Was this what actors felt as they stepped into a new role? Or was she just a born liar who had not yet fully realized her potential?

She could visualize Midge MacKendrick quite clearly: a thin creature with wispy fair hair and slightly crooked front teeth, who was getting married the following year to a man who worked in the same department, up in Strathspey . . .

"Are you going to invite me back for coffee?" Casaubon asked expectantly.

"No."

His face fell. "I'd rather hoped—"

"It's miles in the wrong direction for you."

"I don't mind."

"I do."

"I see."

Cursing herself for feeling any need to soften the blow with excuses—after all, he had shown himself to be an unregenerate male of the most unreconstructed kind—she said, "I have a lot to do before tomorrow. I must have an early night."

"I can't pretend I'm not disappointed," he said.

"Don't be. I'm renowned for my dreadful coffee."

"I'm sure there'd have been other compensations."

Cassie did not bother to reply to this verbal leer.

Driving home, she asked herself if what Casaubon had told her changed anything. Apart from establishing a moment when the Plumptons were still alive, she could not see that it did. If, that is, he was telling the truth. As far as she knew, the police had cleared him, yet there was only his word that he had left Sonia at the door of the Macbeth Room that fatal morning and then continued on to the hotel's swimming pool. Unless, of course, there were witnesses who had seen him in there.

But suppose that instead of heading immediately for the pool, he had followed Sonia into the room, seen the obelisks on the overmantel, and, for some reason still unclarified, had decided to brain Sonia. That still did not explain why the Plumptons had not raised the alarm.

Or how the three strange tricks came to be played, tricks made all the odder by the fact that Casaubon had overheard them being played.

THE cards were on the table, where she'd left them. Once again she set them out as she remembered them, then took the cards left over and placed them separately, as tricks played. She stared at the layout, unable to think straight. West had been Dummy, opposite Colonel Plumpton at East. In South's position, with her back to the windows had sat Mrs. Plumpton. Opposite was North, back to the mantelpiece and the two alabaster obelisks.

▲ MANTELPIECE ▲

North

♣	♦	♣	♥
7	8	K	
6	4	4	
4		2	
3			
2			

D O O R

West (Dummy)					*East*			
♦	♣	♥	♠		♣	♠	♠	♥
K	Q	A	Q		A	A	3	
9		7	10		10	J		
7					9	10		
5					8	6		
3					2			

South

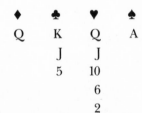

■	♦	♣	♥	♠
	Q	K	Q	A
		J	J	
		5	10	
			6	
			2	

W I N D O W S

Trick 1:	♠6	♠5	♥4	♥3
Trick 2:	♠8	♠7	♥5	♥9
Trick 3:	♠J	♠9	♥8	♥K

■ = 2nd pack of cards

▲ = alabaster obelisk

She was still bothered by the three tricks. Given the hands held by the three players, they made no logical sense. Something else was out of kilter. The second pack of cards, placed to the right of West, meant that Colonel Plumpton had been Declarer. Which also meant that when he laid down Dummy's hand, Diamonds would have been placed on his left, or Dummy's right.

This still did not explain how the three played tricks had been made up. Frowning, she thought back. She took another pack of cards, dealt four hands, picked them up and began to sort them. She like to alternate black/red/black/red, regardless of the fact that diamonds and hearts followed each other in value, and—and then she remembered that not everyone did the same.

Excited now, she thought about it further.

Colonel Plumpton, for instance, usually, though not always, kept his cards in order of value upwards, his Clubs to the left and his Hearts to the right, whereas Mrs. Plumpton liked to place her Trumps, whatever suit that might be, to the left of the cards held in her hand, and *then* alternate red and black. And Dummy had laid its cards down with Diamonds on Colonel Plumpton's left . . . Once more she dealt the hands which had been on the table at the time of the murder.

Yet again she frowned over the cards. Diamonds *must* have been Trumps, because if they were playing in No Trumps, Clubs would have been laid down first. But if Diamonds were Trumps, why had the ♥King been played—or any of the other Hearts for that matter? As Mrs. Plumpton appeared to have led with the ♠6, Dummy should have followed suit—and indeed had done so. North ought to have done the same, leaving

Colonel Plumpton to drop his singleton ♠3. But neither North nor East had played as they should: instead of putting down Spades, they had put down Hearts.

South, presumably having won the trick, then played her ♠8, Dummy followed suit with his ♠7, North should have played his ♠King, and East should have trumped. Instead, both North and East had unaccountably played Hearts again.

Cassie stared at the cards. If they were to be believed, and even if Mrs. Plumpton had not yet had time to arrange the cards in North's hand to her liking, an extraordinary amount of revoking—not following suit—had been taking place. But these were experienced players: it was inconceivable that they would have revoked so often, or that no one would have noticed and the trick would have been collected and placed face downward.

So how had it happened? She thought again about the cards, about the people playing them, about the way they played—and suddenly saw where the tricks must have come from. They were clearly the cards on the extreme right of each splayed hand, plus one from Dummy. It was the only logical explanation.

But why? Why would a murderer have taken time to gather twelve cards, one at a time—and done it three times, then laid them face down to give the impression of played tricks?

She could not come up with any answer but she had an inescapable conclusion. The person responsible for gathering them up—the murderer—had not, *could* not have been a bridge player. Ergo, all you had to do was find a non-bridge player with a motive for eliminating Sonia Wetherhead and you had your murderer.

But her brain ticked on. It always did, when bridge was concerned. Perhaps she was wrong. Perhaps the murderer had not expected anyone to look at the cards. Or perhaps had simply not cared.

So what else could she deduce?

When a thing is not as it appears to be, then it must be something else. Cassie looked at the spread cards and then gathered them slowly together.

Think radical, she told herself. Think lateral. There were three people in that room: suppose, after all, that Charlie Quartermain's jokey suggestion, and her own wild hypothesis, had in fact been correct, and that it was not Sonia Wetherhead who was the intended victim but one of the other two. Suppose Sonia had found herself at the wrong end of an alabaster obelisk simply by virtue of having blundered in, like a moth in homespun, at the wrong moment.

With that starting point, think even more radical. See this as a domestic argument gone tragically wrong, and Sonia reduced to the spectator on the sidelines who winds up caught in the cross fire, the innocent bystander hit by the stray bullet, the runaway omnibus, the fallen scaffolding.

Putting aside such questions as whether any one of us can truly be said to be innocent, whether Man is, as Uncle Samuel would have it, irredeemably sinful, suppose the intended victim was actually one of the Plumptons, not Sonia at all.

What did she know about either of them, apart from the incident—as deposed by Mercy Laughton—of Reggie Plumpton's alleged knicker-waving some ten years ago? He, by his own admission, had been in the

Special Investigations Branch; she, according to newspaper reports, was a former social worker. Hidden behind those two brief biographies might lie any amount of the domestic angst which Cassie knew was one of the hazards of marriage.

Reggie's pipe, for instance. Mrs. Plumpton was already on record as hating it. Suppose he had lit up once too often, puffed one more careless cloud of noxious smoke across the bridge table, and his wife, temporarily unhinged by the thunder somewhere at the back of her skull caused by the Albanian tooth stripper served the night before, had asked him to desist and been refused. Was it not feasible that, maddened by years of marital indifference and argument, she could have risen from her seat, approached her husband, and somehow contrived to kill him? Though Cassie was vague about the details, she did not think it would be difficult to dispatch an old man. Only then, with the Colonel dead, did Mrs. Plumpton become aware that a horrified Sonia Wetherhead was standing at the door, hand to mouth, a witness to the whole scene. It would be the work of moments for the elderly murderess to pick up the nearest weapon, brain Sonia with it, and stagger back to her own seat, feeling distinctly groggy with the excitement of it all. And Nemesis had struck as she reached for her pills; before she could say "One No Trump," she too had keeled over.

Not bad, Cassie thought. She looked out of the window. It was snowing again. A couple of starlings, iridescent, pipped like strawberries, quarreled on the bird table; three mallards from the nearby river flew in lower-middle-class formation across the white sky. She got up, keenness irradiating her bones, and poked at the logs on the fire.

Turn the theory around. Take Colonel Plumpton. Imagine that for some as yet undiscovered reason—mounting debts, an importunate mistress, *anything*—he wanted to get rid of his wife. This might not square with his remarks made at the Bridge Weekend party about the couple having been together for forty years and it not seeming a day too much, but those could have been a cunning ploy intended to cover his tracks. Suppose that, while he was doing exactly that, Sonia had come in.

Vividly Cassie saw the scene. The Colonel in the midst of—what? suffocating? strangling? making terrifying faces at?—his wife, Sonia pushing aside the velvet curtain and entering, her consternation and alarm.

"Stay your hand!" she cries. "What in the hell are you doing?"

At which point the Colonel seizes the obelisk and, somehow getting behind Sonia, brings it down on her skull. The witness silenced, he mops his brow, sits down at the table, and immediately realizes he can give no rational explanation for Sonia's death, thus bringing on a major anxiety attack which proves fatal for him too.

As a theory, it had certain merits. Although he could easily have murdered his wife in their shared hotel bedroom, or even at home, had he done so, then he himself would have come under immediate suspicion. Murder Mrs. Plumpton in the Macbeth Room, and her death might be put down to the excitement of the weekend, or even a delayed reaction to the party the night before. No one in their right mind would choose to kill their wives at the bridge table; ergo: it was a brilliant notion to do so. He had already circulated the story of her illness on Friday evening; when she died, everyone would assume it was owing to natural causes.

Which brought Cassie to the major flaw in her hypothesis. How do you kill your wife and make it look like natural causes? Even if someone has a weak heart, it can't be that easy. And another objection: if Casaubon was just a few yards away down the passage, having just left Sonia at the door of the Macbeth Room, would he not have heard Sonia's exclamations, assuming she had uttered some?

Unless he—or Mrs. Plumpton—had heard her remarks and hastily stationed themselves behind the door, ready to bring down the obelisk on her head as soon as she came into the room.

Yes. The more she thought about it, the more possible it seemed, the more of the eventualities it covered. Going back over the scenario, polishing and refining, she was inclined to cast Mrs. Plumpton in the murderous role. Though vague about methods of murder which left no trace, she knew they existed. She could not help remembering the pathologist who had attended one of her Bridge Weekends last year.

"People talk about the perfect murder as though it were a matter of undetectable poisons or fiendishly clever planning," he had said. "My own opinion is that there are hundreds, if not thousands, of murderers walking round today who have got away with it."

Gasps all around. The pathologist had grinned.

"It's all a question of choosing a method which won't be suspected, and a victim whose death won't be challenged. Forget your locked rooms and your invisible puncture wounds. In spite of the improvements in technology, the pathologist's art is an imperfect one and on many occasions I'm no better equipped than you are to say whether someone died naturally or was helped on their way."

He had stared somberly at Cassie, and then around at the rest of them. "*Murder being once done* . . . but most people only need to murder once. Think of it: I bet everyone here has at least one person in their lives whom, if they could get rid of them without questions being asked, they would."

There had been a murmur of dissent from the others, but Cassie was appalled to see them thinking about it, wondering, some even faintly nodding. She could think of no one she wished to eliminate. The twins were often irritating to the point that she wished them on another planet; she could not for a moment imagine wanting to *kill* them. Not seriously.

The pathologist had smiled knowingly, pulling a cigarette from a pack, lighting it without asking anyone if they minded—she *hated* that—apparently uncaring. But death is serious, death is irrevocable, its consequences permanent, not to be treated lightly. Sarah's death was so far removed from Cassie's present life that she scarcely thought about it. But Dad's? Gran's? She had stared down at her plate thinking that she had been unluckier than most, to have lost, at the age of thirty-two, all those she held most dear.

Which led on to her husband—*former* husband. Not that he was dead. But once she had held him, too, most dear, particularly up to and including her wedding day and for most of the subsequent six years. By the time it was over, the marriage had settled into nothing more than amicable resignation. Not even loathing, simply a kind of weariness. Loathing would have been better, would have implied that there was still some feeling between them. Even the breakup had been without passion: there had been no Other Woman—or Man—no spectacular finishing row, simply the recognition that they no longer wished to live together.

At which point, she had buggered off.

She kicked at the logs again. This was not the time to recall her marriage. Thinking about her husband inevitably led on to thinking about herself, the reasons behind the fact that she lived alone, was childless. And, abnormal though it might be, liked it that way—most of the time.

Turning back to the cards, she exhorted herself to think radical in the extreme. Imagine that there had been three people already seated at the bridge table when Sonia Wetherhead came in: the two Plumptons and A. N. Other, sitting in North's position. Casaubon had spoken of a third person; both he and she had assumed it was the murderer. It might well have been, but perhaps he had joined them in a friendly game first, before proceeding with his murder.

Which still made no sense of the three played tricks.

She picked up the telephone, then put it down. Despite the snow outside, the lowering wintry day, she was restless. The cottage confined her like a cage; she needed to escape. She would drive over to Mercy Laughton's place and see if she had remembered whatever it was she had forgotten about Reggie Plumpton at

their last meeting. And maybe—not that that had anything to do with it—Giles would be there too.

He was. Glaring at her from a window as she pulled
her car in as close as she could to the house before
switching off the engine and running for the porch,
pursued by snow-laden wind. Did she imagine it, or did
the frown on his face momentarily lift as he recognized
her and moved away out of sight, to reappear seconds
later, opening the front door?

He took both her hands in his and drew her in.
"You're frozen."

"I drove here with the windows open."

"Why?"

No point telling a man so newly met that she wanted
to match the inner chill her thoughts had generated
with an outer one. "Is your mother in?" She brushed
snow from herself onto the ugly patterned carpet in the
hallway.

"Yes." He sounded disappointed. "Is that why you
came?"

"Some of why," she said, looking directly at him. "But
by no means all."

Mercy Laughton was sitting at a table set in a square
bay, overlooking a smooth rise of hill crisscrossed by
bare hedges and some sheep. To the right, revealed by
the leaflessness of a creeper which wound itself around a
fence, could just be seen the back of Sonia's chapel, far
enough away not to be in any real sense overlooked, yet
indisputably there.

"Hello, Miss Swann." Mercy looked up from the newspaper she was reading, took a swig from the glass at her side, and felt in the pockets of her long black cardigan for her cigarettes.

"Good afternoon," Cassie said. If the ash scattered down the front of the cardigan was any guide, Mercy had already smoked liberally that day; the air was thick with smoke and the whole room smelled of stale tobacco. Perhaps that explained the anger on Giles's face: Cassie wondered where he had lived before his wife— Amanda, was it?—had left to keep company with Sonia's husband—Perry?

"Has Giles offered you a cup of tea? Or a drink?" Mercy said, folding the newspaper and preparing to be sociable.

"I'm just about to." Giles disappeared in the direction of, presumably, the kitchen.

"Poor boy," Mercy said. She dragged so hard on her cigarette that the end crackled with heat and burst briefly into flame. Leaning back in her uncomfortable upright chair so that one arm hung over the back, she said, "You aren't in the market, are you?"

"What for?"

"Marriage, of course."

Cassie laughed. "I thought the age of the marriage broker was long gone."

"Giles needs a wife—another wife. To be frank, he absolutely hates living here with me, and fond though I am of him, I'm not that thrilled to have him here." Mercy puffed blue smoke upward and brushed at her cardigan. "I mean, you pack the poor little sods off to boarding school as soon as you decently can, and after that, you don't really expect to see much of them except

in the hols, and even then, with any luck, they'll be invited to stay with some chap from school. Then they go off
to university or whatever and you can congratulate yourself on a job well finished and settle down to your own
life again. It certainly isn't part of the plan that they
should be back permanently just a year or two later."

"Why have them in the first place?" Cassie said.

"It was my husband's fault. Always too impatient,
always carrying on about spontaneity," Mercy said.
"Kept saying the cap interfered with things. I used to
say that's what it's designed for, dear, but he wouldn't
listen. It was being so bloody spontaneous got me pregnant both times. The Pill wasn't around much in those
days. After that, I put my foot down and kept my knickers up."

"I hope Giles doesn't know," said Cassie.

"He should—I've told him often enough. Doesn't
stop me loving the poor chap, of course, but I really
would like to have my home to myself again."

That might explain Giles's latent anger, Cassie
reflected. Notwithstanding her anarchic views on moth-
erhood and the hideous surroundings she seemed to
enjoy, there was something disarming about Mercy
Laughton. Cassie looked around the comfortless room.
Despite the clearly impeccable antecedents of its mistress, it was execrably furnished, though there was a fine
desk in one corner, some pieces of tarnished silver and
grubby-looking porcelain on the mantelpiece, a couple
of dusty watercolors which would have set the heart of a
dealer throbbing. But the general effect was drear.

"Hasn't he got a home of his own?" she asked.

"He did have, but it was sold when he and Amanda

broke up. There's nothing to stop him buying another, but he just doesn't seem to have any reason. Whereas if he had a wife . . ."

"And you think I'd make a suitable applicant for the post?"

"As good as any," Mercy said indifferently. "And he's dead keen on you, I can see that."

"He has a son, doesn't he?"

"Yes. Roderick. But he lives with his mother in New Zealand."

"Oh. I thought Lady Comberley said something about him being here."

"He was. They were over here for a few weeks. Amanda was visiting her parents, and Roddy came to stay with us. But they've gone back now."

"I see," Cassie said slowly. In the light of this information, perhaps the antipodean sheep farmers gained new prominence and overlaid her recent theories about the Plumptons. "Where do her parents live?"

"On the west coast of Ireland."

"And she was there the whole time?"

"Not at all. Once they'd dumped Roddy with us, poor little bugger, they were off to tour Europe. By the time they got back, Sonia Wetherhead had been murdered." Mercy reached for her glass and paused with it held to her lips. "I must say Perry took the news surprisingly well."

Giles came back into the room carrying a tray.

Cassie said, "And presumably the tour operators could vouch for the presence of—er—Amanda and Perry."

The tray was put down on top of Mercy's newspaper.

"For God's sake," Giles said irritably. "You don't think they had anything to do with Sonia's murder, do you?"

"Not really. But you have to eliminate—"

"Jesus." Giles began to pour tea haphazardly toward the cups. "Look. When are we having this dinner date?"

"Can I ask your mother about Colonel Plumpton?" Cassie said. The conversation had a kind of wonderland serpentinity about it, weaving from point to non sequitur and back to different point.

"What about him?" Mercy said.

"Last time I was here you were going to tell me something else about him, and then Giles interrupted and it went out of your head. I wondered if it had come back in."

"And you drove all the way over here to ask me that?"

"I was in the area anyway," Cassie said. To her annoyance she felt herself blush.

"I'll bet you were. I think you like Giles as much as he likes you. And if so, I wish the pair of you would cut the cackle and get down to—"

"Mother, *please*." Giles too was red-faced. "Could you answer Cassie's question and not drift off into irrelevancies?"

"Reggie Plumpton. I wonder what on earth it was I was going to say about him."

"When did you last see him?" asked Cassie.

"I told you, in the Strand Palais, about ten years ago. I'm sure I told you this. He was waving a pair of Fr—"

"And dancing the hokey-cokey," Cassie said quickly, looking at the expression on Giles's face."

"That's right. He said he was in London for a regimental reunion dinner."

"I see," Cassie said doubtfully. The idea of Colonel Plumpton waving foreign lingerie about in Piccadilly only ten years earlier was almost beyond belief but for the moment she was prepared to accept it. "But that's what you told us last time. And then you said you had something to say about him."

"So it couldn't have been that." Mercy drank some of her tea, then followed it by a pull at her glass. "Was it to do with his wife? Or his job? Or something about them moving house?"

Cassie and Giles hovered over her, as though she were a prize bitch about to give birth to a litter of expensive puppies. "Well, was it?" Giles said impatiently.

"Don't rush me," Mercy said. She drank more of her tea; drips from the saucer joined the ash on her cardigan. "By the way, did I tell you that during the war he was attached to the same regiment as Hilda Comberley's husband?"

Cassie's reflexes jerked expectantly, though offhand she could not think of any reason at all why this information should be relevant to the murder inquiry. "Oh?"

"Yes. I only discovered that recently. Bit of a coincidence, isn't it?"

"Certainly is. Is that what you were going to tell me when I came before?"

"No. His job. I'm sure that was it. Something about his job." Mercy clapped a hand to her head. "Oh, if only I could recall what it was. But when you get to my age . . ."

"Mother, you're barely sixty," Giles said. "There's no need to pretend you're senile."

"I've had a hard life," Mercy said. "You have to make allowances."

"Do stop acting like Meg Merrilees—"

"My memory," quavered Mercy, "Nobody wants you when you're old . . ." She raised her glass to her mouth and drained it.

Cassie had once—only once—accompanied Aunt Polly on a visit to an old people's home. "You remember perfectly well," she said without sympathy, just as Aunt Polly had. "You're only pretending not to."

"Quite right," agreed Mercy. "What Reggie said was that he'd retired a couple of years before, but to his surprise, he was working harder than ever."

"Doing what?"

"Being a bloodhound was how he put it."

"And did he say what he meant?"

"Someone—I'm not sure if it was the people he worked for when he was still in the Army—had retained him as a special consultant. He went round the country, apparently, searching antique shops and going to auctions, looking for stolen goods. The thing is," said Mercy, lighting a fresh cigarette and dropping the still lighted match onto the newspaper, "people have this idea that as soon as you turn sixty or sixty-five, your mind goes. It's absolutely not true—not that I'm sixty-five yet, not by a long chalk, but I *am* sixty and I can tell you that my brain was as good the day after my birthday as it was the day before—whatever this idiotic government chooses to think."

"Why don't you bloody behave like it, then?" demanded Giles. The newspaper on the table began to smolder and turn black; he poured the dregs of his teacup onto it while Cassie tried not to laugh.

"You just wait until you're consigned to the scrap

heap, my boy," said Mercy. "Labeled a Golden Oldie, of all things, as though you were a pop song from the forties. Eligible for some ludicrous bus pass, even though we haven't had a bus service from the village for the past eight years, thanks to the shortsightedness of the government. People calling you dear and trying to help you across the road. I'm afraid I told the last one that tried it to piss off."

"This job of the Colonel's," Cassie said quickly.

"Yes. Apparently they have this register of stolen stuff, and a whole lot of people like Reggie, who appear to be nothing more than bumbling old-age pensioners, have been hired to turn the full power of their still razor-sharp minds on to the problem of missing antiques. Looking out for them in unlikely places, or listening to people's conversation. Reggie said it's surprising how many you pick up that way."

Is that what had happened at Broughton Manor that weekend? Had Colonel Plumpton overheard something which would lead to the discovery of someone involved in selling or stealing antiques? Was that why he was dead?

Vividly Cassie remembered him approaching her at the Saturday night party, Mrs. Plumpton in tow, and his clearly apparent air of being about to burst. "*Deeply exciting*," he had said, in answer to her query as to whether he was all right. And added, "*Talk about a small world . . .*" What had he seen or overheard that had precipitated his mood?

She tried to remember from which direction he had come, from which group he had detached himself in order to join hers. He had been standing alone, hadn't he? And not looking particularly excited at the time. So what, in the interval, had he overheard? The two young couples had been nearby, and he had stopped for a moment to talk to the solicitor, Joseph Newsome, if she remembered correctly. And then—yes!—to the woman who owned an antique shop in Hereford. In that short time, he had learned something which agitated him. Who from?

Did he know her, through his bloodhound activities? Had she informed him that the picture she had been examining so carefully was in fact part of a haul removed from her own shop? Had he accused her of trafficking in stolen goods, thus triggering his own demise as she frantically sought to cover her own criminal tracks by murdering him?

Paying a visit to Hereford was an obvious next step. But though the news Mercy had given her with regard to Colonel Plumpton's undercover operations could even have moved the investigation a step nearer to what might ultimately be the truth, it did not seem to help much. Even if the Colonel had been the intended victim all along, the same objections held good as had held for Sonia's death: the police would have examined everybody's motives, everybody's alibis. If nobody had had the opportunity to murder Sonia, then equally they did not have the opportunity to dispatch the Colonel. Besides, he was supposed to have died of a heart attack. And did the fact that he had been in the same regiment as Lady Comberley's husband mean anything at all, and if so, what?

The whole thing was deeply depressing.

"**W**E only went two down," Lucinda Powys-Jones said with satisfaction. "I thought it was going to be much worse than that."

"Doubled, though," said Naomi Harris. She pulled her scorecard towards her and filled it in with a certain amount of ferocity.

"I'm terribly sorry, partner." Across the bridge table from Lucinda, Anne Norrington's face was red, as it had been since she laid down her cards as Dummy and saw the expressions on everyone else's face. "I don't know what possessed me to push the bidding so high." She laughed guiltily. "When you opened Clubs, I assumed you must have a five-card suit, and with all the little ones I had, I thought we were safe, even though I only had nine points."

"That's all right," Lucinda said kindly. "I bid 1♣ because I had sixteen points. Too many to bid 1 No Trump, so I had to call my four-card suit."

"I see."

"And when *you* responded with 4♣, naturally she thought you were asking for Aces," said Naomi, her voice scathing.

"I remember the rule now," said Anne.

"Which is how," nagged Naomi, "you ended up in 5♠ with twenty-five points between you and only three possible Spade tricks."

"It doesn't matter," Cassie said soothingly. It was important not to frighten Anne off at this stage. New bridge players often saw themselves as standing on the edge of a huge abyss with no idea of what lay at the bottom except that it was full of complicated things to remember.

"I'm really sorry . . ."

"I'll go over it again with you later," said Cassie. "And don't look so stricken. It's not all that long since some of the rest of us were beginners." Meaning Naomi: and where the hell does she get off, behaving so nastily?

"Seems like a good time to have coffee, ladies." Lucinda got up from the table. "Or something else. Anne? Naomi?"

"I'll have a whiskey," said Naomi. And added belatedly, "Please."

Lucinda raised her eyebrows but went nonetheless to the antique breakfront where her husband kept the booze. It was understood at these bridge afternoons that although strong drink was offered, it was never accepted. Naomi, for some reason, had chosen to break the unspoken rule.

PMS, Cassie thought, though she would have screamed aloud if a man had said such a thing. Or her medication. Only a month earlier Naomi had tripped over one of the three cats she cherished instead of children, which was lying at the top of the steep stairs in her picturesque cottage, and had pitched to the bottom, breaking a wrist and severely damaging several vertebrae.

This was a group with which Cassie played regularly, one of many she had joined as teacher/player, and watched with satisfaction as it flourished and grew strong. Just as Anne would do too if Naomi's attitude did not discourage her at the start. She had taken the place of a woman whose husband worked for a major pharmaceutical company and had been moved up north a month earlier. Perhaps that explained Naomi's unaccustomed brusqueness. If the group had divided at all, Lucinda and Cassie would have been on one side, Naomi and Pat on the other; Naomi probably resented the newcomer. In her mind's eye, Cassie could already see Naomi suggesting that they look for someone else before the next session; in that case, she would have to remind her of her own stumbling efforts to learn the intricacies of the game.

This afternoon they were in Lucinda's house. Which meant fresh-baked chocolate cake, two kinds of home-

made cookies, and some variety of savory sandwich, usually smoked salmon, since Lucinda's husband wasn't
short a bob or two, as Charlie Quartermain might have
put it, though Lucinda herself would never have
dreamed of so doing. The sandwiches would have been
cut into hearts, diamonds, clubs, or spades. There would
be sugar lumps too, in the same shapes; though none of
them took sugar, the handles of the obligatory silver tea-
spoons would have the same symbols at their ends.
Lucinda liked things to be right.

And why not? It was the infinitely expandable nature
of these very accessories which had prompted Cassie to
consider going into the business with a friend. If her
income had not been so suddenly curtailed by Sonia
Wetherhead's death and its subsequent repercussions on
her earning capacity, they would have been discussing it
this coming weekend, going over the figures with an
accountant, setting up meetings with a friendly bank
manager, discussing overheads and suppliers, small
business loans, feasibility.

As it was, she had been forced to telephone her friend
and postpone everything. Bridge was a precarious
enough way to make a living and she was certainly in no
sort of financial position at the moment to be able to
risk plunging deep into debt. If only these damn deaths
could be cleared up.

Lucinda reappeared from her politically correct
stripped pine/Aga-heated kitchen with a laden tray.
Setting things out on the table, by now covered with a
white linen tablecloth embroidered with bridge motifs,
she nodded at Naomi's empty glass.

"Another one?" she asked.

It was one of those questions which, had it been couched in Latin, would have been prefaced by the word *Num*, since it clearly required the answer no. To her surprise—and Cassie's—Naomi said, "That'd be lovely."

Having settled her guests, Lucinda turned to Cassie. "Have the police found out who killed that woman? Sonia somebody or other?"

"Not yet."

"The reason I ask," Lucinda said in her high clear tones, evolved over countless generations to call landed gentry home for sherry, calm restless natives in times of insurrection, or bring to heel large numbers of overexcited golden Labradors. "is that I met someone who was there when it happened at a drinks party the other night."

"Who?" demanded Cassie.

"Vicky someone. She's bought a weekend place somewhere round here—in Whitley, I think—though she lives in London most of the time."

"Vicky Duggan? A publisher?"

"I believe she did say she worked in publishing, but you know me: I probably got it wrong." Lucinda was perceived among her friends as being thick; no one minded in the least because she was also kind and extremely beautiful.

"What did she say about it?"

"She said she—" Lucinda looked around the table and her face grew solemn. "She'd actually seen the murderer leaving the room where it happened."

"And she'd passed this tidbit on to the police, had she?" Cassie asked.

"She said she had."

"So why isn't the case solved?" Naomi said aggressively, before Cassie could ask the same question.

"Because although she saw the person, she couldn't actually identify them. Whoever it was was wearing a dressing gown," said Lucinda. "More tea, Anne?"

"A dressing gown?" said Cassie.

"Yes, please," Anne said. She gazed at Cassie with awe. "Are we talking about that case where three people died in the middle of a game of bridge?"

"Not quite," said Cassie, cursing Thomas Lambert, journalist, for the nth time.

"That hotel has a swimming pool, hasn't it?" said Lucinda.

"Yes."

"And they supply these white toweling things—bathrobes—don't they?"

"Yes. But they—"

"And they've got hoods on, according to this Vicky person."

"Sounds like the Ku Klux Klan," Anne said.

"It does rather, doesn't it?" agreed Lucinda politely, although she clearly had no idea what Anne referred to. "Anyway, this woman—Vicky—was just passing the end of the passage on her way back from the pool, and she saw this person come out of the room where the murders took—"

"Mur*der*," said Cassie—though if her latest hypothesis was correct, the plural was more correct.

"—where it took place, with the hood up over its face, and hurry off in the other direction. She said it absolutely must have been the murderer."

So that was how whoever it was had got away with it,

Cassie reflected. Anyone at that hour of the morning encountering a figure in a toweling bathrobe with the hood up would simply assume that the person had been in the pool and was on the way to their bedroom to change and dry their hair. No need for Groucho Marx irrelevancies, or stocking masks, anything of that nature. The bathrobe was the perfect disguise, and one which would absolutely not be questioned.

"And she couldn't tell whether it was male or female?" Cassie asked. Again it was one of those questions expecting the answer no. Which is exactly what it got.

"No. Someone asked her that. She said it was impossible to be sure: it could have been either," said Lucinda. Her fair skin had flushed; she was not used to being a conversational cynosure.

"Sounds terrifying," said Naomi, with a dramatic shudder.

"I'd have been petrified," agreed Lucinda. "I mean, suppose he'd seen her there. He could have—"

"It might have been a woman," said Anne.

"He or she could have gone after this Vicky person and killed her too," said Lucinda.

"After all, she was the only witness who could identify him," said Naomi. "Or her."

"Except she's already said she couldn't," objected Cassie.

"According to her," Lucinda said, "there was absolutely nothing identifiable about this person: middling height, middling build, no funny walk or anything."

"If only it had limped," said Anne.

"Or had a hunchback," said Naomi morosely, staring into her glass. "Or a parrot on its shoulder."

"Those robes are very long," Cassie said, speaking more to herself than the others. "It would have covered up the legs and feet—Vicky Duggan wouldn't have been able to tell whether it was wearing trousers or a skirt or what."

"Perhaps it was a ghost, not a murderer." Naomi gave a snorting laugh.

"Even if it had been wearing trousers, it wouldn't have meant anything," Anne said. "These days, lots of women do. Jeans and things."

"And when you can't see someone's bottom, it's difficult to tell what sex they are," said Cassie.

"Don't talk to me about bottoms," Naomi said. "John's been nagging on about how much weight I've put on recently. Among all the *other* things he seems to find wrong with me at the moment." She looked defiant. "Can I have another piece of your fantastic chocolate cake, Lucinda?"

"Weight isn't something I have to worry about," Lucinda said, in the placid tones of a much-loved woman. "Tom always thinks I look fabulous, whatever way I am."

Lucky Lucinda. Lucky earth mother, thought Cassie. How many other women could say the same? At least with all this worrying she herself had lost four pounds in the past couple of weeks.

"Have any of you tried that F-Plan diet?" Anne asked. "It's really supposed to work."

"I haven't yet, but I expect I'll get round to it," Naomi said gloomily. "I've tried every other bloody diet that's going."

"Me too," said Anne. The two women looked at each

other for the first time with something approaching warmth.

There's something wrong with a society which asks half its members to aim for the impossible, Cassie thought. Which sets the nagging thorn of inadequacy squarely on their weight, then sits back and lets them suffer, while at same time happily ignoring such faults as beer bellies and balding heads, varicose veins, and hair growing unchecked out of ears and noses. She wished she had the strength to resist the pressure. No one asks men to go on diets: it wasn't fair.

While the others discussed diets, she mused further. Mantripp had asked whether she had used the pool on the Sunday morning, not because he suspected her somehow of murder but simply to eliminate her from his inquiries. She wondered why he had not mentioned the bathrobe-clad figure on his visit to her cottage two days earlier; perhaps the police like to keep some surprise aces up their sleeves—though it couldn't be much of a surprise if Vicky Duggan was going around the Cotswolds telling everyone about it.

Did the murderer know that he/she had been seen?

She had not been home more than half an hour when there was a violent banging on the door, so unexpected, so—since dark had fallen—terrifying, that she shot out of her chair and screamed. It felt really good; if this was what primal scream therapy was all about, maybe she should take it up. The front-door timbers shivered as someone's shoulders thudded against them. Before she had time to register further alarm, she heard a muffled voice shouting something. It was a voice she recognized. She ran to the front door and wrestled it open, first having to shut it again in order to get the chain off.

There was nobody there. At the same time, behind her in the house, she heard the sound of smashing glass. Oh God. She ran back into the sitting room and through to the tiny dining room. Outside the window, of which several small panes had been smashed and the leading twisted to one side by a hand that looked like half a pound of uncooked sausages, she could see a huge balloon of a face, floating in the darkness.

"For God's sake!" she shrieked. "What on earth do you think you're doing?"

"Are you all right?" Charlie Quartermain shouted through the hole in the window.

"Of course I'm bloody all right." Cassie was exasperated almost beyond words. "At least I was until you appeared." She opened the side door and let him in. "Just look what you've done," she said. "Those are the original windowpanes, practically irreplaceable."

" 'S all right, darlin'. I've got a mate with a diamond-paned-window shop." Quartermain winked. "He'll see you right."

"But that's the original *glass*," stormed Cassie. "And will you *please* stop calling me darling."

"All me mate's windows are original glass," Charlie said.

"What in the world induced you to break them in the first place, you stupid idiot?"

"Heard you screaming, didn't I? Thought you was in trouble. Enter Prince Charming to the rescue."

"Charming? You must be crazy. And naturally I

screamed, with you hammering at the door like that. Why can't you knock in a normal fashion? I thought you were a—a crazed axman or something."

"Oh Gawd," he said. He rolled his big eyes up at the ceiling, which lay some two inches above his head. "It's got a lovely face and a gorgeous figure, but it hasn't got much brain, has it? Do you honestly think a murderer would be knocking at the door before he murdered you?"

Put like that, obviously she did not. "Don't patronize me," she said. How had she found herself in the wrong when *he* was the one behaving like a vandal? She wished she had the strength of purpose to tell him just how much she disliked him, and how she wished he would stay away from her. What stopped her was the deep-down recognition that in Charlie Quartermain she saw something of the exuberance of spirit with which her father must have captivated Sarah thirty-five years ago and led her to marry him in spite of the opposition of her family. Sarah had died too long ago for Cassie to remember if her parents had been happy together; she only knew that until then, she herself had been, and that the warmth and love generated by Gran and Granddad, her father's parents, as well as Dad himself, had healed the wound of Sarah's loss without visible scars.

"What did you come round for, anyway?" she demanded.

"Tell you in a minute, gal," he said. He picked up the telephone and dialed a number. "Bert? It's me, Big Charlie. Yer. Gotta bit of an emergency, mate." His voice roughened, the vowels coarsening. "This bird I know—

thass enough of that, don't be filthy, boy—had some windows broke. Any chance of you getting out here pronto? Great." He winked at Cassie, who turned away. "Slight problem, though. It's one of your upmarket Cotswold gems we're talkin' about. Diamond panes and that. Original seventeenth-century glass. Think you can do it? Good boy." He gave the address. "See you soon, Bert. Yer. Yer. Bye."

He put down the receiver and followed Cassie into the kitchen. "That's settled," he said. "Bert'll be out here within the hour. Want me to light a fire?"

The image conjured up was so domestic that she said "No!" with unnecessary vigor and saw perplexity crease the large moon face.

"No need to shout," he said. He turned away. She could see he was hurt.

"Would you like a drink?" she said, trying to moderate the stridency of her tone, though somewhere inside her head another, more aggressive voice asked why she thought she needed to. He was the one who had frightened her, who had broken her windows, who had *intruded*. Why should *she* now feel the need to apologize?

"Thought you'd never ask," he said, and she cursed herself.

They sat on either side of the young fire which reluctantly she had allowed him to build and light, despising herself for her inability to see him off the premises. "What exactly did you come to see me about?" she asked.

"Well." For once he seemed less than at ease. "I got to go to this do in London. Wondered if you'd come with me. The invitation says Mr. Charles Quartermain and guest."

"And you want me to be your guest?"

"Thass right. It's a bit posh, see, so I wanted to take a posh bird along."

How easily she could imagine it: a host of men in the motor trade, wearing navy-blue dinner jackets with cowl collars; ruffled shirts edged in matching blue; gaudy bow ties. If they were anything like Charlie, the bow ties would probably revolve or spray water at you as well. She could remember Granddad saying once, "Never trust a man in a colored bow tie," and she never had.

She said, "Haven't you got anyone," then broke off. She had been going to say "of your own kind," but it was exactly the sort of remark Aunt Polly might have made, quite apart from being politically incorrect in this egalitarian age.

Instead, she finished: "else?"

"Course I have," he said. "But I'm looking for class. Which is what you've got."

"Oh yes?"

"Too right."

"I'm afraid I really can't come," she said.

"You don't know when it is."

"I know. I still can't come."

"Why not?"

Since he was being so blunt, she would be too. "I don't want to."

"Simple as that?"

"Yes."

"Fair enough." He got up and walked about. From a side table he picked up a silver-necked perfume bottle of deeply cut glass. "Very nice," he said.

She did not answer.

They remained mostly in silence—uneasy, on Cassie's part. Quartermain did not seem to be fazed by her obvious hostility. He sat there with a smile flickering across his face, staring into the fire. Once, he said, "You ought to have a dog, you know."

"Why?"

"Living out here on your own, a gorgeous girl like yourself—"

"I'm a woman, not a girl. And perfectly capab—"

"Stands to reason, dunnit, you're asking for trouble."

"I don't want a dog," Cassie said. "I don't like dogs." And somewhere at the back of her mind came a memory she could not remember recalling before, of something soft and russet, with long floppy ears, something she used to hold in her arms and roll on the floor with. She bit her lip. "I don't *like* dogs," she repeated.

A van pulled up in the lane outside. Bert, presumably. The man with the diamond-paned-window shop. She sighed.

It took about an hour, with Bert and Charlie conferring together in the dining room, Cassie mutinously in the sitting room. Even though she was prepared to accept that Quartermain was well-meaning, the man was nonetheless a menace. What kind of person breaks into people's cottages via the window when there is a perfectly good front door? She tried to keep her indignation and anger fueled, but she knew, deep down, that just suppose the situation *had* been different and she had been in the process of assault by some stranger, how thankful she would be to see Quartermain come bursting in. Much more than if he stood feebly outside on the doorstep while some loathsome fetid-breathed rapist held his hand over her mouth until finally the footsteps faded away down the path.

Finally the last shards of glass had been hoovered up and Bert accepted a small whiskey before departing, while Cassie inspected his work. She could find no fault with it. Much though she hated to admit it, the repaired window looked exactly as it had before Charlie had smashed through it, and the replaced glass had all the wavy inexactness that she had loved. Charlie forced her to go outside and peer in at him to make sure before Bert was allowed to leave. There was something distinctly unsettling about peering in through her own windows and seeing the familiar room, the familiar furniture, with Charlie Quartermain in the middle of them. She came rapidly indoors again.

Now she and Quartermain sat on either side of what had become a roaring blaze, searching for things to say. Nothing at all came to mind.

The telephone rang and thankfully she got up to answer it. A reprieve. But it was only a wrong number. How soon could she reasonably start looking at her watch and clearing her throat meaningly? When she returned, Quartermain was holding her Angelica Kauffmann plate again.

"Can't keep my hands off it," he said, grinning in a manner she guessed was intended to be rueful.

"I'll know where to look if it goes missing," she said, and knew she had failed miserably to keep the acid from her voice.

"It's just, I love her stuff," said Charlie. "When I was working in Germany I used to go down the local museum—they had three or four really nice bits there."

"Really?" The plates had been Sarah's and because she had so few reminders of her dead mother, Cassie resented anyone touching them.

"'S right. Not that she painted much of it herself—mostly done from engravings she'd done."

"Is that right?"

"Yer." Charlie put the plate back with reverence. "Not one of your greats is old Angie. But I've got a soft spot for minor figures: the big guys have got plenty of eggheads ready to spout off about them, but who's gonna speak up for the little chaps?"

"I've never thought much about it," Cassie said truthfully.

He sat down again, pulling a pen from the pocket of his jacket. "I have. I reckon we all need a champion—and I'm Angelica's. Anyway, I'm dead keen on what they call domestic art." He filled in a clue in the crossword puzzle and began doodling in the margin of Cassie's newspaper. Without looking up, he said, "I'd like you to see some of my work sometime."

"Gravestones aren't really my line," Cassie said.

"Gravestones? *Grave*stones? Wot you on about?"

"Aren't you a stonemason?"

"Yer."

"Isn't that what stonemasons do: carve headstones for graves?"

"Some may do, I s'pose." He laughed loudly, flinging his head back. Behind him, a yellowing asparagus fern took a distinct turn for the better. "*Not lost but gone before* sort of thing? RIP. *And the trumpets all sounded on the other side*. That what you mean?"

"Well, yes. I—"

"That's a monumental mason, darlin'. I'm a master mason. Quite a different kettle of fish, though I've done some monumental stuff in my time, lettering and that."

"Oh yes." Cassie remembered now, vaguely, though she had not been giving it her full attention, fascinated as she was by the amount of beer he could swallow in one go. Tympana, he had spoken of, one evening over a drink. Gargoyles. Capitals.

"As a matter of fact, I'm involved in a project with a mate of mine who wants to use lettering in gardens."

"Yes?" Cassie raised her eyebrows discouragingly.

"Quite a nice idea. Big rough-hewn stones, sort of thing, set among the plants, with runes and suchlike carved on them. He thinks we'd really clean up. Course, you'd have to have a big garden for that sort of thing, but there's plenty as has."

"It all sounds absolutely fascinating." Just so had Aunt Polly routed ladies who lingered too long over their cup of tea and two digestives, which was the standard vicarage fare when people dropped in around four.

"Yer. It is. But listen, Cass. If you won't come to this do with me—and I quite see why you might not want to, I'm not exactly the sort you'd want your friends to see you with, am I?"

This was so exactly what Cassie *was* thinking that she found herself rapidly backtracking. "I wouldn't say that," she said with unnecessary vigor, "not at all," and was appalled to see him take her seriously.

"OK, then. One Sunday I'll pick you up in the motor and take you over to the vick's."

"This is the Vicar of St. Alphege?"

"Yer. Over at Byfold. We'll have lunch there—I know

they'd love to meet you—and then I'll show you what
I've been doing all these Thursdays."

"Thank you very much," Cassie said, trying to sound
enthusiastic. "Yes. I'd—uh—I'd like that."

"Good." He got up. "I'll give you a bell sometime, fix
it up."

"Super," Cassie said.

He got up from the sofa, his large body creasing with
the effort. "Here. Sorry, I've messed up your paper."

"You have rather."

He hesitated, as though anxious to prolong the conversation. "There was a pair of these once, but one went
missing. The other's in this museum in Germany I was
telling you about."

"A pair of what?" Cassie was dying to look at her
watch.

"Lidded vases, they were. Special presentation commissions."

"They look more like urns to me," said Cassie, peering without interest at the newspaper margin.

"Beautiful decoration on them. Gold line work.
Usually these regimental things are a bit stilted, know
what I mean?"

She didn't really. "Hussars waving the colors, with one
foot on a dead horse," she said, dredging up a memory
of some museum visit.

"And all sorts of military fol-lols. Draped flags, regimental colors, martial drums. The colonel-in-chief
always tried to get in everything but his mother-in-law's
corsets." Quartermain waved the newspaper at her. "But
Angie wasn't the sort to kowtow to colonels. She told
them what she intended to do, and they could lump it if

they didn't like it. And since she was one of the leading decorative artists of the day, they liked it, of course."

"So what did she do in this particular instance?" Despite herself, Cassie found she was interested in what he was telling her.

"They told her they wanted to commemorate the proudest moment in the regiment's history," Quartermain said. "Some battle somewhere—I can't remember where. So she did. But instead of showing blood and guts and heroism, on one vase she showed the women and children standing on the edge of the battlefield, looking at their fallen menfolk, and on the other, the same scene some years later. Marvelous."

"Presumably it wasn't exactly what the colonel wanted."

"Too right. As an antiwar statement, she couldn't have done better. She got all the pointlessness of it, all the futility of war. Some years on, the battlefield is this lush pastoral landscape, green grass with a stream running through. No bodies, no death, just three horses, like there was in the first scene, only this time they're cropping the grass instead of lying shot to pieces. You look at the two paintings and ask yourself what war's all about, what those soldiers died for."

For the first time that evening, Cassie really looked at him. He had dropped his boorish wide-boy persona. Or perhaps he had not. Perhaps it was still there but his enthusiasm for something had brought to the surface a Charlie Quartermain he did not often display. Maybe, she thought, like her he was playing a part, concealing something of himself because he was not sure how he would be received.

"And which is the one that's missing?" she asked, genuinely wanting to know.

"The pastoral." He grimaced. "I sound as if I've seen it, but I haven't. Only read about it. A detailed description was given to the colonel—in those days you had to, of course, not having the benefits of photography for record keeping." As he spoke, he drew several swift strokes, embellishing his doodle.

"So presumably the one in the German museum loses its point without its companion piece."

"To a certain extent."

"When did the second one go missing?"

"Sometime during the mid-sixties. It was sent off to some show or other and never arrived, though its mate did."

"Did someone steal it?"

"More likely some dozy clerk had just taken it out of its wrappings when the old bugles announced it was nosh time." Quartermain put a fist up to his mouth and blew a very creditable "Come to the Cookhouse Door, Boys" through his fingers. "Dah de-de-de de dah dah! The silly sod dropped it in the rush for the bangers and mash and was too terrified to own up, for fear of being hung, drawn, and quartered by the regimental mascot or something."

Cassie laughed.

"You can just see it happening, can't you?" Quartermain said, smiling too.

"Absolutely. What a shame, though."

"Yer." He looked at her as though he wanted to say something more. Then he said, "Better go now, before I overstay my welcome."

"Um . . ." Difficult for him not to, she thought.

"See you next Sunday, then."

"That's when it is, is it, this visit to St. Alphege's?"

He thought, breathing heavily through his mouth. "I got to be in Kilpeck for a couple of days this week, so why not?"

Cassie could think of several reasons why not. She said, "I'll see you there," firmly forestalling any offers to pick her up, since they would necessarily carry the implicit assumption of bringing her back. "St. Alphege's Vicarage in Byfold. I shouldn't think that's too difficult to find."

His big eyes narrowed. "You beat me to the draw on that one, girl," he said quietly.

"I know."

When he had gone, whatever large and discreet car it was that he drove putting quietly away down the lane into darkness, Cassie picked up the newspapers, plumped up the cushions flattened by Quartermain's bulk, took his glass out to the kitchen, stuck another log on the fire.

Peace at last. Pouring herself a small whiskey, she sank down into her armchair. Minutes later, she was asleep.

A mysterious hooded figure. A missing urn. It was the stuff of which gothic dreams are made. Not that the urn—the lidded vase—had anything to do with it. Waking during the early hours of the morning in a chilly room, with the raw taste of whiskey at the back of her throat and the kind of stiffness in her neck which instantly brought visions of infirm old age, Cassie had bundled herself into bed and expected to return to sleep. Instead, she lay wakeful, considering both urn and figure, and coming up with nothing. Lucinda's information about the white bathrobe was interesting in that it explained how the murderer got away undetected from the scene of the crime. Quartermain's input was interesting but irrelevant.

In the end, it seemed easier to get up, even though it was still dark. The cottage was cold, the central heating not timed to come on for another hour. She made herself some tea and went into the sitting room, wrapped in a duvet. The air was scented with wood smoke from last night's fire; she put out the lamp and sat on the window seat in fading darkness, watching the world begin to stir. The sky first: a faint pink edging the line of the rise beyond the hedge at the bottom of the garden. Then birds, exploratory throat clearings giving way to full-blooded song as the light deepened eastward and began to make its way slowly up the sky. A cat from the nearby farm appeared, flowing like a silk scarf around the holly bush which marked the end of her vegetable garden, first its head and front paws, the rest of its lean black-and-white body following, feet delicate on the frosty ground.

It was at this time of day that she most clearly felt the immensity of the universe and her own insignificance within it. Like a giant zoom lens, she could track backward away from herself: a woman in a cottage under a slope near a village and, spreading away from her, the complex roll of field and hill, landscapes succeeding to mountains and thence to great oceans, huge continents, the very edge of the world, and Earth itself insignificant among the galaxies and infinities of space.

A wood pigeon shook noisily out of a tree and dived

at the scarlet berries of the holly. Cassie found the list of addresses she had obtained from the skeletal receptionist at the Broughton Manor Hotel and discovered that the Plumptons had lived at Hay-on-Wye. Was it worth the longish drive over there? Did she seriously hope to learn something which the police, with their superiority in almost every aspect of the sleuthing game, would not already have done?

The answer was a resounding "No!" Did she want to stay home, laze about by the fire, work out a few bridge problems, maybe catch up on some of her lost sleep? "Yes" to all suggestions. Nonetheless, she knew she would have to go. Anything was better than being there to field the telephone calls which kept informing her that she was surplus to requirements. And Hay-on-Wye was not only just beyond Hereford; it was also the place with all the secondhand-book shops. If nothing else, she could buy herself a book.

Finding a place to park her car, she walked toward Hereford Cathedral. The woman with the antique shop was called Margaret Dinnock and, as Cassie remembered her, seemed an unlikely perpetrator of either grand larceny or murder. Fiftyish, she had seemed somewhat self-effacing, surely an undesirable quality in someone hoping to make a living out of salesmanship. And hanging in the neckline of her blouses was a gold cross on a chain, a dead giveaway, Cassie would have thought, when it came to questions of probity. The only stylish thing about her was her bridge game—and remembering that, Cassie quickened her step a little, resisting the temptation to pop into the cathedral and look at the Mappa Mundi, resolutely ignoring the shops.

"Dinnock Antiques": you couldn't really say fairer than that, Cassie reflected, pushing open the glass door and stepping down onto darkly polished floors spread with Oriental rugs so worn that the pattern had almost vanished. The contents of the antique shop were mostly furniture, mostly blackened oak, with here and there a fine porcelain piece, a gleaming copper jug, a satin-wood teapoy. From the back of the shop, Margaret Dinnock approached; she wore jeans and a navy-blue sweater over a blue-and-white-striped shirt with the collar turned up to frame her face. Very middle-class, thought Cassie, for whom the phrase had few negative overtones, unless used by her cousins.

Ms. Dinnock stopped. A faint frown creased her face. "Uh—oh, it's Miss Swann. How nice to see you."

"I was on my way to Hay," Cassie said. "I remembered you lived hereabouts, thought I'd drop in."

"What about a cuppa? I've just made one, actually." Margaret Dinnock gestured vaguely rearward.

"Thank you." Cassie followed her toward the back of the shop. "Actually, I wanted to ask you something about that weekend at Broughton Manor."

"*What* about it?"

"You and Colonel Plumpton," Cassie said.

Was it imagination, or did Margaret's shoulders stiffen? And if they did, was it due to guilt, or surprise, or merely a sudden twinge of sciatica? And how was she to find out which? Cassie realized that she made a hopelessly bumbling amateur sleuth. Anyone with any brains would have had a story prepared, a list of questions to ask, and answers to find out. Instead, she had come wandering in here without any real idea of what she expected Ms. Dinnock to say. On top of which, for all she knew the woman might well be the one who had smashed poor old Sonia's brains in, and as such, prepared to do the same to Cassie if the incisive probing which any minute now Cassie was about to launch into should prove too near the bone.

"What do you want to know?" Ms. Dinnock said cautiously. She poured from a blue teapot into a matching mug and handed it to Cassie. "Presumably it's something to do with those poor people dying, is it?"

"Yes. The thing is, there's some suggestion that perhaps Sonia wasn't the intended victim after all, that possibly one of the Plumptons was the murderer's target."

"How am I involved?"

"Because at the party, the night before, you talked to the Colonel. And shortly after that, he came up to me and seemed pretty excited about something."

"Reggie often got excited," Ms. Dinnock said.

"Reggie?" Cassie raised her eyebrows. "You knew him, then?"

"Indeed I did. Had done for many years."

"What, as a colleague, or something? A friend?"

"As a lover, Miss Swann."

"What?"

"Don't look so surprised."

"But you're . . ." Aunt Polly's training had taken too deeply for Cassie to be able to complete the sentence, which would have almost certainly ended with the word "old."

"Old? Is that what you were going to say?"

"Absolutely *not*."

"People over fifty do *do* it, you know."

Cassie did not ask what she meant. "Of course they do," she said warmly, though her mind struggled to produce a picture of Colonel Plumpton and Margaret Dinnock *doing* it.

"We got to know each other through this shop. He was involved in the antique business, in a peripheral way. We became friends first, then . . ." She waved a hand about. "I miss Reggie terribly," she said, and Cassie saw there were tears in her eyes.

"I'm sure you—"

"The worst thing is not being able to mourn him in public. We kept it secret for so long and so there's no one now that I can share my grief with."

Still trying to contain her astonishment, Cassie asked, "Did Mrs. Plumpton know?"

"Probably."

"Really?"

"I'm sure she did, actually. I think she found it rather amusing, maybe even a little touching. In recent years, she had rather withdrawn from him. In an emotional sense, I mean. And like all of us, Reggie needed a little affection from time to time."

"I see."

"Do you?" Mrs. Dinnock wiped her eyes. "I don't suppose your generation knows what I mean by affection. You think it's all sex and orgasms, but my goodness, there's so much more to loving someone than that."

"I do understand," Cassie said. "And I'm terribly sorry about it all. And I would like to say that *my* generation, as you put it, does understand about love, as well as sex."

Margaret Dinnock nodded, pursing her mouth. "Of course. That was unfair of me. But sometimes I feel very bitter. At my age, the chances of finding someone you can love are much smaller than at yours. And now I've lost him."

The two of them were silent.

Cassie was wondering if this extramarital affair of Colonel Plumpton's could possibly be a motive for murder. But it didn't seem very likely. "When he spoke to you that evening, what did he say?" Cassie asked gently.

"We discussed, as I remember, Webb's Wonder."

"But that's a—"

"Lettuce, yes, I know. Reggie was extremely keen on growing lettuce. I told him about a new variety I'd heard of recently, which the French growers had been developing. Very hardy, multisprouting, good nutty taste. Much better value than Webb's. He was thrilled."

Lettuce? Is that why the Colonel had been puffing out his cheeks and talking about being hardly able to contain himself: because of a new variety of *lettuce*? "He didn't mention stolen antiques?" Cassie said, and even to herself, her voice sounded faint.

"Not then."

"But later?"

"Later, when we were on our way up to bed, the three of us, he did say something about a discovery which was going to set the cat among the pigeons." Mrs. Dinnock looked at Cassie and smiled. "Reggie liked a nice cliché. It was his only real fault."

And how many people could you say that about? Cassie wondered. "Did he say what this discovery was?"

"Something about a lost piece—he called it a piece—being restored to its owners. But it was only a passing remark." Margaret Dinnock sounded surprised. "Is that what this is all about—stolen antiques?"

"I haven't," Cassie said, with feeling, "the faintest idea."

The All Routes signs out of Hereford showed a direction for Kilpeck. The name seemed familiar; she had heard it in the near past, but who from? On impulse she took the road and had gone some miles before she realized that she was going considerably out of her way. She continued, nonetheless, still trying to remember why the name had struck a chord of recognition. The village, when she reached it, proved to be small and unremarkable, except for the church, which she recognized instantly as being a particularly fine example of Norman. Getting out, she wandered around it, gazing up at the curious carved figures which decorated the exterior. Someone out of sight was laughing in an uncontrolled manner, disturbing what would otherwise have been a certain measure of rural tranquillity, one which Cassie felt she richly deserved.

Rounding a corner, she saw two men staring up at the walls of the church. One of them wore a black cassock over tobacco-brown corduroys; he carried a roll of paper which he was scrutinizing, listening intently to the other man, who banged a vigorous finger alternately at it and at the carving above his head, at the same time talking in an unrestrained manner about local stone. The other man was Charlie Quartermain.

Hastily, Cassie backed away. If he saw her, he would immediately assume she had followed him there, that she wished to see him. Turning, she ran for her car, climbed in and drove away, but not before she thought she heard a bellowing voice shout, "Cassie! Come back, Cass."

The Plumpton home was a well-kept little terrace house of grayish stone at the far end of the main street. A low stone wall separated the front garden from the road; on the blue front door a dolphin-shaped brass knocker gleamed.

Cassie thumped it against its plate and, as if in response, the door of the neighboring house, divided from the Plumpton residence by another low wall, opened abruptly. A little woman in a sleeveless overall popped out.

"They're dead," she said.

"I know." Without seeing her birth certificate, Cassie couldn't have been sure but she'd have guessed the old girl was well past eighty.

The woman stared. "Then why're you knocking?"

Good question. "You're Mrs.—uh . . .?" Cassie glanced down at the clipboard she was carrying, as though searching for the information.

"Evans, dear. Mrs. Dolly Evans."

"Ah. Well, Mrs. Evans, I was hoping there might be someone in the house."

"What sort of someone?" Mrs. Evans narrowed her eyes.

"One of the—er—dependents," said Cassie. Did the Plumptons have any? Was it the sort of thing an insurance agent ought to know? She hefted the briefcase she was carrying, assumed an official air.

"He's only got one of those, dear. I mean, you can't really count Josie."

"Josie." Cassie looked down at her clipboard again and nodded judiciously. "How would I get in touch with her?" she said.

"Have to try further up the road if you want to talk to Josie—and even if you did, I shouldn't think you'd have much response. Not from Josie, you won't." Mrs. Evans gave a laugh which was the closest thing to a cackle Cassie had ever heard and shot her upper set of teeth forward, retrieving them in a movement so fast it was reminiscent of a chameleon catching flies. Indeed, Cassie would have doubted whether it had happened at all, were it not for the fact that people don't hallucinate about other people's false teeth.

"Why not?" Even as she spoke, Cassie saw how easily she had been lured into acting as straight man to the other's stand-up comic. She guessed the answer before the old girl, teeth aglint, said, "She's dead too. Buried in the churchyard."

"Oh dear."

"Murdered, she was. They never found out who did it."

"How awful for her parents." No wonder poor Mrs. Plumpton had suffered from a weak heart.

"I suppose it was," the woman said carelessly. "We had the BBC down here and all."

"Did you?"

"Doing interviews with the local populace. Vox pop, and that. I was on meself, seeing as how I live right next door. Very interested in my views, they were."

"What were your views, Mrs. Evans?"

"Can't remember now, dear. Can't hardly remember my own name these days, let alone something I said five years back." She cackled again.

"What about the other—er—dependent?"

"Humphrey?"

Again Cassie did some judicious nodding, this time pursing her lips for good measure.

"Came back for the funeral," said Mrs. Evans. "I've got to give him that."

"Back from—"

"So he can't be *all* bad, can he? The fact that he hasn't seen his parents, not above once or twice a year, for the last ten years doesn't make no never mind. He came back for the funeral and I suppose that's what counts."

"Where did he come back *from,* Mrs. Evans?"

"The United States. I'd have thought you'd have that down on your thingummy. Next of kin and all that." She stood on tiptoe and tried to see what Cassie was reading.

Cassie raised the board higher, to hide the fact that the piece of paper she was perusing was in fact blank. There was more to lying than just lying, she was beginning to realize. You needed props. Next time she went anywhere where there was a possibility that she might need to lie, she would come better prepared.

"We like to have facts confirmed by a third party wherever possible," she said vaguely. "And who better than someone like yourself, who knew the family?"

"What's your interest in the Plumptons, then?"

"I'm from the head offices of their insurance company," Cassie said, hoping some representative had not already been. As though to punish her for her lie (hadn't she promised to give lying up after the Midge MacKendrick episode?), Mrs. Evans said suspiciously, "We already had one of them. Came down last week."

"Which insurance company would that have been?" Cassie asked, smooth as butter.

"Can't remember, dear. One of the big ones: Prudential. Or the Halifax."

"That explains it," Cassie said, bringing the briefcase into play again. "I'm from a much smaller agency. It's to do with a low-cost personal pension plan which Mrs. Plumpton took out many years ago."

"Sensible, she was," Mrs. Evans said, nodding. "You can't be too careful these days, can you?"

"How do you mean?"

"Well, I mean to say, the way men pop their clogs these days, you've got to be prepared, haven't you? And you can't trust husbands to provide for you, can you?"

"I suppose you ca—"

" 'I've done me best for you while I'm alive, Dolly,' my husband used to say. 'I'm blowed if I'm going to waste eternity worrying about you after I've gone. The harp's a complicated instrument,' he used to say, 'and it'll require all me energy to learn it.' Very fond of the harp, my husband was. So I just asked for a bit more housekeeping, told him prices were just wicked these days, and took out me own policy on his life. Quite nicely off, I found meself, when he went." She glanced upward, as though hoping to catch a glimpse of Mr. Evans working on his fingering technique. "Want to go in, do you?"

"I do rather." Cassie looked helpless. "You wouldn't happen to know where I could find someone with authority to let me in, would you? The Council Offices, maybe? Something like that."

"Look no further," said Mrs. Evans triumphantly, as Cassie had hoped she might. The brass knocker had obviously been polished by someone: who more likely than the next-door neighbor with the key? "I used to look after the cats when Colonel and Mrs. P. went off for weekends. No one's thought to ask me for it back. So I'll let you in myself. I'll have to accompany you, though. Just in case there's questions asked."

"Absolutely," Cassie said. "I was going to ask."

In spite of a lingering trace of pipe tobacco, the interior of the house smelled fresh and lived in, as though the Plumptons had just popped down the road for a secondhand book and would be back any minute. Photographs of two children, which gradually gave way to photographs of the two adults those children had become, were set here and there. Pieces of brass and silver shone; the houseplants on the kitchen windowsill were thriving.

"I come in now and then," Mrs. Evans said vaguely. "Give the place a tidy-round. Just because they're gone's no reason to let things go, is it?"

"None at all."

There was a room to the left of the passage which would have figured on the estate agency's specifications as a dining room. The Plumptons had turned it into a study-cum-office, with a large table in the center and a chair at either end, at which they both, evidently, used to work. Was Mrs. Plumpton also in the business of tracking down stolen valuables or did she have some occupation of her own? A social worker: what exactly did that mean, in Mrs. P.'s case, and wouldn't she have stopped doing whatever it was at the age of sixty? Asking Mrs. Evans would make it obvious that she had very little information about a woman who was supposed to be a client. Surely insurance companies knew what kind of people held policies with them.

"Did they keep busy?" Cassie asked brightly, casting a swift eye over the papers still stacked in neat piles on the table. Mrs. Evans had not yet thought to inquire why an insurance assessor should need to enter the house of a dead client, but might do so at any moment.

"Oh yes." Mrs. Evans had pulled a duster from the pocket of her overall and was flicking it over the furniture as she spoke. "Did her prison visiting right up to the end. Not that she knew it was going to be the end, did she, poor soul? But she—"

Cassie reached into her briefcase for another piece of paper, which she attached to her clipboard.

"Do you happen to know which prison she last visited?" she asked. As if it could possibly make the slightest difference to an insurance payout. She thought she might buy herself a pair of glasses: she would feel a lot more authoritative if she could look up over the frames at Mrs. Evans.

"Couldn't say, I'm sure," said Mrs. Evans. "She did tell me, but I can't remember. It's me short-term memory, you know. Goes on and off like an egg timer."

"I don't suppose it matters," said Cassie. She turned to a four-drawer filing cabinet placed directly behind the door and flicked the top drawer open. Neat green drop files hung in alphabetical order. She saw names: Abbott, Burrows, Carswell, Davies; Unwin, Varney, Whitstone, Yorke.

The second and third drawers held more named files; her eyes flicked over Anthony, Bartholomew, Crickson, Dewey . . . Samuels, Thomson, Weedon, Zongole. The bottom one seemed to be devoted to copies of prison journals, police publications, newspaper clippings, and the like. She slammed it shut. Had Mrs. Plumpton had another job besides prison visiting? In newspaper reports she had been referred to as a social worker; was it possible—or, rather, it was not *im*possible that the press had got it wrong yet again, and that by social worker they actually meant prison visitor. And whether they had or not, did it make any difference?

Once again she recalled the Colonel and his excitement over some discovery, some encounter, some overheard scrap of conversation—she would probably never know which—at the Bridge Weekend party. Could Mrs. Plumpton have discovered one of her old lags at the weekend, masquerading as a respectable citizen? But if so, she would surely have come across him or her on Friday night. Or had she overheard someone talking *about* one of her old lags? Someone discussing a scam and mentioning a name she recognized? But surely, in that case, it would have been her who was excited, not the Colonel.

Yet, driving away, she could not help thinking that she held all the information necessary for solving the puzzle of who had killed Sonia Wetherhead. Think of it like a hand at bridge, she told herself. You know some of the cards—those in your hand and those in Dummy. You can make extremely informed guesses as to those held in each of the opponents' hands, especially if either of them have bid. It's just a question of knowing what to discard and what to hold on to.

"**N**INE No Trumps," Colonel Plumpton trumpeted. He was slumped back in his chair, head lolling.

"Our rubber, I think." Lucinda Powys-Jones put down her last card, and knocked back the generous whiskey she had just poured herself.

"Madam, I most splendiferously protest," said Felicity Carridine, sweeping the cards up into his capacious hands; Cassie was acutely aware of the sprinkling of black hairs below each knuckle.

"Your trick," Mrs. Plumpton said. Her eyes were shut, her fingernails deathly blue. "Your trick." Her voice faded, returned more strongly, faded again. "Your trick."

Cassie awoke. Somewhere at the dim edge of hearing, the sound of Mrs. Plumpton's voice still echoed. Dead men tell no tales . . . but what about women? Was this particular dead woman trying to give utterance to a tale she thought Cassie ought to hear? And if so, what was it about?

"Your trick," Mrs. Plumpton had said—briskly, faintly, angrily, accusingly? How exactly had she said it? And did it matter? Perhaps it did.

Cassie dialed Casaubon's number and could tell by his voice that he had been asleep. She did not stop to apologize, or even to feel marginally penitent. "Cassandra Swann here," she said.

"Who? Oh, Cas"—he dropped his voice—"sie." She guessed he was speaking from his bed, and that there was someone occupying the half he did not. Someone female.

"Listen."

"I'm all ears."

"That conversation you heard while Sonia was coming toward you along the passage from the dining room . . ."

"What about it?"

"Tell me exactly what you heard."

"I told you. Nothing really except murmurings."

"Didn't Mrs. Plumpton say something?"

He thought for a moment. "That's right. She said, 'Your trick,' as far as I can recall."

"That's all?"

"I think so. Then this small thudding noise."

" 'Your trick.' Nothing more? Think back."

Another silence, during which she could hear him scratching what she assumed was his head. "Your trick, sir," he said in a wondering voice. "I think she said, 'Your trick, sir.' I remember now, because I *think* I almost remember thinking how odd to call your own husband 'sir.' But of course it's the kind of thing people do all the time."

"The way Felicity Carridine calls people 'madam.' "

"Not me, he doesn't. But I take your point."

"Are you sure about this?"

"No," he said. "Not sure at all."

"What else could she have said?"

Again he thought. " 'Your trick, son?' "

"*Son?*"

"I don't know," Casaubon said shruggingly. "I mean, given that I'm not even sure she said 'Sir,' I'm just as unsure that she said 'Son.' But looking back, I'm reasonably confident that she *did* say something more than just 'Your trick.' "

"How did she say it?"

"I don't quite follow wha—"

"Did she sound angry? Triumphant? Depressed?"

"None of those things. Just sort of neutral, as though she was making a straightforward statement."

"Thanks a lot," said Cassie.

"What made you—"

Cassie put the receiver down. She imagined him turning between crisp white sheets, putting one hand on the curving hip of the slim and lovely body beside him, touching his mouth to a smooth brown shoulder, whispering "I love you" as his hand crept down her flat belly, stroked the triangle between—

"Stop it," she said aloud.

She reached behind her and piled the pillows up under her head. She thought about what Casaubon had said. Was it her question which put the words into his mouth, or had he *really* heard Mrs. Plumpton saying "Your trick, sir"?

And if he had heard not "sir," but "son," was it remotely possible that Humphrey Plumpton (who in their right mind would name a child Humphrey, with that particular surname to follow?), the son who lived in the States and rarely came home, not only could have been in England at the time of his parents' death but was playing bridge with them in the moments immediately prior to it? Logic told her not to be so bloody daft, but just supposing he was, would it not be equally logical to assume that he was the murderer?

And if he was not, there was still the question of whom the Plumptons *had* been playing bridge with. Someone young enough to be called "son" by Mrs. P., that much was evident—if Casaubon was right about what he had overheard. Which included nearly all the males who had been on the Winter Bridge Weekend.

The only way to answer her questions with regard to Plumpton Junior would be to find out whether he had been in England at that time. And the way to do that was either to look at the stamp in his passport or else to check with the airline he flew with. And she did not have the slightest idea how to set about implementing either course of action. She sighed. All the advantages lay with the police. They had the technology, the know-how, above all the authority. She could just imagine what would happen if *she* rang Heathrow asking to check passenger lists. Even if she knew which day Humphrey might have arrived in England. Even if she knew which airline he might have taken. Even if she was sure that he had come directly from the States, rather than from some intermediate stop on the way, like Moscow or Madrid.

Even if she knew he'd been in the bloody country in the first place.

The opposition held all the cards, she thought gloomily. Then she brightened. She was seeing this whole thing as confrontational when it was in fact collaborative. She was *not* Sherlock Holmes making an idiot out of Lestrade, or Wimsey patronizing the lower orders. Nor was Mantripp the kind of plodding village bobby with a bicycle who figured in Agatha Christie novels. All she had to do was call the detective inspector's attention to the fact of Humphrey Plumpton's presence, and he would do the rest.

Wouldn't he?

She wondered if Casaubon had yet informed the police of the conversation he had overheard from the Macbeth Room. She dialed his number again.

"Hello?"

Was it her imagination or did he sound breathless, like a man caught in the middle of pleasurably screwing his current mistress? She hoped so. "Cassie," she said. "So sorry to disturb you again."

"That's quite all right."

"It's just, I wondered whether you'd told Inspector Mantripp what you told me. About hearing the Plumptons playing cards in the Macbeth Room, and your feeling that there was someone else in there with them, just before Sonia went in."

"As a matter of fact, I simply haven't had time," he said.

"Are you going to?"

"Ab-so-lute-ly."

"Because if not, do you mind if I do?"

"Not. At. All," he said. She knew exactly what he was doing. She had been there herself, the telephone clamped to her ear, with Uncle Samuel or Aunt Polly or one of the cousins on the other end, while some man made love to her.

"I hope the earth moves," she said, and put the receiver down.

Detective Inspector Mantripp, when he finally returned her call, did not seem impressed. "A bit dubious," he said. " 'Your trick, my son.' "

"Just 'son,' " said Cassie. "Or possibly 'sir.' "

"Either way, it's not much to go on."

"I thought you wanted to hear everything, however trivial it might sound."

"Yes, yes, I do. Why didn't this witness come forward himself?"

"He said the mere sight of a policeman and he breaks out into a hot flush."

"A common reaction, unfortunately. Makes our job very difficult." Mantripp sighed. "And why don't you want to tell us his name?"

"I'm perfectly happy to do so if you think it's relevant."

"Casaubon, is it?"

"What?"

"The wine merchant chappie."

"I know who you mean. And you're completely—"
About to deny it, she broke off. "Yes," she said.

"We'd better get a man up there to take a statement.
Not that in my opinion this will make much difference.
We've checked all the alibis out over and over again."

"And this person in the hooded white bathrobe—
who's that?"

"Oh. You've heard about that, have you?"

"Yes."

"Ah."

Who says "Ah" these days except a policeman? wondered Cassie. Unless it's someone whose doctor is peering down their throat with a tongue depressor to hand.
"I hope that wasn't the ace up your sleeve, Inspector,"
she said.

"Ace?" Mantripp gave a hearty laugh. "Oh, very
good, Miss Swann. Very apposite."

"Because Vicky Duggan—you remember her?"

"Clearly."

"She's going round telling everybody all about it."

"Oh dear," he said, unconvincingly. So much so that
she wondered if he had in fact hoped that the word *would*
spread, eventually reaching the murderer's ears and caus-
ing him to do something silly and be caught. Or her.

"Have you found out who killed Sonia Wetherhead
yet?" she asked.

"An arrest is imminent," he said smoothly.

"About time too," she said, not believing him. "It's
been weeks since it happened."

"Believe me, Miss Swann, when we charge the suspect, you'll be among the first to know."

Replacing the receiver, she wondered whether there was any significance to the words. "The first to know . . ." He couldn't possibly believe that she herself was responsible, could he? She remembered the hooded bathrobe hanging on the back of her hotel bedroom door: she had worn it to come back from the pool on the Saturday afternoon. Perhaps he was waiting for her to incriminate herself. Perhaps they had followed her to Hay-on-Wye, monitored her entry into the Plumptons' house. Perhaps Mrs. Dolly Evans had been briefed on what to do if she showed up.

She drew in a sharp breath, then slowly let it out. If they really suspected her, they would have grilled her far more ferociously than they had done. Besides, there remained the fact she was sometimes in danger of forgetting: she was entirely innocent.

There were murder cases, of course, where they never discovered who the killer was. She hoped that this was not going to be one of them. In time, she knew, the Bridge Weekends would resume, her peripheral involvement would be forgotten, the country hotels would start to book her again. But by then, she would probably be dead of starvation. Or else well stuck into the "A" Level biology syllabus at some ghastly school. If it came to it, perhaps she should try a boys' school: the smells would be as bad—socks and sweat—but they'd at least be different.

Her spirits lifted with the arrival of the morning post, which contained a suggestion from a shipping line, with whom she had been in correspondence for some months, that she visit their London headquarters with a view to discussing the proposal she had put to them. Either they had not heard about the deaths or they didn't care. Whichever, it would be a terrific morale booster if she could bring it off.

There was also a letter from one of her regular clients (it sounded as though she were a high-class whore), offering her a £500 fee to act as his partner in three weeks' time, when he would be playing at one of the private bridge clubs in London. Below the engraved crest on the back of the high-quality linen-laid blue envelope, she calculated that if she gave up food and drink almost entirely, the money would last her for about a month.

She stared out of the window. It was one of those cold gray mornings when day and night seem to be slugging it out for precedence and neither side wants to give way. One of those days when it hardly seems worth getting dressed. Not for the first time, she considered the advantages of Quartermain's suggestions that she get herself a dog. Not only would it bark at intruders, including Quartermain himself, it would also give her a purpose in life. It would need walks night and morning, which in turn meant slobbing around in a dressing gown all day was definitely not on. It would need feeding and grooming. Something to fill up the supermarket trolley with, apart from the low-fat spreads and the lite drinks and the high-fiber cereals.

Depressed by the thought that if she needed a purpose in life, a dog was likely to supply it, she took a bath. Deep in sudsy water, she thought again of Mrs. Plumpton, up there at some celestial bridge table, taking time off, while Dummy, to break through from the Other Side.

"Your trick," she had said. Or "Your trick, sir," or possibly "son." In imagination, Cassie stood in the tiled passage as Casaubon had done, and recalled Mrs. Plumpton's precise tones. She shook her head. It all boiled down to credibility. A woman like Mrs. Plumpton would no more use the word "son" in that context than she would use a major obscenity. Any more than Cassie would countenance a person who said "lay" instead of "lie," or used the word "Pardon." Mrs. P. did not use the specialized language of the streets any more than she would have used the equally specialized language of the science laboratory.

Hers was drawing-room speech, and drawing-room people did not call other people "son," not even if they were addressing their own male offspring. Such distinctions might seem petty, but in a class-ridden society like England, they were fairly exact. Which meant . . . up to the neck in Raspberry Ripple Bathing Bubbles, Cassie suddenly realized what exactly Mrs. Plumpton must have said.

The theory held together, whichever side she examined it from. Identification might be a problem, but that was something she could leave to the police. She stepped from the bath, raspberry-scented foam rising from her shoulders like angel wings. If she was right, this really was a breakthrough. All she had to do now was test it out.

As though to underline that the mood was up, she caught sight of her body in the mirror and, about to wince, to slide her eyes away, was astonished to see that she really was slimmer than she had been last time she made a mistake and looked at herself.

That was more than four pounds off. Much more. She stepped onto the scales. Good Lord: she had lost nine pounds in the weeks since Sonia Wetherhead's murder. *Nine* whole pounds! Another five and that would mean an entire stone of fat gone. She started to think something along the lines of it being an ill wind—and stopped herself in mid-think. Murder as a slimming aid? Puh-lease.

Midafternoon found her back in Hay-on-Wye, hemmed in on all sides by secondhand books. The air was thick with literary dust; she imagined all the words from all the unread books grinding down over the years into a fine powder. She found a copy of Julia Horatio Ewing's story, *Mary's Meadow*, and started to read through it. It had been a favorite of Sarah's. Although Cassie's first six years lay at the far end of her life, refracted by time, pieces of them still shone like polished glass, catching the reflection of a lost sun. She could remember Sarah's voice vividly. She had been captivated by the thought of being the Weeding Woman.

Mrs. Evans was not at home the first time she knocked at the door, or the second. The town had not substantially changed in the twenty-four hours since her previous visit: tattered banners advertising last summer's literary festival still hung from the telegraph poles, the burnt-out castle still loomed over the town, hills somber and more stark than the Cotswold slopes she saw from her own window still reared upward from the gray little river walk.

Only Mrs. Evans had changed, by not being there. Cassie hoped she had not departed on a world cruise, a visit to some distant grandchild, to the hospital. Before she telephoned Mantripp again, she wanted to be sure of her facts, and to do that, she had to get inside the Plumpton house once more. The more she thought about it, the more she was sure she had finally cracked the case. Mantripp's assurance that he was about to make an arrest was simply standard cop-speak; it was obvious he had no more idea of who was responsible than he had had when the murder first occurred.

There were lights behind Mrs. Evans' lace curtains when she called the third time. "I'm so sorry to disturb you again," she said breathlessly when the old lady opened her door. "But there are a couple of facts I still need to check out next door."

Mrs. Evans was less obliging than yesterday. "First I've heard of insurance companies needing to see the inside of people's houses," she said. Behind her, strong smells of liver and bacon clustered like moths around the red plastic lampshade which hung from the passage ceiling. There was a trace of ketchup in the corner of her mouth.

"I do so agree," Cassie said brightly. "But my superior asked for some further information before he's pre-pared to release the sum insured and I'm fairly sure I saw exactly what I wanted to know on Colonel Plumpton's desk yesterday."

"I don't know," grumbled Mrs. Evans. "Seems a funny way to carry on."

"Red tape, I'm afraid." Cassie smiled, horribly aware of her similarity to Aunt Polly in one of her brisker skir-mishes with Uncle Samuel's parishioners. "We're all martyrs to it, aren't we, Mrs. Evans?"

Mrs. Evans began to feel in the pocket of her apron.

"I don't know," she said again. "Doesn't seem right somehow. You poking about in there, and those two not there to see what you're up to. Ever so particular, she was. Said you couldn't be too careful, not with ex-prisoners about. They looked you up in the telephone directory, she said. You couldn't go handing your address out, or anything like that."

"I already know the address," Cassie said. She leaned forward into the house. "Goodness, I do hope I haven't disturbed you at your tea."

"Well . . ." Mrs. Evans hesitated, casting a longing look backward to the invisible kitchen where her liver and bacon congealed on its plate.

"I shan't be more than a few minutes," Cassie said. "Why don't I let myself in, look up the information I need, and pop back with the key. Five minutes at the absolute outside."

"Oh, all right." Mrs. Evans reluctantly produced the key. "I hope I'm doing the right thing."

"Of course you are." Cassie took it and stepped over the wall dividing the two houses. "Back in a jiffy."

Inside the house, she moved confidently toward the office, found what she was looking for, and attached the information to her clipboard, under the wodge of insurance forms she had picked up from a branch of her own insurance company on the way here. She replaced the file, and was standing on Mrs. Evans' doorstep again within four minutes.

"It's only me," she trilled. "Thanks so much for your cooperation, Mrs. Evans. You've made a difficult task a little easier." How often she had heard Uncle Samuel use the same phrase as he urged volunteer workers into feats of overtime they would not have contemplated for a single moment were they being paid for it.

It was late by the time she was home again. The cottage waited, black against the paler darkness of the sky behind it. There were stars hanging above the hill; she heard the coughing of sheep and the sharp cutoff cry of some hunted night creature. The house was still warm with the residue of the day's central heating. Her first winter here, she had left it on all the time, only to fall into panic when the quarterly bill arrived. Now, she preferred to brave the cold early mornings and keep the log fire banked up overnight. Shivering, she switched on the electric blanket, went downstairs again, and made tea. She took the tray upstairs and snuggled underneath the duvet. Finally, she looked at the papers she had stolen from the Plumpton office.

It was all there. She had been right about having enough information to nail the killer. Here was the proof not only of the reason for the murder but even of the murderer's identity. It was only a matter of proving what identity that person had assumed, since clearly the one in the file on her knee had long since been discarded.

The victim was not and never had been Sonia Wetherhead. Mrs. Plumpton had been recognized by the murderer, and then recognized in her turn the person she had last seen doing time inside. And she had sounded her own death knell by speaking those devastating words—which were not, and never had been, "Your trick," though even before that, the murderer had decided she must be eliminated before she could expose the truth behind the respectable veneer.

With the information in front of her, Mantripp would

have to reinvestigate and almost certainly would find that her death had not been natural as was suspected, even if it was difficult to prove.

She thought about it. Even though his wife was the principal victim, undoubtedly the Colonel had been rumbled as a bloodhound, making it clear to the guilty party that he had overheard an incriminating revelation and intended to dig deeper. Perhaps not just one but both of the deaths of the old people had been unnatural, though it might well be impossible to prove it—unless the person responsible confessed.

And Sonia Wetherhead had been nothing more than a red herring.

Cassie had read somewhere that as society grew more liberal, so the detective story writer found it increasingly difficult to come up with convincing motives for murder to be done. In the old days, when respectability and the good opinion of your neighbors were not only worth having but also necessary for your peace of mind, people were prepared to kill to maintain their reputations. But now, when every peccadillo could be sold to the tabloids for vast sums (*"I Was Pop Star's Mistress," Says Gay Bishop. Why I Ate My Own Mother—the Canonbury Cannibal Speaks Out*), a desire to maintain appearances no longer seems a compelling reason for murder.

Yet, if she was correct, here was that article writer proven wrong. Reading the murky case history, Cassie could see with clarity why the deaths had occurred. Physical abuse, suspected sexual abuse, the subject taken into care at the age of ten after a sibling died of injuries inflicted by their stepfather, picked up for vagrancy at the age of seventeen, with a charge of soliciting allowed to lie on the files. And as the subject grew older, so the charges grew more serious: petty theft, breaking and entering, aggravated assault, assault with a deadly weapon. Then came an early marriage and a child, which was battered in its turn. Then prison. And finally, the turnaround.

Art classes undertaken in prison under the guidance of a dedicated art teacher, with the support of a caring governor. A passion generated and allowed to bloom. Moved from the prison laundry to work in the prison library. The subject's belated recognition that only a radical change of outlook and behavior would ensure the kind of life which would provide satisfaction. And with the help of an enlightened prison visitor (Mrs. Plumpton) and a willing probation service, the final rehabilitation: the leap into respectability via the Army.

Somewhere along the way, there would have been the opportunity to amass some money—some of it perhaps not strictly legal but never too far on the wrong side of the law, not now that the possibility, the advantages of respectability had been glimpsed, and a chance offered to put the past behind for good.

Cassie laid the papers down on the bed. As the years passed, the money would have increased, and so would the ability to indulge in the passion which originated in those prison art classes. And then had come the chance encounter at a Bridge Weekend. An innocent question from the Colonel, the simple statement from Mrs. Plumpton, the overwhelming panic at the startled recognition that the elaborate yet flimsy façade so painstakingly constructed over the years could be brought crashing down.

When she looked at it logically, Cassie could see so easily how murder must have seemed the only way out. Her repulsion for the act itself was mixed with a certain compassion. It was difficult enough to escape from the shadow that the past flung forward onto the present. To see Nemesis in the shape of two elderly people calmly dealing a pack of cards onto a green baize table— though, come to think of it, they must have been seen and maybe recognized before that Sunday morning in the Macbeth Room. On Saturday evening, perhaps, or even earlier. Either way, the threat to the reconstructed life must be eliminated.

She paused. What threat? Mrs. Plumpton would surely have seen fit to congratulate, rather than denounce, her former client. Respectability attained was something to be proud of; to be in a position to show one's former mentors that one had justified their faith was hardly a matter which led on to murder.

Unless the means to the end was in some way criminal—and the Plumptons were in a position to prove it. Cassie frowned. She had read in an Hercule Poirot story that the great Belgian detective felt good bridge players to be ruthless, cunning, and resourceful, prepared to take any risk, as long as it had a reasonable chance of success. Which was fine. Except that if the person in Mrs. Plumpton's file might well be all those things— indeed had proven to be so—it was not because of any bridge-playing abilities.

Before going up to bed, she tidied up. There were several yellowing leaves left where she could not possibly miss them; callously she chucked them into the fireplace without even glancing at their former owners.

After all, she was not running a botanic hospice here, for heaven's sake. As she picked up the discarded newspaper from two evenings before, still lying where it had been left, her eye fell on the Quartermainic doodles. He had drawn the outline of the vase he had been telling her about in firm clear lines, perfectly proportioned, though she would have still have called it an urn.

About to scrumple it up and chuck it into the hearth, ready for tomorrow's fire, she looked at his sketch again. And paused. A missing Angelica Kauffmann vase, he had said. A regimental vase, one of a pair. One was in a museum in Germany. But the other . . .

Unless she was entirely mistaken, she had seen the other, and recently. An urn—sorry: a lidded vase— almost exactly as Quartermain had drawn and then described it. In her mind's eye, she could clearly see the lush meadow, the stream edged with meticulously painted purple iris, the three horses, white, brown, and dappled, moving across thick summer grass, the three trees in the distance. Calvarial against a blue sky set with small clouds.

She looked at the dark pressing against the windowpane. Yes. She had definitely seen it somewhere. And recently. Where on earth had it been?

FRIDAY. The freezing weather continued. A dank cold mist clutched at the garden, making it difficult to see even as far as the shed. Her inclination was to stay in bed, with a breakfast tray and the paper. As always, the realization was accompanied by the delightful subsidiary thought that there was absolutely nothing to stop her doing it if she wished. As a self-employed person (for how much longer?) she could do as she liked.

Turning the pages, reading of atrocities, starvation,

Cabinet Ministers caught with their pants down, the latest murder, she came to the Arts page, which featured an interview with the male lead in *Aces High,* a new political thriller about to open in the West End. Although the accompanying photograph was flatteringly arranged to eliminate some of the lines and enhance the profile, she recognized the face immediately.

The name, too, was familiar, last heard dropping from the aristocratic lips of Hilda, Lady Comberley. She stared at it with rising fury mixed with flooding embarrassment.

"My character in *Aces High* is a gambler," Emlyn Charteris, hard-jawed charmer, trifler with the affections of vulnerable women, alleged wine merchant, was quoted as saying, "and plays bridge for high stakes. Some of the action actually takes place at a bridge tournament, and since I know absolutely nothing about bridge, I've been boning up on it in the past few weeks—enrolling in a couple of Bridge Weekends, sitting in at the Invitation Pairs competition which was held in London recently, that sort of thing. I wanted to try and experience for myself the highs and lows that a fanatical bridge player might feel during the course of intense competition, but unless I knew something about the game, I wasn't going to be able to make the character convincing."

The journalist had asked whether he always gave his parts this degree of commitment. "Always," Charteris replied. "For instance, the last character I played—in the comedy *Pass the Bottle*—was a wine merchant, so I spent as much time as I could spare working at my local off-license, learning a bit about the trade."

A sweat of embarrassment pricked Cassie's underarms. She had thought Casaubon fancied her, when all the time he had been picking her brains as he prepared to play a part. At least it proved that her instincts had been right when she suspected that there was something not quite kosher about him. And how amazingly glad she felt that she had not given in to her other baser instincts and allowed him to come home with her after dining with him. It was particularly galling to have been used, when she would have been happy to give him the information he required had he asked for it.

She ran her eye over the rest of the piece, but there was no mention of Sonia Wetherhead or the death of the Plumptons, which had to be some kind of a bonus.

She reviewed her theory of the previous day and found that it still held up. The dilemma now was: should she tell Mantripp what she knew, what she suspected? To do so might land her in all sorts of dog dirt. She had, after all, entered private premises under false pretenses, and removed property from those premises without authority. She had entered, even though it had been without any accompanying breaking. She had gone equipped with intent to deceive. Committed can't-get-away-from-it theft. Impersonated an insurance agent. They probably threw the book at you for that one alone, never mind all the other offenses which would have to be taken into consideration.

And what about Mrs. Evans? She'd be done for aiding and abetting, at the very least. Even Mr. Evans' indifferent fingers might falter on the celestial harp strings at the sight of the poor old girl being carted off to the nick while the neighbors twitched their curtains in an ecstasy of *Schadenfreude*.

Which meant that she ought to have something concrete to set in front of Mantripp before she spoke to him. Which meant she ought really to go down and confront her suspect. Which raised another question: should she go alone? Confronting the enemy without backup was about as idiotic as jumping from a plane without a parachute and then being surprised at not surviving the landing. On the other hand, she didn't really *have* a suspect. Not as such. For the fiftieth time, she reviewed those people who had been present at the Winter Bridge Weekend: just about all of them had already been eliminated by the police.

Yet she knew she had the information tucked away somewhere in her brain, if she could only hoick it out, like an oyster from its shell.

Once again, she went over the three nontricks. Perhaps she had been overclever in deducing from them that the murderer did not play bridge. There were any number of reasons to explain them. It could have been a bluff, though who or why he was bluffing she couldn't quite work out. Perhaps the murderer did not expect anyone ever to look at them, or if they did, not to start trying to deduce things from them. Perhaps they had simply been a panic reaction, a never very realistic attempt to throw the police off the scent, or gain extra time, to suggest that the Plumptons had been playing for longer than they really had.

Beside the bed, her telephone bleeped.

"Felix Ryland here," she heard.

"Yes?" she said coldly. Why should she be polite to the sod?

He coughed. "I know you've been having some trouble since the—uh—unfortunate incidents which took place here recently."

"Trouble is one way of putting it," she said, her tone lowering the temperature even further. She could be very unforgiving.

"I want you to know that I personally don't blame you in any way—"

"That's *really* good of you, Mr. Ryland." You dick, she thought. "I appreciate that *enorm*—"

"—and in fact I've had so much positive feedback in spite of what happened that I'm wondering if we could start discussing a couple—or even more, depending on your availability—of weekends in the autumn."

"The autumn?"

"Between September and Christmas. We're working on the autumn brochures now, you see. How do you feel about it?"

"Well . . ." She was backtracking now, trying to sound more friendly. "Naturally I think it seems like an extremely good idea."

"Splendid." Ryland coughed again. "Would it be asking too much for you to drive over here to discuss it with us?"

"Us?"

"Kevin, my manager, and I.".

"When?"

"Whenever's convenient. But sooner rather than later."

Cassie looked out of the window. "This afternoon," she said reluctantly. "Or tomorrow." It might have turned a bit warmer by tomorrow.

"Tomorrow afternoon," Ryland said. "Teatime-ish? That'll give me time to go through my figures."

*　　*　　*

There was a man standing by the side of the ditch as she drove down the lane. His car was parked by a gate; he had the casual air all men assume in a similar situation. Cassie slowed down. Should she go and embarrass him by pointing out that, whatever he might think to the contrary, this was not a public urinal, and that, what's more, this was not the first time she had seen him there, in similar pose? A gust of wintry wind shook into the car as she rolled down the window and opened her mouth to shout. A thought struck her. Was she going to turn into one of those cantankerous old ladies who walk down crowded pavements banging the backs of people's legs with their walking sticks? Was she going to end up taking books out of public libraries in a coat which smelled of mothballs? Would she be one of those moaning old biddies who seem to have a grudge against the human race, who terrorize small noisy boys and hiss at young mothers with baby buggies? Had she, indeed, already become one? She rolled the window up again and drove on.

The Broughton Manor Hotel looked much as it had a few weeks earlier. Some kind of small convention seemed to be in progress: a lot of bronzed men in royal-blue jackets were wandering about the passages and sitting on the chintz sofas in the reception hall. Many of them had antipodean accents and wore enameled ostrich-shaped badges in the lapels of their jackets.

"We'll go upstairs to my private sitting room," Ryland said. He seemed more relaxed than on the previous occasions she had met him. "I'll have some tea sent up."

What sort of tea? A full Devon cream tea? A cucumber-sandwiches-with-the-crusts-removed tea? A two-kinds-of-cake tea? Any or all of the above sounded acceptable, Cassie thought, following him up the wide oak staircase leading from the front hall.

His large sitting room had four bay windows, each with a window seat, overlooking the parkland which spread behind the hotel. Beyond a line of trees rose frosted Cotswold hills, plowed fields, black trees. Cassie shivered, hunching her shoulders. Too much country-side made her feel unprotected, agoraphobic. Give her a crowded urban environment, a modicum of bricks and mortar, and she was a lot happier. She surveyed the pleasant room, set with sofas and comfortable easy chairs, low tables, and some fine objets d'art, displayed carelessly here and there, as though they were the every-day stuff of life, rather than special pieces to be kept behind glass. She had only been here once before, and then for no more than a few panicky seconds. Nonetheless, she was aware that something about it was different.

A log fire burned boisterously under the painted overmantel, which was loaded with more bibelots of var-ious kinds. Ryland saw the direction of her gaze and said, with a deprecating laugh, "Clutter, clutter. I'm afraid families like mine rather go in for it."

"Nice clutter, though," Cassie said.

"Most of it." He picked up a navy-glazed cup with a bouquet of spring flowers hand-painted on it. "This, for instance. It's Coalport: worth something if we had the saucer too. I wonder where it's gone—my mother always kept it on her dressing table, for her loose hairpins."

Why was she embarrassed by his remarks? Was it the contrast between his family background, rooted in tradition and longevity, and her own? She was aware that the veneer of respectability imposed by her years at the vicarage was growing thinner and more etiolated as she grew older; she envisaged a time when she would revert to type, become increasingly like Gran, increasingly unlike Uncle Samuel. Perhaps she would lean on beer-ringed bars and burp along with the best of them. Perhaps she would revert to frilly nylon blouses which revealed her cleavage, and call total strangers "love." And if she did, it would only confirm Aunt Polly's worst fears.

"Have you spoken to the police recently?" Ryland asked politely.

"Not very. Have you?"

"Not for weeks."

Cassie could see herself in the Venetian mirror on the far wall, the mantelpiece behind her, the firelight's glow lending her an all-over halo. You'd never mistake her for a celery stick but, on the other hand, the suggestion of pinchable flesh around the hip and under the chin had vanished. Taut, she thought. Rangy. Or was it just that particular mirror, with its mercury backing long ago melded with the glass to produce a flattering oyster opacity? She studied her reflection again. Whippetlike was another adjective which sprang very much to mind, but she did not possess the mental agility to handle it. *Whippetlike*, for heaven's sake. Who did she think she was kidding?

Ryland went over to an elaborately inlaid bureau which stood against the wall to the right of the fireplace. Several files were stacked on the pulled-down front. he picked them up and laid them down on the low tables between two armchairs placed in front of the fire.

"Let's have a look at dates," he said. "You brought your diary, I trust."

"Yes." But she had no intention of letting him see it, or the empty blanks with which it was filled. She might not bear much resemblance to a greyhound, but she still had her pride.

He opened one of the files, riffed through it, held a pencil poised above a sheet of paper. "How are you for October?

Cassie held the diary up, turning the pages. How she was for October was unengaged, unbooked. Free. Likewise September. *And* November. "Uh—which dates in October did you have in mind?" she asked.

"The first weekend," Ryland said.

Cassie gambled. "Sorry, I can't make that. Nor the last one."

"Then how about the third weekend?"

"Fine." Cassie penciled it in.

"And what about November?"

They fixed another weekend in there, and a further possibility in December, Cassie biting back remarks to the effect that it was good of him to engage her. "We can talk fees and arrangements nearer the time," she said briskly.

It was hard to see why Ryland had asked her to trek cross-country on a bitter winter's day for something which could equally well have been dealt with over the telephone. Nor, she realized belatedly, was there any sign of Kevin.

Ryland got up and walked over to the windows. "Looks like more snow," he said.

"Mmm." Cassie did not do weather forecasts.

"It's west of here that they really get the heavy weather. The Wye Valley and so on. Do you know it?"

"Not very well."

"Ever been to any of these towns like Ross or Hay-on-Wye?"

"No," she lied, wondering why he was asking. "Should I have done?"

"Only if you like secondhand books. Or meddling in other people's affairs."

The change in his voice was sudden and very violent.

"What?" She half turned in her armchair to look at him, as he came across the room toward her, his footsteps very light on the carpet, very menacing.

"Interfering cow."

"I *beg* your par—"

"What the hell does it matter to you anyway?"

Cassie tried to stand up. Belatedly she had realized that she was up here alone with him and that something was wrong, though she had not quite worked out what. "Does *what* matter? I'm afraid I don't quite—"

He pushed her back into the chair and kept a heavy hand on her shoulder, making it difficult to move. Fear cramped the muscles in her foot so that it was impossible to keep it still.

"You middle-class wankers," Ryland said in a low sneering voice. "Think you own the bloody place, don't you? Not one of the bloody lot of you've ever known what it's like to be cold or hungry, or to hate where you live, or the people you live with. Especially the swine who calls himself your stepfather and beats you up every time he comes home from the boozer with a skinful."

"I'm not middle-class," Cassie said.

"Sure you aren't." He grabbed at her hair and pulled it upward, as though trying to lift her from the seat.

"I grew *up* in a boozer," she quavered, but he didn't hear her, lost in some hellish memory of his own.

"Ever been swung round by your hair and smashed against the wall?" he asked conversationally. His speech patterns had coarsened. He pulled harder at her hair.

"N-no. But—" Tears of pain rolled down Cassie's cheeks. She tried to wipe them away but more came. And more. It felt as though the top of her scalp would part company with her skull at any moment. If she twisted, it only hurt more.

"My mum was. Regular as clockwork. He'd start in on me and my brother, and then he'd do her over." To Cassie's relief, Ryland let go of her hair and came around to stand in front of her. "Ever been kicked in the stomach when you're eight months pregnant?"

"I've n-never been—"

"That's what he did to her. She lost the baby." His voice was matter-of-fact. "And that's not all he did, the shit. Not by a long chalk." He stood over Cassie, leaning his hands on the arms on either side of her so that she shrank down into the seat of the chair. "Not by a long fucking chalk."

"Look, I—"

"So some self-important old bag comes along and takes us into care, me and my brother. La-di-das about the place, patronizing us, sneering at my mum, says we've been abused, takes us away from her, sticks us in—" He sniffed suddenly, and his eyes glistened. "We never saw her again, after that. She left my stepdad, jumped off a bridge somewhere. If that old bat hadn't turned up—"

"I'm really very—" Cassie began futilely.

"I didn't get this far on any silver bloody spoons," Ryland said. He waved one hand at the comprehensive views beyond the windows and then replaced it on the chair's arm, as effective as a steel bar so far as any chance of Cassie getting away from him was concerned. "There wasn't any money from Mummie or Daddy waiting for me when *I* turned twenty-one, believe you me."

"Nor me," Cassie said, but he did not appear to hear.

"I had to earn it any way I could—and some of the ways you wouldn't want to know about, you really wouldn't."

"Mr. Ryland, you've got it all wro—"

"And then that old git Plumpton comes poncing in," Ryland said savagely. " 'Ay say, Rayland, some jolly faine stuff you've got in heah.' I knew what he was on about, soon as he said he'd been in this room. And then the old girl pitches in, staring at me like I was the Second Coming or something. I could see my number was up unless I did something about it PDQ."

Trapped in the chair, Cassie said nothing. She had read too much crime fiction not to know that the longer you can keep the suspect talking, the more chance you have of surviving. Not that she was keeping Ryland talking: he was doing that himself, his eyes not quite focused, resting on her only to glance away, seeing her not as a person, but as the paradigm of a class he blamed for all his childhood troubles. Though in that case, why strive to imitate them? she wondered. And then thought: Is that what I do too? Try to be something which by both upbringing and inclination I really am not?

Ryland straightened, still standing very close to Cassie. "One thing they teach you in the Army," he said conversationally, "is different ways to kill a man so that it looks like a natural death." His eyes were as shiny and expressionless as marbles. "Ever read detective novels?" he continued.

It was like being at the dentist, the questions asked without expecting any answer. She shook her head.

"All those elaborately set-up plots," he said contemptuously. "Poison and arson and that. The best way to eliminate someone is to squeeze the side of their neck."

Is that what he had done to the Plumptons?

"Looks like natural causes then, you see," he went on. "Nobody suspects a thing."

It dawned on Cassie, for the first time, that he actually intended to kill her. The realization sent the blood draining from her face. She lay back in the chair, glad of its support, feeling faint and weak. She said nothing.

"Made a bad mistake, didn't you?" Ryland said levelly. "Should have left the detecting to the cops—they're really not much good at it."

"Whereas I am?"

"Too bloody right."

She would know where to come if she needed a reference . . . "How do you know?"

"Because I followed you, didn't I? Down to Hay-on-Wye, saw you chatting up the old bat next door, getting her to let you into the Plumpton's place. Knew you must be on to me."

"On to you? I really don't know what you mean." But she did. Looking around the room, her eye caught the overmantel again, and she was able to put the last piece of the jigsaw into place. Since placatory cowering was not getting her anywhere, she decided to go on the attack. "You killed the Colonel because he recognized the Angelica Kauffmann vase," she said boldly.

Ryland seemed suddenly unnerved. "You know about that as *well*," he said. "Did old Plumpton tell you?"

"I figured it out," said Cassie.

"How could you possibly? Nobody knows."

"Colonel Plumpton obviously did. So did I."

"And you worked it out on your own?"

She was about to nod. Then the realization struck her that if she were to claim credit, if she were to lie once again, she would be signing her own death warrant. "No," she said quickly.

"You're lying."

"I'm not. I'm really not. A—a friend of mine is an expert on Angelica Kauffmann. He knows all about the missing urn thing." Ryland was staring at her with a sneer of disbelief. "There was a pair of them, commissioned by a particular regiment," she said, desperately wishing that she had paid more attention to Charlie Quartermain's explanations. "And then in the nineteen-sixties, they were sent to some military exhibition and one of them never arrived. Or so it was believed." Watching his face, she added, "I bet the orderly or whatever who was unpacking the artifacts was *you*. I bet it was you who nicked it."

It was his turn to stay silent.

"Anyway, I told this friend of mine that I was coming to see you and that I knew you had the ur—the lidded vase, because I'd seen it when I dashed in here to fetch help for poor Miss Gunn." She remembered again how she had dashed along the corridor from the old lady's hotel bedroom to Ryland's private quarters, had turned the door handle to reveal an empty room, had taken in the details in a single sweeping glance before turning again and running toward the stairs leading to the reception area.

A terrible idea struck Cassie. Surely Ryland could not have—

"There was another interfering old biddy," Ryland said. "Kept staring at me, couldn't quite place me. I remembered her from years ago, but she wasn't quite sure she remembered me."

"So you killed her?"

"Disposed of her, yeah." Ryland grinned, showing even yellow teeth. "It wasn't too difficult."

Cassie said, trying to sound in control, "I expect my friend will be contacting the police if I don't get home soon. So you really can't afford to do anything to me."

He laughed. "After what I've told you, you don't bloody think I'm letting you go, do you?"

She stared at him wordlessly.

"And don't think I believe all this stuff about *friends* and *contacting the police*, because I'm not buying it."

"You won't get away with this, you know." The sentence sounded as lame emerging from Cassie's own mouth as it always did when someone said it in a film.

"I'm going to have a bloody good try," Ryland said. "With you out of the way, I ought to be in the clear."

To which the stock reply, in all the B movies Cassie had watched on the telly, all the Golden Age crime fiction she had ever read, was: "Don't be too sure, my man," or words to that effect, usually uttered in the kind of drama school voice which would send a class-warrior like Ryland right up the wall.

She stood up carefully, watching him. "Wanna bet?" she said.

"It's a risk I'm prepared to take."

"In that case—"

In that case what? Kill me, I'm yours? Cassie was spared any further thought by a sudden violent banging at the door.

"Mr. Ryland! Mr. Ryland, are you there?"

She recognized the sullen peacock screech of either Miss Skin or Miss Boanes. After this is over, she thought, I'll buy that girl a whole head of lettuce and she can pig out on chlorophyll. She opened her mouth to scream but before she could do so, Ryland had grabbed her and clamped his hand over her mouth.

"Mr. Ryland! One of the conventioneers has been taken ill. I've sent for an ambulance but . . . Mr. Ryland: are you *there*?"

Crushed against his chest, Cassie closed her eyes in despair. The powerful muscles of his upper arms held her rigid. If only she *had* told Charlie Quartermain where she was going. Or anyone. But no one knew she was here. All Ryland had to do was use whatever method he'd employed to dispatch Colonel and/or Mrs. Plumpton and then walk out of the room to deal with the sick man.

She recognized that he could not afford to let her go. She recognized, bleakly, that she was in terrible danger. Above her head, Ryland called out, "I'll be there in a moment, Felicia. Go down and tell them I'm coming."

Cassie began to kick at him, clawing at his arms. If she could only scream . . . He shoved her bodily across the room in front of him and grabbed something from the desk in the alcove beside the fireplace. He manhandled her back into the big armchair.

"Bitch," he hissed into her ear. "Fucking bitch."

Behind her head she heard a tearing sound. The next minute he was winding paper tape across her mouth and around her head, as though she were a parcel. Beneath its sticky folds she mewed like a kitten, gazing up at him, pleading, begging.

He did not meet her eyes as he methodically went on to tape her wrists together behind her back and then her ankles and knees. Mummified, she knew there was no way she could escape from the stuff; she had spent too many hours doing up parcels of bridge accessories not to know just how strong and untearable it was.

He used the rest of the roll of tape to truss her inside the chair, as though it were a cage.

"I shan't be long," he said, grinning at her. "And then we'll finish off our chat, all right?"

He opened the door. She could feel sweat rolling down her back; her stomach heaved and she fought it, knowing that if she vomited, she would in all likelihood suffocate. Tears blinded her. She knew with a desperate clarity that she did not want to die.

There was a sudden swirling thumping. She blinked the tears away as Ryland came flying backward into the room and crashed to the carpet. At the same time, Charlie Quartermain thundered in after him. He kicked Ryland brutally in the ribs, three times, then leaned down and lifted him by his collar and swung one massive fist into Ryland's face. The crack of bone was clearly audible above the scream of Felicia.

"What are you doing? What on *earth* do you think you're doing?"

"Get the police, darlin'," Quartermain grunted.

"Don't worry, I most certainly shall."

"Get a move on, then."

"Mr. Ryland, are you all right?" Felicia's voice was sharp with anxiety. She did not seem to be afraid of Quartermain.

"All right? Course he's not. And likely to be a lot less so for the next twenty years or so, isn't that right, Ryland?"

Ryland stared up at him, eyes glaring in his bloodied face. Then, with extraordinary agility, he leapt up from the floor and head-butted Quartermain, at the same time bringing up his foot to crotch level and shoving hard.

"*Oof!*" Charlie Quartermain doubled over. At the same time the momentum of Ryland's push sent him staggering toward the wall.

"Stop it!" screamed Felicia Boanes. "Stop it! Help! Stop it at—"

She caught sight of Cassie in her winding sheet of mushroom-colored plasticized tape and broke off. One emaciated hand rose slowly to her mouth.

At the same time, three of the royal-blue blazers burst into the room.

"Whut the hick's goin' on?" one of them said.

Ryland whirled, ran toward them, began pushing between them.

"Don't let him go," Quartermain gasped. "He's a murderer."

They seemed bewildered but complaisant. Two of

them grabbed Ryland, the third walked over to Cassie and stood looking down at her. "Blimey," he said. "How in Gawd's name do yuh work airt the postage on *this* pahcel." He began to unwind the tape around Cassie's mouth.

Charlie came over to her, using a curious crablike motion. "Are you all right, darlin'?" he said urgently.

"Fine, thanks," Cassie said as soon as she could speak. Her lips felt as though they had been torn off along with the tape, her scalp ached, her stomach was close to rebellion. "Don't I look it?"

He leaned down and kissed the side of her face. With her arms still taped, there was nothing she could do to stop him. "You look gorgeous," he said with fervor.

"Would somebody mind explaining what's going on here?" Felicia Boanes said indignantly. "And why are you two holding Mr. Ryland prisoner like that?"

Cassie spoke from the depths of her chair, wreathed in tape like some ancient cobwebbed priestess. "That's not his real name."

She turned her head toward Ryland, slumped between the two hefty men in their bright jackets, the blood from his broken nose dripping onto the Chinese carpet, and said, as Mrs. Plumpton must have done several weeks earlier, "You're Crickson."

DRESS the Rev. Cyril Briggs in a suit of lights or as a pantomime dame and he would still have looked exactly what he was: a clergyman. More specifically, a rural vicar, high of forehead, fluting of voice, solemn of specs. He had a large and serviceable mouth, which he was currently packing with the ginger-colored shepherd's pie and boiled sprouts that was the vicarage supper that evening.

Cassie had met him before, a thousand times, each version slightly different in terms of height or weight but all substantially the same. The same benign gaze, the same unworldly approach, the same matey relationship with God.

"We're so fond of Charlie," Mrs. Vicar—Enid—was saying as she handed more sprouts around the table.

Cassie smiled. No way was she going to agree that she was too, although it was clearly what they expected, not even though she would probably be lying at the bottom of some rubbish tip, or even being eaten by pigs—she had read somewhere that pigs were partial to a bit of human flesh—if he had not burst in at the eleventh hour and rescued her from whatever Ryland/Crickson had in mind for her.

"Yes, indeed," the Rev. Cyril chimed in. "And he's been so good to us."

"That's nice," murmured Cassie. Good? Did they mean Charlie Quartermain assisted at Holy Communion, or led prayers at eleven o'clock service? Hard to imagine. Very hard.

Charlie himself was vigorously knocking back the contents of one of the two bottles of wine he had brought with him, swilling the stuff around his teeth as though it were mouthwash and then swallowing it gulpingly down. "Yeah, well," he said. He glanced over at Mrs. Vicar. "Nice nosh, Een."

Enid smiled gently at him. "Nothing very special, I'm afraid."

"Nothing like good home cooking," Charlie said. "Don't you agree, Cass?"

"Absolutely," Cassie said. If it was *good* home cooking you were talking about, which was a category into which this shepherd's pie definitely did not fall.

In the way of such places, the vicarage was gently shabby, the carpets worn by the feet of countless parishioners, the furniture scuffed and dented. Comfortless was the word which sprang to Cassie's mind, and she immediately despised herself for being so materialistic in the face of the Briggsian evident spirituality.

"Frankly, I don't know where we would have been without Charlie," the Rev. Cyril confided to her. "The cost of renovation these days—and we're only a small congregation. The Church Commissioners have so many claims on their purse too, and in these times of recession, it's particularly hard to increase the fund. So he's been quite literally a godsend to us." He smiled across at Charlie, who smiled back. He looked suddenly very different: almost, Cassie thought with astonishment, lovable.

"I hope you have fully recovered from your ordeal," Enid said, turning to Cassie. "Charlie told us all about it."

"Yes, indeed," sighed the Rev. Cyril. "We have been praying for that poor man."

"Poor man!" snorted Charlie. "Nothing poor about him. He's murdered at least four people—old people too, apart from poor old Sonia. People who couldn't put up any kind of a fight against him." He drained his glass as though it contained water. "I don't hold with that."

"It's all right if they're young and vigorous like me, is it?" asked Cassie.

He looked at her with serious eyes. "Listen, girl. If he'd done anything to harm you, I'd have killed him myself. Straight up."

"Please, Charlie. Don't say such things," said the Rev. Cyril. "The man came from terrible beginnings. He never had much of a chance in life, we must forgi—"

"Don't give me that crap," Charlie said. "Why should he be forgiven?"

"As I understand it, he was abused by his—"

"So was I," Charlie said. "A real sod, my stepfather. Didn't turn *me* into a thief and a murderer. Besides, once he got into the Army, things started to go right for him. He killed those poor old people in order to keep up the pretense he was a nob, nothing more than that."

"And Sonia got in the way," Cassie said. "I suppose she was too big for him to try that trick with the carotid artery or whatever it was. So he grabbed the alabaster thing and hit her with it."

The Rev. Cyril closed his eyes as though in pain. "Terrible," he murmured. "Truly terrible."

"Let's not talk about it," Enid said brightly, beginning to clear away the plates.

"But there is one thing," Cassie said, looking apologetically at the Vicar.

"Yeah?" said Charlie.

"I still don't see how you managed to burst in on Ryland like that. I mean, how you even knew where I was."

Charlie tsked and slowly shook his head. "Didn't think I was going to leave you on your tod, did you? Not after the way you've been playing at Miss Marple."

"I see," said Cassie coldly, wondering whether to be annoyed at his patronizing tone or not.

"There's a lot of social undesirables knocking about out there. So I've had Nasty Norman keeping a friendly eye on you for the last few days," continued Charlie.

"Nasty Norman?"

"Didn't you notice the bloke taking a leak by his car

every time you went out? Got trouble with his water-
works, has Norm. Blends in nicely with the scenery."

"And he's been following me, has he?"

"That's right."

"And he's been reporting back to you?"

"You bet, sweetheart."

Cassie would have made some crushing retort if had
not been for the undeniable fact that, whether she liked
it or not, Charlie had actually saved her life. She
remained silent.

The shepherd's pie was followed by an apple tart.
The apples were watery, the pastry marmoreal. Cassie
looked at the Rev. Cyril with new respect as he compli-
mented his wife without the slightest trace of irony.

Later, Charlie shoved back his chair. "Come on,
Cass," he said. "I'll show you what I've been doing."

"And there'll be a cup of tea waiting when you get
back," said Enid, as though they were children being
sent out to walk off their lunch.

They walked side by side down the vicarage path and
out onto the green around which the village was set.
Between plane trees could be glimpsed four dignified
Georgian houses with elaborate fanlights and maroon
brick fronts. Several pretty cottages faced them, together with a mixture of dwellings built from the local
honey-colored Guiting stone. St. Alphege's was a fine
medieval structure, attached to a Norman tower and set
in a graveyard of crumbling antiquity.

Although a bitter little breeze zipped through the yew
trees which stood here and there, there was nonetheless
an underlying warmth in the air which spoke of spring
in the not too distant future. Sparrows chittered on

gravestones; a couple of magpies strutted superciliously away from them down a path of old stone flags.

"There's some splendid strapwork inside," Charlie said, gesturing at the church as it squatted among the lichened headstones. "Elizabethan."

"Mmm," Cassie said. She felt remarkably at peace with the world, but then the world had made its peace with her. With Ryland cast into the outer darkness of formal charges and remand prison, her engagement book had suddenly filled and overflowed. The bridge sundries business was being examined by an accountant with a view to purchase if he recommended it as a going concern.

Charlie flourished a large medieval iron key. "I'll open up," he said.

She followed him into the timbered porch and into the church itself. Cold seeped out as soon as he had opened the door, and with it the smell of dead flowers and dust. It was gloomy inside, the stained glass ("It's only Victorian," said Charlie, who seemed to know about these things, "but not too bad for all that") casting a dim polychromatic light over empty pews, brass lecterns, carved font and pulpit.

"This way." Charlie beckoned her after him toward a curtained doorway. He opened another door, using another key, and began to climb upward, Cassie stumbling after him. When she tripped, he reached down one huge hand and took hers. It seemed easier, frankly, to let him.

They passed the belfry, long ropes hanging like nooses in the dusty gloom, each one banded in colored plush, like a surgical stocking. Finally, they came to the roof of the tower and stepped out.

"Parky, innit?" Charlie said.

"Very." Cassie walked to the edge and looked out between crenellations. Below her the Cotswolds stretched toward Worcestershire and Gloucestershire, the fields and woods threaded with rivers and gradually giving way to blue-hazed slopes and rounded hills. She turned. "So, Charlie. Show me what you brought me up here for."

He took a step toward her and she thought, in panic: I hope he didn't take that as a come-on.

"Face like an angel," he said softly. "Soon as I saw you, knew it was what I needed."

"How do you mean?"

"Look." He pointed and she saw a series of carved cherubic heads gazing blandly down. "What do you think?"

The one nearest Cassie had been weathered into almost total obliteration, but the others had recently been renewed, cut in high relief. The features had been carved with the utmost delicacy; no two expressions were quite the same. She looked at them more closely and felt tears prick her eyelids. Stone curls drifted about their cheeks, their mouths smiled, a suggestion of angelic wings fluttered behind their heads.

And the face of each one was, unmistakably, the face of Cassandra Swann.